The Thirteenth Tower

Works by Sara C. Snider

The Tree and Tower Series

The Thirteenth Tower
A Shadowed Spirit

Other Publications

The Forgotten Web
Hazel and Holly
a web serial at saracsnider.com/hazel-and-holly/

THE THIRTEENTH TOWER

SARA C. SNIDER

Double Beast Publishing
Stockholm, Sweden

Book design by Ray Rhamey

Cover art by Ferdinand D. Ladera

For my family

CHAPTER 1

EMELYN AWOKE, AS ALWAYS, in darkness. She lay still, savoring the quiet solitude. She felt hidden, protected, and, for just a moment, like she existed someplace else entirely. The house above her would fade away, and in that heartbeat she could imagine that she had a family, that she was loved.

But it was only a moment.

Fearing the inevitable rebuke if she was found loitering in bed, Emelyn cast off her blanket and put her feet to the hard earthen floor. Her room had no windows, only a pallet, a table large enough for a candle and cup, and a chest containing her few possessions.

She walked to the chest and pulled out a change of clothes. Her fingers brushed against the fabric of her fine muslin dress that she wore for special occasions. Tonight was the Harvest Festival; she might get to wear it, provided she finished all her chores. Her heart felt heavy at the thought of missing yet another one. Fallow's yearly festivals were rare occasions where she almost felt happy.

She smiled at the thought of all the dancing and food and people that the festival would bring. Derron would probably be there, too, and she smiled all the more as she pictured his quirky grin—

A cold shiver struck the image from her mind. She drew a long, shaking breath and, suddenly eager to leave the darkened room, Emelyn wriggled out of her night-dress and pulled on a working dress. She slipped on a pair of stockings and reached into the darkness to where she knew her boots to be. She tied an apron around her waist and, using her fingers as a comb, tied her hair back with a ribbon as she walked through the door.

She made her way across the sprawling, darkened basement. High on the wall, cracks of light peeked through shuttered windows. Emelyn pulled back the wooden slats, allowing dim morning light to fall into the room.

The Mansell residence was one of the grandest houses in Fallow. Emelyn reminded herself that she ought to feel grateful for living there. She knew of servants who would have been eager to trade positions with her. Such knowledge ought to bring her comfort, but it never did.

She knelt in front of the hearth and scooped out the previous day's ashes into a metal pail. Restocking the fireplace with wood and kindling from a nearby box, she set it aflame with the help of a tinderbox. She had managed to get the fire burning when a bell near the staircase rang. Emelyn started at the sound. It would be Miss Cook—the master and mistress rang either Miss Cook or Tilly when they needed something. But why would she ring? Wiping her hands on a corner of her apron, Emelyn hurried up the stairs.

Pale light streamed through the leaded windows along the outer wall of the kitchen. Miss Cook stood at a table in the middle of the room, kneading a ball of dough. She was a sturdy woman with a thick oxen-like neck and hands like mallets. Her formidable frame always made the dresses she wore look out of place, bordering on ridiculous.

"You took your time," Miss Cook said as she worked. She picked up the dough and cast it back onto the floured tabletop.

"Yes, Miss Cook."

"I need you to run over to Mr. Hibberly's and fetch some eggs. There were none to be had in the henhouse and the mistress requires onion custard with breakfast."

"What about the water?" Emelyn had not yet put the morning washing water on to boil.

"Tilly will see to it. Mr. Hibberly won't have opened shop yet, so be sure to knock loudly and tell him it is a matter of emergency."

"Yes, Miss Cook."

"And no dillydallying." Miss Cook stopped kneading long enough to point a thick, doughy finger at Emelyn. "You head straight there and back again. We've a lot of work to do and I'll not have you idling about."

Miss Cook needn't have told her, especially today of all days. "Yes, Miss Cook." Emelyn fetched a woven hand basket hanging from a shelf, then walked to the door and hung her apron on a peg in the wall. From another peg she took a knitted woolen shawl that she wrapped around her shoulders.

The morning was sharp and dewy, and the chill air bit at Emelyn's skin like pinpricks. She drew the shawl around her as she hurried down the path leading to the road. They lived on the outskirts of town, and Fallow was about fifteen minutes away by foot.

Emelyn walked by prim clapboard houses and painted fences. Smoke drifted from chimneys, spicing the chill autumn air. She passed farmland and fields, some dotted with newly harvested grain that had been bundled and left to dry. In the distance, the tall shadow of the Magister Tower spiraled out of the surrounding forest like the tail of a great serpent.

Fallow was constructed in a globular fashion, with cobblestone roads that led like spokes in a wheel to the town square, which in this case was distinctly circular. Shops and businesses lined the streets, the most prominent among them found near the center—Mr. Hibberly's store among them.

Rounding a corner, Emelyn came upon a little girl peeking in the window of Mr. Wainwright's carpentry shop. The girl had long, dark hair and wore a dress of rough leather with colorful little beads that clicked when she moved. On bare feet, she stretched to her tiptoes as she peered through the glass.

"Hello, there," Emelyn said.

The girl turned and looked at her but gave no reply. Her eyes were grey like the clouds overhead, much like Emelyn's own. They looked striking against her dun-colored skin. Emelyn had thought her own skin dark, but now felt fair by comparison. The girl regarded her, unfazed and unblinking. It was . . . unsettling.

"Are you all right?"

The little girl said nothing. Then she turned and ran down the street, her dark hair trailing behind her like wild shadows.

Emelyn watched her run, listening to the click-clack of the beads as they faded into silence. She lingered a moment, staring at the empty road before she continued walking. The girl must be a traveler here for the festival. Yet Emelyn still worried for the lone child in the cold with no shoes.

She made her way to Mr. Hibberly's shop and rapped on the door. When no answer came, she rapped again as hard as she dared, her cold hand stinging from the effort. After a few moments, a pale face appeared in a window in the door, distorted by the thick, cloudy glass. The door cracked open and Mrs. Hibberly poked her head out, her long nose and protruding mouth reminding Emelyn of a large rodent venturing out of a hole in a wall.

"Yes? What do you want? We're closed, you know. Come back later." Giving Emelyn no time to respond, she shut the door.

Emelyn knocked again. The door reopened to reveal Mrs. Hibberly's withering, weaselly glare.

Emelyn curtsied in hopes of lightening that scowl. "Begging your pardon, ma'am, but Miss Cook sent me over from the Mansell residence. It seems we're out of eggs, and Mistress Mansell was expecting onion custard this morning. Would you happen to have any on hand?"

Mrs. Hibberly said nothing, peering at Emelyn through the crack in the door with her dark, beady eyes. After a lengthy moment of uncomfortable silence, the door swung open and Mrs. Hibberly motioned for her to come inside.

The morning light streaming through the front window of the shop was too weak to illuminate the vast room. The pigeonhole shelves that lined the walls disappeared into darkness as they stretched towards the ceiling. Sacks and barrels cluttered the floor in shadowed heaps while a wrought iron ladder clung to the wall like some great skeletal beast. The air was heavy with the aroma of leather and spices, oil and dust. A familiar smell, one that brought Emelyn comfort.

Mrs. Hibberly picked up an oil lamp burning on the counter near the door. She held it to Emelyn's face, peering at her with narrowed eyes. "You're the little whelp that got left on Torrence Mansell's doorstep all those years ago."

That Emelyn had been abandoned as a baby hurt her more than she ever let on. The notion that she was somehow abnormal, unworthy of the love of her own parents haunted her. It was a thought she struggled to keep buried, but it was always there, deep down. A nagging fear that she was, and always would be, inadequate. Love could never be anything more than an unattainable idea, a fanciful feeling of which the likes of her would never know.

But she kept dreaming. Emelyn still hoped she would one day find her parents. It was a day in which all her questions would be answered; a day in which her heart would feel whole.

"Yes, ma'am." Emelyn shifted her feet, uncomfortable under Mrs. Hibberly's critical gaze.

"Raised by Merridan, of all people. Hmph. I knew her before she had a last name. I shouldn't have thought her capable of raising a child."

Emelyn blinked. She was unaccustomed to hearing Miss Cook called by her first name.

Mrs. Hibberly pursed her lips together as she continued to peer at Emelyn, looking her up and down. "I suppose you turned out well enough. Though you're bigger than you ought to be. How old are you, girl? Thirteen?"

"Seventeen, ma'am." That's what she figured, anyway. Birthdays were never celebrated at home, at least not among the servants. But Miss Cook had told her she was ten the year she officially started working for the Mansells, and that had been seven years ago.

Mrs. Hibberly grunted. "Haven't amounted to much, have you?"

Emelyn stiffened her back and set her jaw, grateful when a door at the far end of the room opened.

In walked Mr. Hibberly, holding a candle to light his way. He wore a gold and blue striped vest that stretched at the seams over his rotund body. His long mustaches grew along his jowls and to his ears, giving him a perpetual grey, bushy smile.

"Well now, what have we here?" Mr. Hibberly said as he strolled over to his wife. "Why didn't you tell me we had company?"

"She's not company," Mrs. Hibberly said. "The girl needs eggs for her mistress' breakfast. Apparently it's too important to wait until a decent hour."

"Well! Why didn't you say so? You're in luck, my dear girl, as we have eggs aplenty, kept especially for this moment!" He gave a flourish of his hand and bowed slightly at the waist, undoubtedly all that his ample frame would allow.

Emelyn smiled behind her hand, not daring to laugh under the scornful gaze of Mrs. Hibberly.

Mr. Hibberly turned to his wife. "I can take over from here, my darling. You get dressed while I help our young customer and then we can breakfast together before opening shop. It's going to be a busy day today, I reckon, what with the festival and all. You best rest up while you can. Off you go!" He escorted Mrs. Hibberly to the door leading to their residence while her mouth worked in silent, wordless protests. He swept her through the door.

With the matter of Mrs. Hibberly resolved, Mr. Hibberly turned to Emelyn, boasting a bright, toothy smile broad enough to match the grey, bushy one. "Now then, Miss Emelyn, about those eggs. I've about a dozen, will that suffice?"

Emelyn nodded.

Mr. Hibberly shuffled behind the counter and rummaged through a crate filled with sawdust. "They should still be nice and fresh. I bought them about a week ago from Mrs. Troller, but they have been kept cool and secure in the sawdust there." He took Emelyn's basket and filled it with sawdust. He then added the eggs, arranging them so they wouldn't break. He handed the basket back to Emelyn.

"Will you be going to the Harvest Festival tonight?" he said.

"Maybe. If I can get my chores done."

"Well, you best get to it, then. They say this year's festival is to be the best one yet. Wouldn't want you to miss it."

Emelyn quailed inwardly at the news. It would be her kind of luck to miss the biggest and best festival the town had seen. She was even more eager to get home and get on with her chores.

Mr. Hibberly said, "I'll put the eggs on your bill, as usual."

Emelyn nodded. "Thank you."

She left the shop and hurried through town. She had nearly made it home when two men in scarlet robes appeared on the road ahead. Her breath caught. Magisters.

Magi were imposing figures, unmistakable among the common folk of Fallow with their long red robes, embroidered with intricate patterns in gold thread. One had long white hair woven into a single braid; the other was bald with a round pair of spectacles perched upon his nose. Emelyn was tempted to turn around and head back into town, anything to avoid walking by them. But she was pressed for time, and the rumors were surely nothing more than idle chatter, spread about by bored housewives and unscrupulous servants. She didn't have anything to fear.

Still, Emelyn tensed as the Magi walked by and, when the bald man looked at her, she averted her gaze. She glanced at the distant Tower. What business could the Magi have in the outskirts of Fallow?

She reached the house and followed a pebbled walkway around to the side entrance. Tilly was there, shaking out a carpet from upstairs.

"Emmy," Tilly said. "Did you see the Magi pass by a little while ago?"

Emelyn nodded. "I walked right by them. One of them looked at me."

"Really?" Tilly gasped, feigning fear. "Why do you think they've come all the way out here?"

Emelyn shrugged.

"Maybe they're here to steal children," Tilly whispered. "Like the old wives say." She giggled.

Emelyn frowned. She didn't find such jokes amusing.

"Oh, Emmy! You're always so serious!"

Emelyn forced a smile. Tilly was her dearest and only friend, but sometimes her antics were tiresome. "We should get back to work."

Tilly's merriment faded. She continued shaking out the carpet as Emelyn stepped inside the house.

Once she had left the eggs with Miss Cook, Emelyn set about doing her daily chores. She worked as quickly as she could, determined to get everything done in time for the festival. Luckily, the master and mistress weren't entertaining that night. They sometimes did on festival days, making a grand event of the occasion. Such events always made it impossible for Emelyn and Tilly to get away.

Emelyn swept and scrubbed, dusted and polished. When mealtimes came around, she took them in the kitchen with Tilly and Miss Cook, as she always did. Mealtimes were generally quiet—Tilly never dared gab when Miss Cook was around. But today they were even more terse than usual. Emelyn was eager to get on with her work and get it done; she suspected Tilly felt the same.

Morning passed into afternoon and then to evening. Emelyn was in the basement, up to her elbows in hot soapy water washing a pile of dishes, when the bell to the kitchen rang. She cringed. The hour was growing late and she still had to finish the dishes, help Miss Cook with supper, clean up afterwards, and anything else that might need doing. She hoped that Miss Cook wouldn't choose tonight to clean and take inventory of the larder, or mention the pile of clothes that Emelyn still needed to mend.

She wiped her hands on her apron and rolled down her sleeves before heading up to the kitchen.

Miss Cook stood at the table peeling potatoes. "Mr. Witherby has slaughtered a couple of chickens for supper tonight," she said when Emelyn walked in. "I need you to go out and pluck them."

Emelyn wrinkled her nose—she hated plucking chickens. "Yes, Miss Cook."

"Best be quick about it."

She stepped outside and passed through the hedged garden until she came to the henhouse near Mr. Witherby's cabin. He was close by, pulling weeds from a flowerbed and casting them into a wheelbarrow.

On a chopping block lay two white chickens, their necks broken. Emelyn picked one up and, crouching to the ground, began plucking out the feathers. She worked quickly, eager to have it done.

Faint music drifted on the air, a sweet melody tinted with a strain of sadness. Emelyn paid it little mind, thinking it was Mr. Witherby whistling. But as the music grew louder, she could hear that it was an instrument and not whistling lips that produced the melody. She stood and looked around. Mr. Witherby was also on his feet, looking around as he scratched his head. Emelyn, straining to listen, heard the distinctive pitch of a fiddle. She smiled. It was probably someone from the festival, playing as they walked along the road. She crouched back down to finish plucking the chickens so that she, too, could attend.

Mr. Witherby passed by, his gaze fixed straight ahead as he wandered out of the garden. Emelyn frowned. It wasn't like him to shirk his duties, especially for something so frivolous as music. She told herself to keep working, to focus on the work at hand and get it done. Yet she remained still, watching the hedges where Mr. Witherby had disappeared.

Maybe she would take just a quick peek. Emelyn hastened through the garden, following the music as it lilted through the air. She rounded the house and came upon a group of people trailing behind a lone fiddler. Mr. Witherby was there, walking alongside Miss Cook, who was swinging her skirts, gadding about without a care.

Emelyn stopped and gaped. Miss Cook never attended the festivals, nor was she one for carousing of any kind. When Emelyn saw Tilly in the crowd, she ran after them.

"Tilly!"

"Emmy!" Tilly clasped her hands to Emelyn's arm a little too firmly. "We're going to the festival! Won't it be grand?"

Emelyn frowned, looking at Tilly's flushed cheeks and glazed eyes. She looked unwell. "I don't understand, I thought we were to finish our chores first."

Tilly laughed. "Don't be silly! We're all here, even Miss Cook. When we get there, I'm going to buy one of Mr. Cowan's meat pies and I'm going to dance until I fall!" Tilly twirled around.

Miss Cook, seeing Tilly, also spun around, her skirts flaring outwards as she laughed like a girl half her age.

Emelyn stifled a gasp. She started to back away when Tilly grabbed her arm.

"I bet you Derron will be there," Tilly said, a playful spark in her eyes. "Everyone knows he's sweet on you."

Emelyn scowled as her face burned.

Tilly laughed again. "I bet he'll ask you to dance. Maybe even kiss you." Tilly pulled Emelyn close and pressed her fevered lips against Emelyn's cheek.

Emelyn jerked free, wiping her cheek as Tilly laughed and moved on. She looked at the others. There was Mr. Gatwick, the dairyman, walking arm in arm with their neighbor, Mrs. Bower. Master and Mistress Mansell were parading like peacocks as though they were in the Queen's entourage. The music trilled, quick and merry like a warbling songbird. But something within the notes made Emelyn want to cry, calling to mind memories best left forgotten.

She walked ahead to look at the fiddler. It was a woman, dressed in a pale, gauzy dress that did nothing to conceal her lithe body. A bone mask in the shape of a deer's head hid her face, with antlers that twined and branched high above her brow. The fiddle she held at her shoulder was little more than a piece of twisted wood, the green leaves growing from one end hinting that it shouldn't have been able to produce sound at all.

Emelyn stopped walking as her curiosity congealed into a cold shiver of fear. This was all very wrong. Why didn't the others see it? Did they even care?

She returned to Tilly. "We need to go."

Tilly latched back onto her arm. "Don't be silly! We'll have so much fun. You'll see."

Emelyn swallowed the lump rising in her throat. She wanted to pull away and run. But the fevered blush in her friend's cheeks gave her pause. Tilly was ill, and oughtn't be out in the cold. She needed someone to look after her and, like Emelyn, had no one else.

Emelyn let herself be pulled along. Maybe it was nothing; maybe she was overreacting and Tilly was right—they'd have lots of fun. That was what she told herself as they walked down the road. Yet somehow, she couldn't bring herself to believe it.

CHAPTER 2

THE SUN WAS SETTING by the time the group made it to town, the golden sky growing dark with twilight. Torches had been lit along the road leading to Fallow, creating a path of flickering firelight that the group followed until they reached an open field. Tents and pavilions had been erected out on the grass, illuminated by torches, braziers, and hanging lamps. The fiddler stopped playing and music from the festival drifted over. Mr. Gatwick and Mrs. Bower strolled towards the pavilions, as did Master and Mistress Mansell. Miss Cook, hiking up her skirts, ran through the knee-high grass laughing, while Mr. Witherby shuffled after her.

"Come on!" Tilly grabbed Emelyn's hand and pulled her towards the field.

Tilly giggled as they ran through the damp grass. Emelyn scrutinized everyone and everything, looking for anything peculiar. There were many familiar faces, though it seemed just as many were unfamiliar. Normally, Emelyn would have been delighted over so many visitors having come to Fallow. Now she only felt suspicious and afraid. She envied Tilly and wished she could share her friend's enthusiasm.

They passed booths and tables with merchants selling colorful ribbons, pumpkins, pies, and carved wooden figurines. There was Mrs. Troller, selling apples and jars of preserves. Mrs. Gatwick, the dairyman's wife, had a booth with an assortment of butter, cream, and cheeses on display. A massive keg of ale surrounded by a group of rowdy men marked Mr. Cowan's booth, as did the heady aroma of meat pies that hung in the air. Tilly hurried by. Looked like she didn't want a pie, after all. Emelyn might have insisted they stop to purchase one had she not left her money at home.

Tilly turned to Emelyn, a broad smile stretching across her face. "Dancing!" She yanked on Emelyn's arm and pulled her in a new direction.

Tilly grinned as she pushed her way through a throng of people, elbowing anyone who got in her way. Emelyn, appalled with her friend's behavior, murmured apologies to those they passed. Not that it mattered. Anyone who found a sharp elbow in their side spared them only a cursory glance before turning away. Emelyn frowned.

They reached the front of the crowd, coming to an open space populated by a group of dancers. Men and women were paired up, holding hands as they danced to a lively tune played by a couple of squat musicians. The women were dressed much like the fiddler had been, with diaphanous dresses of silver and grey that flowed in the wind like woven smoke.

The men were clad in well-tailored black waistcoats, the silvery chains of pocket watches glinting in the firelight. Below the waist the men were unclothed, their erect penises protruding from thatches of thick, dark hair. Both the men and women wore pale bone masks wrought in the likeness of animals—antlered deer for the women, snarling wolves for the men.

Emelyn gasped at the sight of them and turned her head. Looking around, she was troubled that no one else seemed shocked by the dancers' impropriety, least of all

Tilly. The girl looked on with wide eyes while fidgeting with her hands. Emelyn wanted to leave; this wasn't how it was supposed to be.

The music stopped and the dancers turned to the audience, their hands extended.

"Emmy! They're inviting people in!"

Emelyn shied away when Tilly tried to pull her forward.

"Let's join them. It will be fun!"

"No." Emelyn tried pulling her arm free, but Tilly's grasp was firm.

"Come on, how often do we get to dance?"

"No!" Emelyn's voice pierced the air and the dancers and audience alike turned to look at her.

Tilly's brow furrowed as the haze in her eyes cleared and the color in her cheeks faded. She looked around, her expression puzzled as if she had just woken from a deep slumber. Then, just as quickly, her cheeks again flushed and her eyes glassed over. "Fine." She turned her back on Emelyn and took the outstretched hand of a dancer.

Others from the audience stepped forward until all the dancers had been paired. The music piped up, the men bowed, the women curtsied, and the dance began. Holding hands, the pairs pranced in circles—the women around the men, then the men around the women. They wove around each other, switching partners before finding, once again, their original mate. They glided and twirled, moving with a fluid grace that was unexpected for such rustic participants. Emelyn had never seen anyone in Fallow dance in such a manner, yet it looked as though they had rehearsed the performance for weeks.

The music escalated, and, on some unspoken cue, the dancers joined hands to form a circle. Around and around the people danced, laughing and singing like children on a summer's day. Then the music grew louder and the tempo increased. What had been a merry ring of dancing soon degenerated into a fervent and crazed dash. Beads of sweat dripped from foreheads while cheeks deepened their rosy hues. The singing stopped, leaving only the hysterical laughter of those who could spare the breath. Shirts darkened and grew heavy with sweat; hair flew loose in wild, dampened strands. On and on the music droned, ever promising an end that did not come.

A woman collapsed, her laughter crazed and shrill as her cheeks and neck blushed with fever. The masked partners on either side of the woman helped her to her feet and the dancing resumed as fervently as before. Soon others fell and they, too, were pulled to their feet and forced to continue. The music had grown so loud that Emelyn covered her ears, swallowing the bile that rose in her throat. She wanted to leave, but not without Tilly.

Powerless, Emelyn watched as her friend ran in the circle, listening as her hysterical laughter hung in the air. When Tilly fell from exhaustion, Emelyn's heart stopped. She stepped forward, wanting to help her. But within the blink of an eye, Tilly was pulled to her feet and the dancing resumed.

Emelyn's stomach lurched as the music drilled into her skull. She turned and pushed her way through the crowd, no longer caring about being rude. Once clear from the throng, she kept walking until she had left the tents and torches of the festival, and the music from the dance had faded. She bent over, resting her hands on her knees as she listened to the crickets chirp. Wind stirred the grass, cooling her face and calming her nerves.

Tilly . . . Emelyn felt helpless. She didn't know what was happening, didn't understand why no one else seemed to think anything was wrong. In the span of an hour, Emelyn's simple life in Fallow had tilted, sending all that she knew into a tangle of confusion and fear. There must be someone who could help. They couldn't all have lost their wits . . . could they?

Emelyn straightened and turned towards the town. Maybe Mr. Hibberly could help, or Mrs. Hibberly. If anyone could keep her senses, it would be Mrs. Hibberly. Emelyn knew it was unlikely they were in town, that they were probably at the festival with everyone else. But she couldn't bear to turn back. Hope that she could find someone to help her was all that kept Emelyn's feet moving.

She gave the festival tents a wide berth. The grass swished against her legs, the dew dampening her skirts. She thought of her fine dress, the one she had planned on wearing to the festival. It was just as well. Would have likely been ruined in this grass and mud. The thought was little comfort.

"Hello, darlin'," a voice said.

Emelyn started, snapped out of her reverie.

A man no larger than a child gazed up at her with bulbous eyes. His hooked nose hung over sneering lips while a tiny white spider crawled within a cavernous nostril. His clothes were mottled green and brown as though someone had woven together a sack of leaves and moss. Bright red berries hung from the hem of his garment as pearls might hang from a fine dress. On his feet he wore two hollowed gourds, the ends removed to allow his long toes—with even longer, yellowed nails—to dangle freely. He grinned at her, showing rows of darkened teeth that looked of rotten wood.

"Care for a dance?" He wheezed as he spoke, his breath dank and earthen like an old, forgotten cellar.

"No, thank you," Emelyn said as she tried to walk around him.

He grasped her arm with a cold, clammy hand. "Aww," he sneered. "You hurt my feelings." He showed his teeth again, accompanied by a rattling in his chest that Emelyn feared to be laughter. The outburst dislodged the spider from his nose, sending it scrambling along a gossamer thread.

Emelyn wrenched her arm but the man held her fast.

Cackling, he dragged her through the field, heading towards a circle of torches.

Emelyn dug her heels into the earth as she struggled. It was little use—the man was surprisingly strong and had only to yank her arm to pull her forward. As they drew closer to the circle, Emelyn saw Mrs. Gristman standing naked in the grass as squat men lathered her body with mud, pressing leaves and moss onto the sticky substance. Mr. Torvel, the alchemist, sat on the ground while several of the imps danced around him, adorning his pate with a crown of berries, leaves, and twigs.

There was even Patrice, a servant girl from a neighboring household, balancing on one leg while one of the men fitted her raised foot with a hollowed gourd. She looked tired, bored, as if struggling to tolerate the imp that scampered about her. There were others in the field—all sitting or standing, some with thinly veiled expressions of annoyance as if they had somewhere else to be. But there was no struggling, no attempts at escape. No one gave any indication of being held there against his will. Except for Emelyn.

She renewed her efforts, scratching at her captor's hand, but his skin was rough and leathery, and Emelyn's nails were trim and meager. Realizing she couldn't pull her arm free, Emelyn stopped resisting and walked close to the man. Holding her breath, she stomped as hard as she could on his exposed toes. She heard and felt the crack as the imp's long nails broke. The skin around his bulbous eyes tightened and his mouth twisted into a contemptuous grin. His grip on her arm tightened, his nails cutting into her skin. Emelyn cried out as her blood welled beneath his filthy fingers.

He showed his wood-like teeth. "Now there's a lovely song, that. Maybe we've got ourselves a pretty little songbird, after all." Another rattling, guttural laugh.

His revelry ended when a branch dashed against his head, sending him to the ground in a lifeless heap. Emelyn jerked her arm out of his slackened grasp and put a hand over her cut skin.

"Are you all right?" a young man asked, taking a step towards her. He held a long, knotted branch; stringy strands of the imp's dark hair clung to the bark.

Emelyn stared at him, not yet understanding what was happening. Behind him the imps gathered, pointing at their fallen companion. In a cacophony of grunts and yelps, they charged through the grass. Emelyn took a step back.

The stranger turned around and put himself in front of Emelyn, brandishing his club before him.

Most of the imps were unfazed by his display, though some slowed to let others charge ahead. As the squat men reached him, the stranger stepped forward, swinging the branch in wide arcs as though scything wheat. The branch met each imp with a dull, sickening sound that made Emelyn's stomach sink.

The display was an effective one. The imps who had yet to be culled ceased their advance, baring their teeth while hissing from a safe distance. The stranger hissed back, causing the attackers to fidget and glance about. One by one, they shuffled off, growling and sulking into the shadows.

The man watched them leave. Only when the last one had faded from sight did he lower his guard. He turned back to Emelyn.

"Are you all right?" he asked again.

Emelyn tensed, ready to run.

The man smiled, placing a hand on his chest. "My name is Corran." He glanced around at the bodies strewn about him and cleared his throat. "I know how this looks, but I assure you I'm quite harmless. Unless you are a squat and filthy little man that smells of dirt and attacks young women, that is." He tried to laugh but didn't quite succeed.

Emelyn said nothing.

Corran shuffled his feet.

"You're not from around here, are you?" she finally said.

Corran looked relieved. "Not exactly. I used to apprentice for Mr. Wainwright some years ago. I'm currently looking for work and knew the Harvest Festival would be going on around this time. I thought I'd stop by to see if there was any employment to be had."

Emelyn looked at him askance. "Mr. Wainwright hasn't had any apprentices for nearly twenty years. You would have still been in your swaddling clothes."

Corran frowned, a look of confusion plain on his face. Then he looked hurt. "I would have been much too old for swaddling clothes twenty years ago. I was quite well on my way to wearing big-boy shirts and breeches, thank you."

Emelyn scowled, not appreciating the joke. "Then how could you have been his apprentice?"

Corran ran a hand through his sandy brown hair and shrugged. "I don't know. Maybe I've come to the wrong town. I'm sure there's more than one carpentry master with the name 'Wainwright.' Stranger things have happened than a man traveling astray." He looked around. "Stranger things seem to be happening right now."

Emelyn also looked around—she had almost forgotten the squat men, the disturbing dance. "Do you know what's happening? Who . . . *they* are?" She pointed at one of the bodies in the grass.

Corran hesitated. "I only just arrived, so I can't say what might be happening. As for these fellows," he nodded at an imp, "well, they sort of have the look of a boggan."

"Boggan?"

"Foul little men that like to steal children, sometimes leaving a basket of leaves in its place. Quite fond of shiny things, though. Where I'm from, superstitious wives will leave a coin or silver spoon in the crib so that should a boggan arrive it will take that rather than the babe." He chuckled. "Silly. And yet . . ." He waved a hand at the bodies around him.

Emelyn stared at the man, wondering if he was having fun at her expense. She opened her mouth to ask another question when a man's startled cry interrupted her.

Corran's smile faded as he lifted the branch onto his shoulder and ran towards the sound.

Not wanting to be left alone, Emelyn followed. They ran through the darkened field and came upon an elderly bald man in a red robe wielding a staff. He wore a pair of round spectacles, and Emelyn recognized the Magister she had passed earlier on the road. He flailed his staff, struggling to fight off a group of imps that danced around him. They hissed and grunted, baring their teeth as they dodged the staff whenever it swung their way.

Emelyn glanced at Corran, thinking he would step in to help as he had for her. But the man lowered his branch and settled into watching the Magi with eyes that had turned hard and cold. Confused, Emelyn turned back to the Magister. He managed to crack an imp upside the head with his staff, causing the creature to skulk away as others took his place. Emelyn tensed, remembering how one of the little men had tried pulling her into the field against her will. She could not stand idly by and watch as these creatures tormented someone else.

Bending to the ground, she picked up a stone and threw it at an imp. Her aim was off and the stone soared into the darkness. She picked up another and threw it, and the stone thumped the back of a dark, shaggy head. The imp turned, startled over the impact. He bared his brown-stained teeth at her and hissed.

Emelyn stiffened, her heart pounding as she readied herself for the imp's attack. But before the creature could take a step, the grass beneath his feet glowed red and orange. Blades of grass licked at his toes like flames licking at kindling. Yet for all its similarity to fire, the grass did not seem to be burning.

The imp showed no signs of pain, only intense curiosity at the ground beneath his feet. The other creatures soon took notice. Forgetting the Magister, they all crouched to their hands and knees, pressing their long noses to the glowing grass.

Then one of the imps barked and jumped back. Then another. Soon they were all scrambling, yelping, and hopping as if bitten. Or burned. The grass flickered and twined like wildfire; maybe it also burned like fire. Whatever it was, the imps no longer wanted anything to do with it. Like a pack of wild animals they ran off, their yelps and grunts echoing into the night.

The Magister closed his eyes and exhaled.

Emelyn stared at the Magi, her mind tangled with a mixture of amazement and fear as she tried to understand what she had seen. Part of her wanted to turn and run, to hide until daybreak when, she hoped, everything would return to normal. Yet another part of her was strangely curious, and her desire to understand surpassed her fear.

Another Magister stepped from the shadows, his long, white braid almost luminescent in the moonlight. "A shameful display, Aldren, especially for one of your standing. I half expected the vile beasts to carry you off before you finally acted."

"I was caught unaware. There were so many of them. And the smell . . ."

The white-haired Magister smiled, his gaze flicking to Emelyn and Corran. "And what have we here? A pair of lovers out for an evening stroll?"

Emelyn stiffened when the Magister's gaze fell upon her. From Corran's sharp intake of breath, she suspected he felt the same.

"I must say, you displayed a fair amount of courage for so young a lady," the Magister said.

Emelyn grasped for words as everything she knew flew out of her head. "I . . . it was nothing. I only threw some stones."

The Magi smiled. "You give yourself too little credit. After all, you took action while others stood feebly by." His gaze shifted to Corran.

Corran bristled. "Magi can take care of themselves."

The Magister's mouth flicked into a smile, though there was no warmth in his eyes. "Quite right."

The other Magister, the one called Aldren, watched the exchange. With wide eyes, his gaze darted from Corran, to Emelyn, to Corran again, his face looking much paler than it had a few minutes ago. He looked as wary of them as she was of the Magisters.

"But forgive us," the older Magister continued. "We have not been properly introduced." He turned and extended a hand towards his companion. "Allow me to introduce my friend and assistant, Aldren Keller, High Magister of the Twelfth Tower. I am Percival Lacreld, also a Magister of the Twelfth Tower, one who has been fortunate enough to serve in the grandest of capacities." He lowered his head and tilted at the waist.

"You're the Grand Magister," Corran said, his voice flat.

Percival lowered his head once more.

Emelyn watched the exchange, unsure of what it meant. She had heard of Magisters, even seen a few. Beyond that she knew little else. "My name is Emelyn." She gave a short curtsey, more from habit than any conscious effort to remember her manners. "Do . . . do you know what is happening tonight, lord Magister?"

Percival regarded her as though weighing whether or not he should answer. "Yes."

They watched each other in silence. Emelyn wanted to ask him to continue, for him to tell her all that he knew, but she could hear Miss Cook's scolding voice in her head, telling her to mind her own affairs.

Percival smiled. "Come." He turned and walked away. Aldren followed.

Emelyn hesitated, unsure if he had been speaking to her. She glanced at Corran. The man had relaxed at the Magisters' departure and looked to have no intention of following them. If the Magisters knew what was happening, maybe they could help. Taking a deep breath, she gathered up her skirts and ran after them.

They came to the forest's edge, little more than a wall of shadow in the moonlit night. To Emelyn's relief, the Magi stopped and sat down in the grass. Emelyn looked back at the festival, to the firelight flickering in the darkened field. Everything was so quiet, so calm. She could almost convince herself that nothing had happened, that everything was as it should be. With a heavy heart, she sat down opposite the Magisters.

Aldren put out a hand, a small stone resting in his palm. He spoke an unknown word and the stone glowed with a gentle light.

Emelyn gasped. "How did you do that?"

Aldren smiled and shrugged, looking a little embarrassed. "We Magisters are trained in such matters." He set the stone on the ground, the surrounding grass causing the light to throw wild and erratic shadows.

"Is it magic?"

"Some would call it that."

"What would you call it?"

Aldren remained silent as he gazed at the glowing stone, leaving the wind rustling in the trees to answer.

Emelyn watched the Magisters, looking from Aldren to Percival and back to Aldren again. The light shining from the stone on the ground illuminated the Magi's faces in an unsettling manner, giving them a gaunt and sinister appearance. Emelyn fiddled with her hands, wondering if anyone was going to speak or if they were to simply sit there in the damp grass, staring at each other in the eerie light.

Twigs snapped and Emelyn turned to find Corran walking towards them. He sat down next to her, glaring at Percival from across the glowing stone. "If you know what's happening, then tell us and let us be done with it."

The Grand Magister looked at him, his face void of expression. "A creature of magic, I fear." He spoke airily, as though discussing the weather.

Emelyn stared at him. Creatures of magic existed solely in the bedtime stories of children, usually as cautionary tales to discourage unwanted behavior. She should have laughed at the notion, waggling her finger at a man who should know better than to spread such nonsense. It's what Miss Cook would have done. But instead of shock or fear or a number of other feelings Emelyn thought she should have felt, she only felt that strange sense of curiosity. It was like the Magister's words confirmed that which she already knew in her heart to be true, but could never bring herself to acknowledge.

Corran folded his arms, unmoved. "What do you mean 'creature of magic?' We have seen a good many creatures this evening. Which one do you mean?"

"None of the ones which you have seen," Percival said. "This creature is a great distance hence, far to the north. These other . . . *things*," he waggled his fingers towards the distant festival, "are simply here by her will."

Corran raised his eyebrows. "*Her* will? It is a female creature?"

The Magister studied Corran with narrowed eyes before replying in a hushed voice, "Indeed."

Emelyn glanced at the men sitting around the light. "I don't understand. Why is this happening? Why is this creature tormenting us? How is it even possible?"

Percival smiled, though his eyes tensed. "It would be impossible to explain all the details. It would be beyond your understanding and we simply do not have the time. I cannot say why it is happening, only that it needs to be stopped. That is a task entrusted to Aldren and me."

Emelyn licked her lips. "My friend, Tilly . . . she was with them . . . the creatures. She . . . wasn't herself." Emelyn swallowed the lump rising in her throat. "I need to find her."

The strain in Percival's eyes softened, his voice gentle. "You cannot help her, child."

"I . . . I need to. I can't leave her."

"You must understand—she has fallen under the creature's spell, as have all of Fallow. You alone seem to be unaffected, aside from my brethren and myself. There is nothing you can do for her."

Emelyn frowned. "Corran isn't affected, there must be others."

Percival's mouth tightened. "Our fellow Magisters have been charged with seeing to the town's safety. I am sure your friend will be quite all right, as will the others. Aldren and I, however, must see to stopping the creature from causing more harm, and we have no time for delay."

Emelyn looked back at the festival glowing in the distance. She wanted to go home, but not while those creatures still roamed around. Nor did she trust that all really would be well, despite the Magister's assurances. "What am I supposed to do? My home is there . . . I have nowhere else . . ."

"You will come with us."

Aldren shot a sharp glance at the Grand Magister.

Corran bristled. "I think not," he said, rising to his feet.

The Magisters also rose, as did Emelyn.

Corran turned to Emelyn. "You have your answers. Now let us leave this place."

"I don't understand," she said. "Where would we go? I don't even know you!"

Corran took a deep breath. "I know you don't know me," he said, his voice tight with strained patience. "But you don't know them, either. I know their kind, and I know they cannot be trusted!"

Emelyn stood dumbstruck, unsure of what she should say or do. Corran was right—she didn't know the Magisters any more than she knew him. She had no desire to go off with anyone; she just wanted everything to return to normal.

"I know who you are, Emelyn." Percival's voice rang clear in the still night. "I know where you come from. I know your parents. You must have wondered about these things. A young woman with no prospects other than a life of servitude, you must have wondered if this is the life you are meant to live, a life in darkness. I can help you find answers about yourself."

Emelyn's heart thundered in her ears; she was surprised she could hear anything at all. All her life she had wondered about her parents—who they were, why they had left her. She had grown up shadowed by these questions, never finding any answers, only a sense of incompleteness, of not belonging. Now this man dangled the promise of answers before her like fish before a stray cat.

"Why would you do that?" she asked, her voice barely above a whisper. "Why would you help me?"

Percival smiled. "Let us just say that I see potential in you—potential that is wasted in a life of menial service.

Whether or not you wish to realize it is up to you, as is your choice to come with us." He glanced at Corran. "Can he offer you the same?"

Emelyn blinked at Corran. What potential could she possibly have? She was a servant, her existence revolved around fetching water and scrubbing floors. Her talents were few and the idea that her life could be something more was a desire reserved solely for her dreams.

"Make your decision quickly," Percival said as he picked up the glowing stone and handed it to Aldren. "We must leave immediately. This field is no place to linger." With that, he and Aldren turned and headed into the darkened forest.

Emelyn felt a stab of panic as the Magisters disappeared into the shadows, realizing from the quickening of her heart that she had already made her choice. Without looking back, she picked up her skirts and ran into the forest after them.

CHAPTER 3

EMELYN TRUDGED THROUGH the woods, putting one numb foot in front of the next. They had walked through the entire night, the sky now lightening with the first rays of dawn. She yawned. For the first hours of their journey, Emelyn had tried to study their surroundings, trying to understand where they were headed while keeping an eye out for noticeable landmarks should she need to pass that way again. But it had been wasted effort—the forest was too dark and her own sense of direction too poor. Now she no longer cared, she only wanted to change out of her filthy clothing and lie down to sleep.

Yet as tired as she was, she still couldn't help but wonder at the trees around her. She had never ventured into the woods around Fallow and she remembered the stories of the forest people she had heard about as a child. Was this where they had lived?

The disappearance of the forest people was a mystery for which numerous rumors abounded. Some declared that their unnatural way of life out in the woods had led to their demise, either from sickness and disease or by being devoured by some vicious beast, depending on who was doing the telling. Others claimed that they had brought about their own downfall through warring amongst themselves, which many assured had happened, for the forest people were said to be uncivilized in nature. Some whispered a different story altogether, saying that the Magisters had gathered the forest people up and taken them into their Tower, where they were never seen or heard from again. It was these stories, told in hushed voices behind closed doors, that made Emelyn feel cold.

Now she was following a pair of Magisters—men that were rumored to steal livestock and curse fields if a man looked at them crosswise. She watched them as they walked in front of her. Small globes of light hung from their belts on leather thongs, bobbing like a pair of leashed fireflies. Was it true they knew of her parents? Or had she been foolish in her haste and was now following them towards some terrible fate? Emelyn hadn't ever really thought the rumors about the Magi to be true. But now, trailing after them through the darkened forest, she no longer felt so sure.

Behind her, Corran's heavy footfalls crashed through the brush. Emelyn had been glad when Corran followed her into the forest. She didn't know why—the man was as much a stranger to her as the Magisters. Maybe it was because he had defended her from the imps. Maybe she was simply grateful for his relaxed nature. Even with his open dislike of the Magi, Corran had a carefree way about him that was a refreshing contrast to their stiff formality. It helped Emelyn feel more at ease.

The Magisters stopped walking and Emelyn leaned against a tree while they talked in hushed tones. She had made the mistake earlier of joining the Magisters when they stopped to confer—an activity they had done repeatedly throughout the night. A withering glare from Percival, however, had made it clear that such meetings were private.

Corran stopped alongside her and gave a wan smile. He looked as tired as she felt.

"How far do you think we've walked?" Emelyn said.

Corran shrugged. "Hard to say. Maybe seven, eight leagues." He put his hand on the tree. "We've been heading south, though. You can tell by the trees. The moss tends to grow thickest on the northern side."

Emelyn studied the tree, running her hand over the thick, green moss that coated the bark like a verdant beard.

"If I'm not mistaken," Corran continued, "there should be an inn nearby, on the main road that leads to Sunbridge. I'd wager we're headed there. We're going to need supplies for the journey and, if Fallow is no longer an option, then the inn would be our best course."

They continued for about half a league before coming to a clearing in the forest. Tall, golden grass waved in the wind, cloven by a long, flat road that stretched from one end of the clearing to the other. A grey stone building sat alongside the road, recently thatched with pale straw. A thin trail of smoke twined from one of the chimneys, and Emelyn's heart soared at the sight of it.

Aldren turned to Emelyn and Corran. "The two of you go to the inn and see if you can find some provisions for our journey. The Grand Magister and I have business to attend to, so you may want to arrange for sleeping quarters until our return."

Emelyn fidgeted with the skirt of her dress. "I haven't any money."

"Do not concern yourself with such matters. The Grand Magister and I will see to it." Aldren eyed Emelyn's filthy dress. "You may also want to inquire if they might have any proper traveling attire."

Emelyn looked down at her clothes as her cheeks grew hot. She felt ashamed that this dingy dress had been the cleaner of her two work dresses, and that she needed to depend upon the Magisters' charity.

Aldren and Percival turned back towards the forest. Emelyn watched as they left, wondering what business they could possibly have among the trees. Corran, however, did not seem to share her concern. He walked into the grassy field and made his way toward the inn. Emelyn hurried after him.

Golden light from the rising sun gleamed through the tops of the surrounding trees. As she walked, Emelyn ran her hands over the waist-high grass, allowing dewdrops to moisten her fingers. Reaching the inn, they found a wooden sign swinging overhead that depicted a black bird with a bright red breast, declaring the inn as "The Meadowlark." Corran opened the door and they stepped inside.

The room was dark; the shutters covering the windows had not yet been opened. Once Emelyn's eyes had adjusted, she saw a spacious common room interspersed with empty tables and chairs.

At one end of the room a hearth stood dark and cold. The other end held a counter, behind which several large wooden casks had been stacked next to a door. The air, though a bit stale, smelled of ale and roasted meat. Emelyn's stomach grumbled.

The door next to the kegs opened and in walked a portly woman holding a broom, her grey hair swept into a bun atop her head. She stopped when she saw Emelyn and Corran and smiled.

"Yes?"

When Emelyn hesitated, Corran spoke. "Good morning, my lady. We are a pair of travelers, in need of a hot meal and warm beds while we wait for our companions to join us."

"You've come to the right place, then," the woman said as she bustled around, opening the shutters. Once finished, she walked up to Emelyn and Corran and looked them up and down. Her gaze lingered on Emelyn. "I can wash that dress for you, if you'd like, while you wait for your friends."

Emelyn felt like crawling into a hole and hiding. Her first trip out of Fallow and here she was, penniless and filthy for all the world to see.

"Uh . . . yes," Corran said. "We were hoping you might have a spare set clothes that my friend here could use. Something more suitable for traveling on foot. We'll also need some food and supplies for our journey, if you have anything to spare."

"Not to worry, business has been sparse lately, so there's food aplenty. I might even have a spare set of clothes that will do for our young lass, here. But we'll see to that later. First you sit down and I'll fetch you something to eat." The woman set her broom aside and disappeared through the door from which she had come.

Emelyn walked to a table near the hearth. She looked at the darkened fireplace and at the pile of wood in a nearby box. The innkeeper would undoubtedly get the fire going as soon as she fetched their food, but Emelyn didn't like the idea of waiting for someone else to do it while she sat and did nothing.

She stocked the hearth with wood and kindling, just as she did every morning at home, and lit it with the tinder-box sitting on the mantle. She tended the flames and, once the fire was burning, lingered in the warmth as the cold and stiffness melted from her bones.

"Well, aren't you handy?" the innkeeper said when she returned with a tray of food. The lines around her eyes deepened as she beamed at Emelyn. She set the tray on the table in front of Corran, then turned to Emelyn and patted her on the hand. Returning to the counter, she retrieved the broom and started sweeping the floor.

On the tray were two bowls of hot stew, a loaf of bread, a pitcher of steaming, spiced cider and two wooden tankards. Emelyn sat and breathed in the aroma—earthen and sweet and peppered with herbs. Her mouth watered. She picked up the loaf of bread, still warm from the oven, pulled off a chunk and used it as a spoon to dish up the stew to her mouth. A thick, beefy broth with dark mushrooms and pale turnips, it tasted as good as it smelled.

They ate in silence, leaving the popping of the fire and the swishing of the innkeeper's broom to serve as conversation. Upon finishing her stew, Emelyn pushed her empty bowl aside and poured cider into the tankards for herself and Corran. She sipped the sweet and spicy beverage as she eyed her companion, who slouched in his chair as he rubbed his eyes.

"What do you think they're doing?" Emelyn said. "The Magisters, I mean. What business could they have out there in the woods?"

Corran blinked at her with red-rimmed eyes before shaking his head. "I don't know. I don't care. If we're fortunate, they won't return." He drank some cider.

"Why do you dislike Magisters so much?"

He stared into his cup. "My reasons are my own."

Emelyn frowned. "And yet you expect others to mistrust them for reasons you won't share."

Corran looked at her, his eyes stern. "I expect nothing, only hope to spare others from falling victim to them, as I have." He emptied his tankard before standing and walking outside.

Emelyn watched him go, his departure leaving her with more unanswered questions than she had before. After a while, the innkeeper returned and offered to show Emelyn to a room. Emelyn nodded and thanked the woman as she followed her up the stairs.

The upper floor was little more than a loft with a narrow landing and low roof that caused Emelyn to instinctively duck even though the beams weren't low enough to pose any real threat to her head. A round window on one wall let in a stream of light, though the landing still felt close and dim. The innkeeper walked to a door, swung it open and motioned for Emelyn to step inside.

The room was narrow and sparsely furnished, but it was clean. A bed was pushed into one corner, covered with a patchwork quilt that looked thick and warm. In the opposite corner stood a table bearing a clay pitcher and bowl for washing. A square-paned window adorned the outer wall, overlooking the golden grass of the meadow that stretched to the surrounding forest.

"I'll fetch some water so you can wash up, and bring a change of clothes you can wear while I wash that dress of yours." The innkeeper turned and walked from the room.

Emelyn continued to look out the window as she wrung her hands. It was strange for her to be waited on—it was usually she who did the fetching. Emelyn thought of Fallow, of what she would be doing right now were she still at home. Master and Mistress Mansell would likely be breakfasting, perhaps even have finished. She would then sweep out the room before moving outside to sweep the steps. Miss Cook would be preparing lunch and Emelyn would secretly guess what she was cooking, judging by the smell. Miss Cook had been preparing chicken last night . . . Then Emelyn remembered that Miss Cook had never made supper last night; she had gallivanted off with the strange fiddler, along with everyone else in the house. Tilly would not be airing out the beds this morning like she usually did; all of Fallow might very well be changed. The Grand Magister had told her that other Magi would be looking after the town, that everything would be all right, but Emelyn had difficulty believing it in her heart.

The innkeeper returned, carrying a bucket of steaming water, a clean towel, and a neat pile of folded clothes. She set the towel and clothes on the bed before walking to the table and pouring the water into the washbasin. She turned to Emelyn and brushed away a stray lock of hair that had loosened from her bun.

"I found some clothes that I think will suit you. One is a nightdress, should you wish to sleep. The others are an old pair of breeches and a shirt that used to belong to my son. He's long since grown from them, and I've not had any use for them until now. You're welcome to them, if you'd like." She smiled, showing rows of crooked teeth that, on her, were charming.

Even with her heavy heart, Emelyn found herself smiling back at the woman. "Thank you, Mistress . . ."

"Call me Beryl, it's my name, after all."

"Thank you . . . Beryl," she murmured, feeling awkward over using her first name. "Emelyn." She gave a short curtsey.

Beryl smiled again. "You get some rest, now; you look as though you've had a long night. Hang your dress outside the door and I'll wash it while you sleep." With a firm nod of her head that showed she would brook no nonsense, Beryl walked from the room, closing the door behind her.

Emelyn remained by the window, staring at the empty room. She had grown up trying to imagine the world outside of Fallow, playing out stories in her mind of what it would be like to leave, to go on a grand adventure. She used to think about running away deep into the forest to live there in secret. She had always been enamored by stories of the forest people, and sometimes she imagined finding them and they would take her in and teach her in the ways of fishing and hunting. Sometimes she imagined finding her parents, who would have been searching for her all these years and when they found her they would hold her tight and kiss her forehead, just as she had seen other parents do.

Emelyn closed her eyes. Before, she had always enjoyed these brief moments of quiet solitude. The times when she would lie on her pallet, alone in the darkness, and send her mind to explore the different possibilities, dreaming of what could be before drifting off to sleep. Yet now that she found herself in the midst of one of those possibilities, the only thing she felt was fear and loneliness. She opened her eyes and looked out the window, wondering in which direction Fallow lay.

Emelyn turned away and changed out of her dirty clothes and into the clean nightgown Beryl had left for her. She didn't bother to wash up first, nor did she hang her dress outside for Beryl to clean. Instead, she crawled under the quilt on the bed, finding comfort in its heaviness and warmth. She stared at the stones in the wall, running her fingers over the rough masonry. This time there were no dreams of things to come, no imaginings of grand adventures. There was only the stinging of tears in her eyes as sleep slowly came to take her.

CHAPTER 4

ALDREN FOLLOWED PERCIVAL as they wound their way through
the forest. He kept his eyes to the ground, taking care to
not trip or snag his robe on a stray branch. Magister robes
were made of the finest fabrics, adorned with labyrinthine
runes of gold. They were not tailored to accommodate the
adventurous Magi, as Aldren had come to know firsthand.
He had spent much time in the mud and bracken of forest
and field and had, on more than one occasion, damaged a
robe beyond repair. Given that he had no hope of obtain-
ing a new robe while away from the Tower, he took care
not to ruin the one he had.

On occasion, Percival would stop and tilt his head to
the side as if listening to the wind. Whispering a rune,
he would wait and listen before continuing, adjusting
his course accordingly. Aldren knew for what the Grand
Magister searched; he only hoped they would soon find
it. The previous night had been long and Aldren was not
accustomed to forgoing sleep.

The morning waned, and, as the sun rose in the sky,
the crispness in the air lessened. Even within the shadows
of the forest, the air was noticeably warmer, reminiscent of
a summer now past. When the morning had grown into
afternoon, they stopped to rest. Percival settled himself on
a large mossy stone while Aldren perched on the trunk

of a fallen tree. The Grand Magister closed his eyes and turned his face towards the sky to bask in the mottled sunlight. Aldren polished his spectacles with a sleeve of his robe as he waited until his master was ready to resume.

Time crept by in heavy silence and Aldren, although a patient man, began to grow weary. While reluctant to disturb the Grand Magister in his contemplation, he was anxious to know their course of action.

"Are we any closer, my lord?"

Percival opened his eyes and looked him. "Yes," he said and closed his eyes again. Yet his concentration must have been disturbed for, a short while later, he opened his eyes, exhaling a long and weary sigh.

"We are closer," he said, as though their conversation had not been interrupted by several minutes of silence. "Yet I can no longer sense in which direction we must travel. She seems to be everywhere and nowhere, all at once. I fear we must wait here until our course becomes apparent."

Aldren nodded and rose from the trunk of the tree. "The day grows long and we have not yet eaten. I will see what food I can find."

Percival waved Aldren away as he closed his eyes, undoubtedly to resume his contemplation.

The wind rustled in the treetops as Aldren tramped through the underbrush. Autumn was a particularly abundant time of year where the forest provided for the hungry traveler—given that one knew where to look, which Aldren did. Although his propensity for reading books was not an uncommon trait among Magisters, Aldren's passion for the natural world exceeded those of his robed brethren. He would spend hours in the great library within the Tower, reading dusty tomes of the land's flora and fauna by flickering candlelight. With the light of day he would venture outside to examine leaves, twigs, and beetles, investigating the various phenomena he had read about, all the while scrawling notes of his own with pencil and paper.

For years he had carried on in this manner before accumulating his vast knowledge into a tome of his own: *On Herbage and Animalia: A Treatise on the Natural World of the North Reaches, by Magister Aldren Keller.* It was his life's work, of which he was immensely proud. It was the first book of its kind to have been written in the past two hundred years. Such naturalist texts had fallen out of fashion in the Towers in favor for glossaries of runes and discourses on the various ways in which they could be inscribed. The Grand Magister himself had lauded his work as "compelling," "comprehensive," and "essential." Aldren had, on numerous occasions, attributed his advancement within the Tower to the success of his work. For, even though he was a capable Magister, he had always felt his ability to wield the Art lacked in comparison to many of his colleagues.

Aldren took a knife from his belt and carefully trimmed off a shelf of brown fungus from the trunk of a tree. The passage he had written in his treatise came to mind. *Pullus Calvae, commonly known as hencap, a name attributed to the dark brown, feather-like pattern found on the cap of the mushroom.* In addition to providing information on the various flora and fauna of the North Reaches, he had also taken care to provide practical, often culinary examples of the ways in which each item could be used. *If eaten raw, the mushroom has a gelatinous texture that is unpleasing upon the palate. It is advised, therefore, for the conscientious cook to heat the mushroom thoroughly, whereupon the flesh firms considerably and adopts a most pleasing, nutty flavor. Thusly cooked, the hencap pairs well with butter or cream, generously applied.* There would be no butter today, of course, but the mushroom would still be delicious as well as provide essential sustenance. He placed the mushroom in the pouch on his belt.

Aldren continued to forage. He found some fire berries, named for their brilliant red color. They were extraordinarily sour and not particularly pleasant, but edible all the same. When he stumbled upon a patch of wooly nettle, Aldren grinned. *Urtica Lanata, commonly known as wooly nettle. Deemed as little more than a troublesome weed amongst the industrious countryside dwellers, this prolific plant thrives in various locales. Care must be taken to pluck only the new and tender leaves that sprout in the spring and autumn, as the older leaves develop a thick, almost fur-like covering that renders the plant inedible. Such leaves, however, are still valuable for medicinal poultices.* Aldren was quite fond of the young and tender nettle leaves, and he mourned the lack of proper cooking equipment and seasonings that would allow him to prepare a delectable, if humble, meal from his foraged goods.

With his belt pouch filled, Aldren turned back. He had only taken a few steps when the shrill laughter of a little girl pierced the calm of the forest. Aldren's stomach sank. He knew why they were there, knew what they were searching for. But somehow it still surprised him, dashing his secret hope that they would find nothing. He turned in the direction of the sound—northwards, not far from where he stood. Adjusting his spectacles, Aldren crept towards the laughter.

He walked for a short time before coming to a hollow. He ducked behind a nearby tree, allowing him to look down into the hollow unobserved. There was little girl with long, dark hair. She wore a dress of rough brown leather though her feet were bare. With her was a little boy, his sandy hair a tousled mess. He wore a plain shirt and trousers, and black, sturdy boots—common attire among boys of the working classes. Together they ran, chasing each other in some kind of game. Their laughter was wild and exuberant—the way that only children can laugh.

Aldren frowned, wishing he didn't feel the weight of sadness spreading through his heart.

Percival walked up beside him and he, too, watched the children play. His face was still, void of expression. Together the Magisters watched in silence as the children frolicked in the hollow, their peals of laughter echoing off the surrounding trees. Several minutes passed in this fashion until the girl, with a loud squeal, darted up and out of the hollow, disappearing into the forest beyond. The boy gave chase and soon all that remained were the fading echoes of their laughter.

The Magisters lingered, looking down in the hollow as though the children were still there. Aldren broke the silence. "Do you think the young man knows?"

Percival was quiet a moment before answering. "No. But he will, soon enough."

"What should we do?"

"We wait. And see."

Aldren opened his mouth to ask another question, but the Grand Magister interrupted him.

"The day grows long, Aldren, as you said. Let us rest here for the night and we will meet with our companions on the morrow."

Aldren closed his mouth and nodded. With one last glance towards the hollow, he began to prepare their camp for the night.

CHAPTER 5

IT WAS DARK WHEN Emelyn awoke in her bed at the inn. Accustomed to waking in darkness, she felt at home. Emelyn sat up and swung her feet over the edge of the bed, preparing to perform the morning ritual that she had done countless times before. Yet when her feet dangled in the air rather than meeting a cold earthen floor, the burden of reality came back to her. She lingered on the bed, replaying in her mind all the events that had led her here, trying to reacquaint herself with this strange new life. She didn't know what to make of it. The Grand Magister said he knew her parents, but he had gone and she was left here. What was she to do while she waited? What was she to do when he arrived? She thought about crawling back in bed, of drifting off to sleep so that she might, once again, forget all that had happened. But years of toil had run deep into Emelyn's bones, refusing her the luxury of lounging in bed.

She put her feet on the floor and fumbled in the darkness for the clothes that Beryl had left for her. Once she located them, Emelyn hesitated. Never before had she worn a shirt and breeches. She found them confounding and floundered for some time before managing to put them on.

Having at last succeeded, she pulled on her boots and groped around on the floor until she found her work dress. She felt the coarse fabric and dried patches of mud that crumbled to the floor at her touch. Part of her wondered if the dress was worth salvaging. Would she even return to Fallow? If she did, she knew it wouldn't matter that she had ruined one of her work dresses. An extended absence on her part would likely leave her out of work, and it wouldn't matter in the least whether or not she had misplaced a dress. Regardless, it wouldn't do to leave it in a filthy heap on the floor.

Emelyn rose and opened the door. Light streamed in from a lamp in the hallway, accompanied by a strain of music. She hesitated. The last time she heard music it had been followed by a nightmare of an evening, landing her here, afraid and alone. She took a deep breath. She was at an inn, it was probably only a visitor whiling away the time with a bit of music. Emelyn hung her dress on the edge of the door and crept down the stairs.

Firelight flickered on the common room floor. The tables and chairs were empty but for one near the hearth. Corran sat there, holding a flute to his lips. A floorboard creaked under her foot. He stopped playing and turned to look at her.

"I didn't know you played," she said.

Corran looked at the flute in his hands. "Something I picked up long ago." He set the flute on the table. "I learned as a boy how to make them. Seemed only fitting I learn how to play one, so I taught myself."

"You play nicely."

Corran smiled though sadness shadowed his eyes.

The fire snapped as Emelyn walked to a nearby table and sat.

Corran was silent a long while as he studied his hands. "I had a wife, you know. A daughter." He hesitated. "Magisters . . . took them from me."

Emelyn frowned. "Took them?"

He nodded.

"Why would they do that?"

Corran shook his head. "Iyen, my wife, was . . . gifted. The Magi developed an interest in her and so they took her. Took them both."

Emelyn's eyebrows shot up. "Can they do that?"

Corran looked up from his hands and stared at her, his eyes sharp. "Magi do as they please, with little regard to anyone else. You would do well to remember that."

"What happened to them?"

He lowered his gaze to the floor. "Dead."

Despite the warm fire, Emelyn shivered. "Did the Magi . . . ?" She couldn't bring herself to finish the words.

Corran shrugged. "Don't know. Maybe it was highwaymen while they were traveling. Maybe she tried to run and they killed her for it. It doesn't matter, they were taken and then they were dead. The Magi are to blame, no matter how it happened."

Silence settled around them. Emelyn wished she knew what to say.

After a while, Corran spoke again. "I'm sorry if I was gruff before. I sometimes forget that not everyone knows about the Magi, of what they are capable."

Emelyn floundered. Here was a man who had just told her of losing his family and was now *apologizing* to her. "It's all right," she said, not knowing what else to say. "I'm sorry about your family."

Corran nodded. "You remind me of her, in a way. Your eyes . . . they look just as hers did on cloudy days." He picked up the flute. "We knew each other as children. As a boy, I used to play the flute for her, to cheer her up whenever she was sad. No matter how upset she was, she would always smile and laugh whenever I played."

Corran smiled, his eyes distant with the memory. "As I grew older, I thought my childhood fancy of playing the flute foolish. But I could never give it up, simply because it would still bring a smile to her face. Now . . . now I play to remember her." He tucked the flute away into a pocket.

Beryl bustled through the door behind the counter and stopped when she saw Emelyn. "Ah, you're awake. And wearing the clothes, I see. Good. Good. Are you hungry? I can fetch you supper if you'd like to eat."

Emelyn glanced at Corran, who was smiling at the jovial innkeeper. "Supper would be nice," she said, rising to her feet. "I can help you fix it up, if you'd like." She didn't want to be waited on.

Beryl scoffed, waving her hands. "Nonsense! I'm the innkeeper, that's what innkeepers do. You sit down and I'll fetch it, quick as can be. Go on, sit!"

Emelyn sat back down.

Beryl smiled. "There's a good lass." She turned and disappeared behind the door.

"So," Corran said, "how does it feel to be liberated from the confines of skirts and petticoats?"

Emelyn swung her legs. "It feels strange, truth be told. Like someone has swaddled my legs with coarse fabric." She paused to consider. "A lot less drafty, though."

Corran grinned.

Beryl returned, carrying a tray laden with a plate of cheese, salted beef, a loaf of bread, two apples, and two mugs of beer.

She set it down in front of Emelyn and turned to Corran. "Now there's enough for the both of you, should you have a mind to eat. The kitchen fire's gone out, so I'm afraid it's a cold supper tonight." She beamed at Emelyn and patted her on the cheek before leaving the room.

Corran walked over and sat opposite Emelyn.

Emelyn picked up an apple and bit into it, the juice sweet and tart. Corran piled meat and cheese onto a chunk of bread.

"So how did you know what those things were back in Fallow?" Emelyn said. She finished her apple and munched on salted beef. "Boggans, I think you called them."

Corran stopped chewing a moment and then shrugged. "I didn't know. I still don't. I only said they had the look of a boggan. As far as I know, boggans don't exist outside of superstition and fancy."

Emelyn frowned. "So, then, you don't think they were boggans?"

He smiled. "What I'm saying is, while I don't know for certain if they were boggans, I'm not discounting the possibility that they could have been." He took a bite from his sandwich.

Emelyn frowned harder still. "But you just said they are things out of stories and superstition."

"And who's to say the stories don't hold some truth?"

Emelyn's mouth hung open; she was at a loss how to answer.

Corran put down his sandwich and wiped his hands on his trousers. "You must understand, where I'm from, stories about things like boggans are rampant. We cling to the old ways, and with that comes a healthy dose of superstition."

"What do you mean 'old ways'?"

"I mean the ways in which people lived before the Magi came."

Emelyn stared at him. As far as she knew, the Magisters had always existed.

Seeing her confusion, Corran continued. "The Magi are not from around here originally. They came from the south, over the Randen Sound and settled in Sunbridge. Over time, they've continued to travel northwards, building their Towers wherever they go. Fallow is one of those places. Tirenfor, near the Myrwind Sea, is not. That's where I'm from. I don't know how many Towers the Magi have built, but I do know they have not come near enough to Tirenfor for their ideas of 'rational illumination,' or whatever they like to call it, to take hold.

"Our ways are the ways people lived prior to Magisters, and we continue in them through the telling of stories. Some of these stories speak of things like history, keeping events long past in living memory. It's how we remember that there was a time before the Magi. Other stories speak of other things, like boggans. As silly as some of these stories might sound, there isn't a person in Tirenfor that doesn't believe that these stories have, however small, a grain of truth. That, even if they aren't true now, they used to be, once upon a time."

Emelyn looked down at her food, feeling very small and very ignorant. There was an entire world outside of Fallow, people with different beliefs, a different way of life. She was suddenly aware of how little she knew, of how little her world extended beyond the Mansells' doorstep. It saddened her.

They finished the rest of their meal in silence and then Corran, declaring fatigue, went upstairs to his room. Emelyn wasn't tired. She had slept through the entire day, leaving her awake and alert despite the late hour. What was she supposed to do?

She eyed the door behind the counter, the one Beryl always walked through. Maybe she would see if she needed any help. Emelyn walked over to the door and nudged it open.

She entered a darkened hallway, lit by the flickering of firelight from a room at the far end. Emelyn wandered through the darkness and stopped when she came to the patch of light spilling onto the hallway floor. She peeked around the corner.

The room was snug and windowless. Beryl sat at a lone table, sewing by lamplight. She looked up as Emelyn peeked in, a smile blooming across her face when their eyes met. She waved her in.

"Come in, child. Come in. You enjoyed your supper, I hope?"

Emelyn stepped inside, placing her hands behind her back—an old habit she had developed while speaking with Miss Cook. "Yes, ma'am."

"Beryl."

"Yes . . . Beryl." Emelyn wondered if she would ever grow accustomed to addressing the woman by her given name.

Beryl studied Emelyn's face and chuckled. "It makes you uncomfortable, saying my name."

Emelyn nodded, unsure if Beryl was asking a question or making a statement.

"I understand, child. I know well the rules of propriety that townsfolk insist on upholding. But we are on our own out here and in my inn, I make my own rules." She smiled as she gauged Emelyn with narrowed eyes.

"Let me guess. You come from a nearby town, maybe Fallow or Timmerfell, where you work as a housemaid, perhaps? Or maybe as a serving girl?"

Emelyn nodded. "A housemaid."

"I thought as much. A young woman like you, very proper and polite, could only be a girl in service. And, if I'm not mistaken, this is your first time away from town."

Emelyn shifted her feet, uncomfortable that Beryl seemed to know everything about her.

"Not to worry, child. We get people like you passing through here from time to time, eyes wide and jumping at their own shadows." She laughed. "I daresay I used to be like you, having grown up in service myself. It wasn't until I married and we built this inn that I was finally able to . . . well . . . be *me*."

Her smile deepened, as did the creases around her eyes. "But enough about this old woman. What can I do for you this evening?"

"I . . . was wondering if you had any work that needed doing. You've been so kind, it's the only means I have of repaying you."

Beryl set down her sewing—an old brown coat—and looked at Emelyn. "All right," she said, rising from her chair. "You know how to sew?"

Emelyn nodded.

"Well, then. Take my seat if you'd like and continue on mending that coat there. It's fairly old and has more than a few tears and missing buttons, but it will be fine enough when patched up."

Emelyn nodded again as she sat in Beryl's chair and took up her sewing.

"I'll fetch another chair and more clothes to be mended." Beryl walked to the door and stopped at the threshold. She turned around. "You know how to salt fish?"

Emelyn nodded. "Yes, ma'am . . . Beryl."

Beryl eyes sparkled as she smiled. "My husband and son are away fishing at the river and are expected back tomorrow. I could use some help salting the fish they bring back. The task usually falls to my boy, but if you step in he can be put to other use."

"Yes . . . Beryl . . . ma'am."

Beryl nodded before turning and walking out the door.

Beryl's husband and son returned early the next morning. But Emelyn, having gone to bed late the previous evening, overslept. When she finally made her way downstairs, Beryl had already begun preparing the fish.

Emelyn was familiar with the process, having often been given the task of preserving fresh fish by Miss Cook. First the heads were removed, followed by opening the bellies and cleaning out the entrails. The fish were then lathered with salt and placed in a shallow crate where they would be left to cure for several days. It was filthy, smelly work, and Miss Cook had always been happy to hand off the task to her underling. Emelyn was accustomed to executing such tasks alone, but she found working alongside Beryl a welcome change. She listened as the woman chattered about apple harvests and the best methods for baking a pie. Beryl had been in the midst of discussing the proper proportion of apples to sugar for a perfectly sweet yet tart pie when a tall and broad-shouldered young man came into the kitchen to announce that two new guests had arrived.

Beryl wiped her hands on her apron. "Royen, this is Emelyn."

Royen gave a nod of his shaggy head and shuffled back out the door.

Beryl sighed. "That's my boy. He's not much for conversation. Takes after his father in more ways than just his name." She walked to the pot hanging over the fire and ladled stew into two bowls. She put together a lunch tray of stew and bread with warm cider, just as she had served to Emelyn and Corran the day before. Beryl carried the tray out to the common room.

Emelyn continued to decapitate and gut the fish, placing the severed heads into a separate kettle that Beryl would use later for stock. The innkeeper returned and resumed her place at the workbench. There were only a few fish left to prepare. When the last one was salted and placed in the crate with the others, Beryl returned to the stewpot and dished up two bowls of food for Emelyn and herself. She placed the bowls on the table and indicated for Emelyn to sit down.

Emelyn slurped down her food. She had missed breakfast—this was her first meal of the day. Beryl joined her, though she ate with less vigor. After a few bites, Beryl eyed Emelyn over her spoon.

"You haven't asked me about the visitors that have arrived. Aren't you curious if they are your companions?"

"I'm sure it's none of my concern," Emelyn said between bites. "And if it was, you would tell me."

"Well, they've arrived, should you wish to go out to meet them."

Emelyn nodded and continued to eat.

"I'm curious," Beryl said, "how two Magisters came to be traveling with a housemaid. Not the most likely of traveling companions, you must admit."

Emelyn's spoon froze halfway to her mouth. "There . . . was trouble in Fallow. The Magisters helped me." The lie felt strange on her lips. It was Corran who had helped her in Fallow. She had only followed the Magi for the promise that they knew of her parents.

"Oh?" Beryl's eyebrows arched upwards. "What kind of trouble?"

Emelyn pushed her bowl of food away, no longer hungry. "Strange things. The Magisters say it was the work of magic, and that they intend to travel northwards to stop the creature causing it."

Beryl's eyebrows threatened to disappear into her hair. "I've heard some fanciful tales in my time, but nothing like what you've just told me." She chuckled. "And what role do you play in all this?"

Emelyn looked down at the table. "None, really." She hesitated. "They just . . . they said they knew of my parents. That's why I followed them, to find out what they know."

Beryl's smile faded. "You're an orphan?"

Emelyn nodded. She didn't like to speak of it. In Fallow, knowledge that she was an orphan was usually met with pitying glances and uncomfortable silences. Yet, despite the stigma that she was somehow abnormal or unworthy of love, Emelyn had kept the idea of her parents close to her heart. Such thoughts had often given her comfort during many cold and lonely nights. But these things were not to be spoken of to anyone, not even kind innkeepers.

Beryl patted Emelyn on the hand. "I understand, dear. Had I been in your place, I reckon I'd have done the same." She stood, readjusting the apron around her ample waist. "Well, your spectacled friend mentioned that you'd be needing some supplies for your journey. I could use some help putting them together, if you wouldn't mind the extra work."

Emelyn smiled and nodded.

They spent the remainder of the day packing the supplies that Emelyn and her companions would take with them. Cheese and dried meats, apples, potatoes, onions, and flour, all gathered into canvas sacks. Emelyn wondered how they could possibly carry it all when Beryl assured her that the Magi had also purchased a mule that was stabled outside. According to Beryl, the animal was "an ornery old thing" and hadn't been much good to her family for some time, and she hoped that the Magi would get better use out of him.

The day had grown late by the time the supplies were packed and it was decided that they would depart the following morning. Emelyn woke early, as did Corran, who was already sitting in the common room eating when she came downstairs.

"Did I oversleep again?" Emelyn asked as she approached him. She was used to waking long before breakfast was ready.

Corran shook his head. "No, there's time yet before we need to leave." He crunched on a piece of bacon and pointed to the empty chair across from him.

Emelyn sat down, eyeing the tray of food as Corran pushed it towards her.

There were rashers of fried bacon, a bowl of boiled eggs, warm bread from the oven and two clay crocks—one with butter, the other with creamy, copper-colored apple preserves that smelled of sharp spices. Corran poured for her a cup of hot tea from a teapot. Emelyn's stomach rumbled as she pulled off a chunk of warm bread and lathered it with butter and preserves.

Corran nodded in agreement with her stomach. "Beryl has outdone herself this morning. Said that only a proper breakfast would do to see us off on our journey." He dipped a piece of bacon into the apple preserves before stuffing it into his mouth.

"When do we leave?"

"As soon as the mule is packed and ready. Beryl's husband and boy are out in the stable seeing to it. The Magi are out there as well, no doubt scrutinizing the poor men rather than letting them get on with it."

Emelyn grinned. She was quite fond of animals and had often wished she were employed in a house with a stable—preferably one with no boys so that the task of caring for the animals would fall to her. A silly fantasy— one she had given up on long ago. Or so she had thought. The idea of traveling with a mule filled her with a child-like giddiness she had not expected. Emelyn spread butter and preserves onto another piece of bread, taking a large bite as she rose from her chair. She grabbed some bacon and an egg before heading to the door. She glanced behind her to see if Corran was following, but he had settled himself comfortably in his chair, pulling the plate of bacon to him.

Outside, the air was sharp and cold. Much colder than it should have been, given the previous day's warmth. It would be a harsh winter. Emelyn bit into the boiled egg. It was loosely cooked, the yolk sticky on her tongue. She walked as she ate, realizing that this was her first time outdoors since she had procured her new traveling clothes. It was strange not hearing the rustling of her skirts as she walked through the grass. Stranger still was being out in the open dressed like a boy. Miss Cook would have been beside herself with indignation, had she been there to see it.

A man's voice saying, "Now you pull while I push this flea-bitten relic," drew Emelyn out of her thoughts. She ate the rest of the bacon and hastened towards the commotion. She rounded the corner of the stable and found Royen and his father, Royen senior, with a pack-laden mule. The Magisters stood nearby, watching with detached interest as the younger Royen tugged on the reins, trying to pull the mule forward while his father tried to push the animal from behind. The mule brayed, showing rows of long, yellow teeth.

"Blasted beast!" the elder Royen cried, slapping the animal on its haunches. The mule brayed again, kicking its back legs out in retaliation. Royen stumbled out of the way even though he hadn't stood in the path of the kick. Frustrated and shaken, he tore off his brown felt cap and crumpled it in an angry fist. He pulled a handkerchief from his pocket and was mopping his sweaty brow when his eyes fell on Emelyn.

"Good morning to you, miss," Royen said as he stuffed the handkerchief back into his pocket. "Pardon the ruckus. We're just trying to get this miserable animal to move, seeing as your companions there paid good money for the foul creature." He looked at the Magisters. "I warned you, good sirs. Told you that the wretched thing would give you nothing but trouble. I can't in good conscience take your money for him."

He turned back to Emelyn. "Had I my own way, he would've been used to make mincemeat pies long ago, but the missus is keen on the stupid beast for reasons I can't figure."

Emelyn frowned. It pained her to hear him speak of the animal so harshly. "Why won't he move?"

Royen scratched his balding pate. "Take me if I know. He's an old bugger. My guess is he just wants to stay in his stall and eat hay all day. It's all he's done of late, to be sure."

Emelyn walked past the Royens to a pile of hay stowed in a corner of the stable. If the animal wanted hay, give him hay. She grabbed a handful, ignoring the feeling of discomfort on having four sets of eyes upon her. She was annoyed at the men's stubbornness to remedy, in her mind, a simple problem. Emelyn walked over to the mule and held the hay to the animal's nose.

The mule's nostrils twitched and his ears perked with interest. He nibbled carefully, then, when there was no trickery, chomped on the hay and pulled it out of Emelyn's hands. She smiled, petting the mule on his long and bristly nose. She lowered her head close to the animal.

"It's all right," she whispered. "They don't understand, but I do. We need to keep together, you and I, and look out for each other."

Having finished the hay, the mule nudged Emelyn's hand, looking for more. She laughed. Picking up the dangling reins, Emelyn gave them a gentle tug. The mule followed.

"Well, then," Percival said. "It would seem our little problem is solved. Aldren, if you would be so good as to inform our remaining companion of our imminent departure, we can be on our way."

Aldren bowed his head and walked towards the inn, his gaze lingering on Emelyn and the mule as he passed by.

The elder Royen shook his head. "Well, can't say I'm sorry that the trouble is over and done with. Come on, boy, we've work to do." He straightened out his rumpled cap as best he could, placing it atop his head as he walked from the stable. The younger Royen trailed after him.

Emelyn lingered behind, feeding more hay to the mule. She realized she hadn't asked for the animal's name and decided that Ferrin would be fitting.

Aldren returned, followed by Corran, who was eating a boiled egg. Beryl trailed closely behind, a brown coat draped over one arm while in her hands she held a leather satchel. She walked to Emelyn and gave her the bag.

"I've packed you some extra provisions, along with some apples for Old Jack, there," she nodded to the mule. "He's an ornery beast and could try the patience of a stone. But he's got a good heart and I've never been able to get rid of him. I'm glad to see you getting on nicely together."

"I . . . thought I might call him Ferrin," Emelyn said, hoping she wouldn't offend Beryl by renaming her mule.

Beryl smiled and patted Emelyn on the hand. "Ferrin is a fine name." She held up the brown coat. "Here, I want you to have this. I've patched it up as best I could and taken it in so it would fit you better. It's nothing fancy, but I thought with winter coming you would need it."

Emelyn's face fell. "I can't accept that. Not without paying for it."

Beryl scoffed, pushing the coat into Emelyn's hands. "Nonsense. You've left your dress behind. It's a fair enough trade, not to mention all the help you've been to me the past couple of days. Given that your friends here have paid for your room and board, the way I see it, I'm the one who's owing you."

Emelyn took the coat, feeling the coarse, thick fabric with her hands. "Thank you," she murmured.

"It's been mighty nice having you around. I love my boy dearly, but part of me has always wished for a daughter as well. You're welcome here anytime, should you ever find yourself in these parts again."

Emelyn looked down at her hands. "You've been so kind . . ."

Beryl lifted Emelyn's chin with a chubby finger. "Keep your head up, girl."

Emelyn looked into Beryl's gold-flecked eyes and nodded.

Beryl patted her cheek, her eyes crinkling as she smiled. "Good." She turned to Ferrin and patted the mule on the head. "You be good, old boy. Don't give the nice young lady too much trouble." Turning back to Emelyn she added, "I hope you find what you're looking for." She gave Emelyn one last pat on the cheek before turning and heading back to the inn.

Emelyn watched her go, feeling an inexplicable sadness spread through her heart. She glanced at her companions. The Magisters were conferring amongst themselves, seemingly uninterested in the affairs of others. But Corran had been watching, leaning against a post near a stall. He smiled. Emelyn gave a small smile back and slung the satchel across her shoulders. The Magisters approached.

"I trust that all affairs have been tended to?" Percival said.

"The innkeeper has been paid for the supplies and services rendered," Aldren said. "We can leave at once, if all are ready."

Both Magisters looked at Emelyn.

"I'm ready," Emelyn said.

Corran thinned his lips and remained silent.

"Very well." Percival turned and walked from the stable. Aldren followed close behind.

Emelyn picked up Ferrin's reins and tugged. The mule followed. She smiled, suddenly looking forward to the journey ahead.

CHAPTER 6

THE FIRST DAY PASSED uneventfully; the weather remained clear, the road empty. As evening drew closer, they made camp off to the side of the road. Emelyn was apprehensive. She had never slept outdoors before and she had heard tales of highwaymen and other outlaws that menaced the roadways even during daylight. What, then, might happen after dark?

"Do you think it's safe here?" Emelyn whispered to Corran as they set up camp.

Corran looked around. "Probably not the best location for a camp, I'll grant you that. But it wouldn't do to wander too far from the road, only to have to find our way back again."

Corran's words brought Emelyn no comfort.

He must have seen her apprehension, for he smiled before adding, "It will be all right. I've slept outdoors on more occasions than I can count. More often than not, the night passes quietly."

"But not always."

Corran shifted his feet. "No, not always. But no one's gotten the better of me yet, plus we have them." He jerked a thumb at the Magi. "Chances are if anyone is out there looking to cause mischief, they'll likely see us as more trouble than we're worth."

Emelyn glanced over at the Magi and their embroidered robes. It was whispered that a single Magister robe would fetch a high enough price to feed a family for a year, and here there were two. Despite Corran's words, Emelyn still worried that someone would be rash enough, desperate enough, to risk the danger for such a valuable prize.

Her fears were unfounded, however, for the night passed quietly, just as Corran had said. They awoke early, made a breakfast of cheese, dried meat, and apples before packing up and resuming their journey.

The road remained quiet and deserted. Morning passed into afternoon, and Emelyn thought they would have another uneventful day when a figure appeared on the road ahead.

"Hello!" the man called as he drew closer. He was short and stocky, his chin covered with a thick black beard. Following him was a dark brown pony laden with bags and sacks. "Road has been mighty barren of late, to be sure!" His beard split to show rows of surprisingly white and shiny teeth.

"Yes," Percival said, his voice lacking amusement. "Have you come from Timmerfell?"

The man bobbed his bushy head. "Quite right, quite right. Making my way to Sunbridge with old Dolly, here." He patted the pony on the neck. "I've wares to sell and the missus says I'm not allowed back till I've got the coin to show for it."

He leaned in closer to Percival. "Though, between you and me, she's doing me a kindness. I may surely perish if I have to eat another of her ill-concocted cabbage soups." The man elbowed Percival in the ribs as he roared with laughter.

Percival frowned, rubbing his side as he stepped away.

"But where are my manners? Name's Werren Worsby." Werren advanced on Percival. "Say, you look like a man of means. Perhaps I could interest you in a finely crafted wooden pipe. Or maybe something for the missus . . . say, a lovely beaded bracelet?"

Percival's lips thinned as his jaw clenched shut, and he gave the man a withering glare.

It being clear he would not make a sale out of the Magister, Werren turned to Emelyn. "And what about you, young miss? I've a lovely scarf, the color of spring blossoms. Just the thing for you, I think, with your complexion. You'd be the envy of all the dance parties!"

Emelyn smiled, wondering what color "spring blossoms" was supposed to be. "I'm afraid I haven't any money."

Werren deflated, his face crestfallen.

"We are heading towards Timmerfell," Aldren said. "What might we expect on the road?"

Werren considered the Magi as he scratched his bristly cheeks. "Well now, hard to say. A man's got to make a living, and, seeing as my wife has all but kicked me out of the house, I'm left to wander in the cold until I sell off my wares." He looked at Aldren pointedly. "The cold can do mighty strange things to a man, make him forgetful and such. I can't rightly say what I've seen on the road. If, say, there was some glimmer of hope, some indication that I'll one day see my lovely wife again, then maybe I'd remember something."

Aldren stared at the man, looking confused.

Werren cleared his throat. "You, sir, look like you could use a charming wooden figurine. Such a purchase would undoubtedly raise my spirits and help me remember the trials of my journey."

Aldren's look of confusion faded, replaced by one of understanding, and then shock. His mouth worked in soundless indignation as he turned to Percival. The Grand Magister closed his eyes and waved his hand, seemingly eager to be done with the business.

Turning back to the stout man, Aldren reached into his belt pouch and pulled out a coin. He handed it to Werren.

Werren snatched the coin. He bit the edge and, smiling, stuffed it into a pocket. "An excellent choice, good sir. You won't be disappointed." He rummaged through one of his packs and pulled out a small figurine carved and painted into the likeness of a raccoon. He handed it to the Magister.

Aldren held the figurine at arm's length as though it might bite him.

"Well now, let's see," Werren said. "I've not seen much out of the ordinary. Ainar Stone was passed out at the waterwheel from too much drink, though there's nothing out of the ordinary with that!" Werren guffawed and tried to elbow Aldren in the ribs, but the Magister dodged the jab.

"Other than that," Werren continued, "not seen anyone on the road except for you good folk." He paused. "There *was* a girl. Small thing, about so high." He held out a hand at his waist. "Strange little mite, kept staring at me like she'd never seen a man before. She was dark, kind of like the young miss here, only darker still. I showed her that raccoon there. All little girls love those carved animals, but not her. She just stared at me without blinking before running off." He shook his head. "Children these days, they're reared without any sense of manners or decency. Well, I was right glad to be rid of her, let me tell you."

Aldren glanced at Percival. "I see. Well, thank you, Mr. Worsby."

Werren flashed another toothy grin. "Always a pleasure to help a customer. When you get to Timmerfell, tell Gunther at the inn that Werren sent you. He'll see to it that you're properly taken care of." He picked up the reins of his pony and continued down the road, whistling as he walked.

Aldren stared at the figurine. Walking over to Emelyn, he held out his palm. "Here, take it. I have no use for such . . . trinkets."

Emelyn eyed him and then, seeing no ill intent in his expression, took the raccoon from his hand. She had always wanted such an item but could never justify spending money on frivolity. Her festival dress was her most frivolous purchase, yet even that had a purpose.

"Thank you," she whispered, surprised over how much she cared about something so silly. She put it in her satchel for safekeeping.

Aldren's eyes softened. He cleared his throat before giving a crooked smile and returned to Percival's side.

They traveled for three more uneventful days before coming to the outskirts of Timmerfell.

Corran said, "The town is known for its lumber mill, and provides timber for the towns along the road and river to Sunbridge. Originally, my parents wished to send me here to apprentice. But there were few carpentry masters in Timmerfell and none were accepting new apprentices, so I was sent to Fallow instead."

Emelyn frowned. As far as she knew, Corran was mistaken in that he apprenticed in Fallow. "How could you have apprenticed there? Mr. Wainwright hasn't had any apprentices for nearly twenty years, remember?"

Corran glanced at her out of the corner of his eye. "So you say. But I remember apprenticing there. You must be mistaken."

"I don't think so."

"I don't see why not. Were you so involved in the all the details of Mr. Wainwright's apprenticeships?"

"No, but—"

"Then you are mistaken. I apprenticed there and apparently you just didn't know it."

"It's a small town. Everyone knows that Mr. Wainwright stopped taking apprentices long ago."

Corran sighed and looked at her. "I don't know what you want me to say. I remember apprenticing there. That's all I know. The only explanation I can give is that everyone else must be wrong."

Emelyn frowned again; it was a poor explanation. But she didn't want to argue, so she remained silent.

They cleared the forest and came to an open field dotted with tree stumps. Beyond, the town of Timmerfell lay on the horizon, dark and grey against the ashen sky. Emelyn disliked the look of it. She couldn't figure out why, exactly; maybe because it wasn't like Fallow.

They followed the road as it twisted through the field. Parts of the field were devoid of stumps, the soil plowed and cultivated. Other parts remained unworked, overtaken by long, wild grass. The road wound through all of it and it occurred to Emelyn that it wandered entirely too much for a road in such a wide and open space. Maybe it was an old road that used to wind through a forest rather than pastures.

"This road that we have been traveling upon is actually rather old," Aldren said as though answering Emelyn's thoughts. "It dates back to the first settlers, who traveled northwards to conquer the wilds of the North Reaches and tame it for civilization. The road predates the town of Timmerfell, just as it predates most towns north of Sunbridge, and has allowed the light from the south to spread forth to the darker places of the world."

Emelyn watched Aldren as he spoke, how his face lit up as he recalled the tale. It didn't seem to bother him that neither Percival nor Corran were paying any attention; he seemed to simply enjoy speaking of it, even if no one was listening. Emelyn, however, was grateful for the story. There had been a time when she thought herself knowledgeable. She knew how to read, taught by Miss Cook herself. It was a skill not every servant could claim. Yet the further she traveled from Fallow, the more she realized that her ability to read was not as much an accomplishment as she had once thought. She thirsted for knowledge, but she didn't have the courage to ask the Magister to continue when he lapsed into silence.

The road snaked its way to the river, running alongside the murky waterway that flowed past the town. As they walked, Emelyn eyed the stone buildings of Timmerfell, especially the mill at the river's edge. The great wooden wheel turned, creaking and groaning as it churned the water. Emelyn frowned, feeling uneasy. Something was wrong. She slowed and scanned the town as she tried to find the source of her unease. She told herself that she was being foolish, that it was only her nervousness at having left Fallow that was causing her palms to sweat and her heart to race. But her assurances did nothing to calm her frayed nerves.

The road turned and they crossed a bridge leading into town. They passed the mill, coming to the stone buildings of the town proper. It wasn't until they had stopped walking that Emelyn finally understood what was wrong: it was too quiet. There were no dogs barking, no children playing in the dirt roads. There were no women beating their carpets, no men chopping firewood. Windows stood empty and dark, chimneys cold and smokeless.

"There are no people," Emelyn said, shocked that she had not noticed it earlier. "The town is empty."

Percival turned his cool eyes upon her. "Indeed."

Emelyn wavered under his gaze. "What . . . what happened to them?"

"What makes you think something happened?"

"I . . . I don't know." Then she remembered Werren. "The peddler on the road, he came from here, didn't he? He didn't mention anything about the town being empty. In fact, he told us to speak to the innkeeper."

Percival smiled. "You are perceptive. Good." He turned towards the town. "Something does seem to be amiss, but we must not come to any conclusions prematurely. Let us investigate so that we might draw such conclusions logically." Percival and Aldren walked off, leaving Emelyn and Corran behind.

Corran frowned as he watched the Magi leave. "I want to look around as well. Will you be all right here?"

Emelyn glanced about. They were at the mill just off the road. She nodded.

Corran hesitated.

"I'll be fine." Now that she knew the source of her unease, Emelyn's fear had faded—though it hadn't gone entirely.

Corran considered her for a moment and nodded. He walked away and disappeared into a nearby house.

Timmerfell was a dreary town. Grey stone houses crowned with slate roofs set against a steely sky. There was no grass, no trees with golden and auburn leaves, no plump, red rose hips clinging to barren bushes. There was no life, only a wintering coldness of drab stone and muddy streets. Emelyn was glad to have the mule with her—a warm and gentle creature that helped remind her that life still breathed in the world. She rummaged in the satchel Beryl had given her and pulled out a vibrant red apple. She held it out to Ferrin, smiling as the mule chomped on the fruit. As he ate, she pulled out the wooden raccoon Aldren had given her. She wondered about Werren's wife, if she was well. She hoped when the peddler returned home, he would find it as it always was.

Once the apple was consumed, Emelyn turned her attention to the mill. She watched with curiosity how the wheel groaned and turned with the rushing river. She had never seen a lumber mill before. She had, on occasion, visited Mr. Gristman's mill that ground wheat into flour. That mill had been much smaller and had used oxen to pull the stone that ground the grain. Emelyn decided to investigate.

The mill had no doors, only open archways that provided a clear view inside. The smell of sawdust hung in the air, reminding Emelyn of Mr. Wainwright's workshop back home. She had gone there once to fetch a set of wooden spoons that Miss Cook had ordered. Emelyn remembered being mystified over the numerous tables cluttered with tools. The air had been so heavy with sawdust that she had to brush her clothes clean before reporting back to Miss Cook. Most of all she remembered the smell—earth and pine, sharp and clean like newly fallen rain. It was a smell that reminded her of Mr. Hibberly and the few occasions she had been allowed to unpack crates of goods. It had been exciting to sift through the soft sawdust, wondering all the while at what she might find. It was a happy memory, one of few.

Emelyn stepped inside the mill—a largely barren space save for the long table that ran the length of the building. A log lay upon the table, close to the jagged teeth of a saw. It was as though the men that worked there had suddenly left without taking the time to cut this last piece of timber. In a corner of the room stood a table and chair. Upon the table was a tankard of ale, a thin layer of sawdust floating on the surface of the dark liquid. A black workman's cap hung from the back of the chair, serving as a ghostly reminder of those who once lived there. Feeling uneasy, Emelyn hastened back outside and found Corran standing next to Ferrin.

"There you are," he said. "I saw the mule standing here and was wondering where you had gone."

"I wanted to look in the mill."

"Find anything?"

Emelyn shook her head. "Wood and an old hat. You?"

Corran scratched his head. "Nothing remarkable. Not really . . ."

"What?"

"Well, I found food and clothes. If the people left town, why didn't they take their food or clothes with them?"

Emelyn considered the question.

"It's probably nothing," Corran said. "It's possible they took only what they needed and left everything else behind. The animals are gone, which could be a good sign. Anyone leaving town would not willingly leave their livestock."

"Livestock?" Emelyn did not see any indication that there had been any.

"A town like this would have oxen to pull the wagons of timber. It also stands to reason that people would have kept pigs, chickens."

Emelyn nodded, feeling silly that she hadn't noticed something so obvious.

"The oxen are gone, yes, but the wagons are still here."

Emelyn turned towards Percival's voice.

The Grand Magister continued. "Nor are there any tracks, aside from a smattering of footprints. If the whole town left, there would be visible traces of their leaving."

"What does it mean?" Emelyn asked. "Did something happen to them?"

Percival spread his hands open. "There is no indication of violence. Food, clothes, and what little valuables these people had all remain behind. Whatever happened to them happened by unusual means. Aldren and I will need to reflect further on the matter. In the meantime, however, let us sleep here for the night. The hour grows late and we need time if we are to understand what has happened."

Emelyn felt a stab of panic at the idea of sleeping in an abandoned town—especially one where its inhabitants had vanished by "unusual means."

Percival smiled. "Not to worry, it should be quite safe. Whatever happened here has passed and is not likely to occur again. Come, Aldren." The two Magisters turned and walked towards the town.

Emelyn's stomach sank.

"It will be all right," Corran said. "If Magi hold to only one thing, it's making sure they are right. It allows them to look down their noses at us small folk if we ever dare suggest they are wrong. I have it on good authority that looking down their noses is their favorite pastime, right next to boisterous drinking games and fiddly bouts of hop-scotch."

Emelyn put a hand over her mouth as she giggled.

Corran smiled. "Come on, then. We better find where we're going to sleep tonight."

They headed to the inn. The sign swinging over the door claimed it to be "The Drunken Jack" and showed a painted man with an axe in one hand and a tankard in the other. They found a stable in the back where she and Corran unloaded Ferrin, leaving him with a pile of hay and a bucket of water. Inside, the inn was clean, though just as empty as the rest of the town. Corran rummaged around until he found firewood and tinder and lit it with a flint and steel. He stood back, admiring his work.

"I reckon we have free reign of the place," Corran said as he warmed his hands by the flames. "It will be nice to sleep in a bed for a change. You can choose which room you'd like first."

Emelyn hesitated—she didn't like the idea of sleeping in an abandoned inn. "I think I'd like to sleep out here, by the fire. I don't mind sleeping on the floor."

Corran raised an eyebrow but said nothing.

They ate a supper of fried bread with onion and turnip stew before Corran headed upstairs to sleep. Emelyn made a bed for herself on the floor in front of the hearth and settled down in the warmth of the fire. She looked at the door, wondering where the Magi were. She hadn't seen them since they arrived in town and she wondered where they were spending their time. What's more, she wondered about her parents and why the Magi hadn't told her anything about them. It had been nearly a week since they left Fallow. Yet in that week the Magisters had been distant, speaking to her only when needed. Why hadn't they said anything to her? Did they really want to help her, or did they have other reasons for bringing her along? Emelyn's stomach sank at the idea that she had made a poor decision in leaving Fallow, in trusting men she didn't know. There was little she could do about it now, though. She couldn't turn back and, for good or ill, would have to see it through.

Emelyn lay down and watched the flames flicker against the hearthstones. The door opened, sending a draft of cold air into the room. Emelyn sat up as Percival headed upstairs. Aldren remained behind, fidgeting with a sleeve of his robe. Did he want to speak with her? Hope stirred within her that she would finally get some answers.

Aldren gave her a crooked smile before heading into the kitchen. She listened to the clinking of plates and spoons as he dished up some food before reappearing, plates in hand. Seeing her eyes upon him he murmured, "Goodnight," and disappeared upstairs.

Emelyn watched as he left, her hopes dwindling with the fading of his footsteps. Then her disappointment turned to irritation. Would she have to plead with them to tell her something?

The idea of it made her uneasy. There had been times in the past where Emelyn had asked about certain matters—Master Mansell's occupation, why the master and mistress didn't have any children. In answer Miss Cook would box her ear or rap her knuckles with a wooden spoon and tell her to mind her own affairs. After several such incidents, Emelyn had learned to hold her tongue and to speak only when spoken to. But how long could she remain silent now? How long until the Magi decided they didn't need a servant girl trailing after them and cast her aside?

Emelyn lay back down. The walls of the inn creaked as though the building was also settling down to rest. Despite her troubled thoughts, Emelyn's eyelids grew heavy and she soon drifted into slumber.

The fire had burned down to glowing embers when Emelyn awoke. The inn was quiet; the creaking had stopped. She suspected the others still slept, given the silence. A glance at the barren windows showed only darkness outside. Unsure if dawn was approaching, Emelyn considered if she should get up or try to go back to sleep. Years of waking before dawn told her to rise out of bed, but the heaviness in her eyes argued for more rest. She wasn't a servant anymore. She didn't need to put water on to boil, or sweep the steps, or shake the carpets. If she got up before the others, she would have nothing to do other than sit in the dark, alone.

She had nearly convinced herself and was about to let her eyes close when she heard a noise outside. Emelyn bolted upright, all fatigue forgotten. She held her breath, straining to hear, but all was silent. Just as she was about to breathe, she heard it again; Ferrin was braying out in the stable. She exhaled, relieved it was only the mule. But why was he braying? She and Corran had left him with plenty of food and water, and the mule had always been silent during previous nights. Should she fetch Corran? Or the Magisters? She didn't like the idea of waking the others, especially if the disturbance turned out to be trivial. Convincing herself that it was nothing to worry over, that Ferrin was lonely or braying at the moon, Emelyn rose and walked outside.

The night was dark, devoid of moon and stars. Emelyn thought of fetching a lamp, but decided against it. She wasn't sure where she could find one and she had Ferrin's braying to guide her as much as her hindered vision. She crept towards the stable. Groping with her hands, she found the wide wooden doors, pushed one open and walked inside. She shuffled forward, her arms outstretched until she found Ferrin.

"Hush now," she said, stroking his mane. "Why are you crying? Are you lonely out here?"

The mule calmed at her touch, though he stamped his hooves as if restless.

Emelyn was patting his neck when a faint light flickered through one of the stable's windows. The others must have woken. She walked to the window and peeked out. From around a corner of the inn came the wavering light of a lamp. It was probably Corran, coming to look for her when he saw she was gone. She thought about calling out to him when Ferrin stomped and paced in his stall. She returned to the mule, trying to calm him, but the animal would not be soothed. Through the window the light seemed brighter, closer. Emelyn left Ferrin to find her way to the door. She pushed it open a crack. She had been right: the light was closer. Behind it, other orbs of light glowed in the darkness. Had the Magisters also come?

Magisters didn't use lamps.

Emelyn closed the door. Her heart bolted as she hoped she hadn't been seen. By whom? The townspeople? Had they returned? Something within Emelyn told her it wasn't the residents of Timmerfell she saw out in the night. She crept back to Ferrin and threw her arms around the mule's thick neck. She wasn't sure if she was trying to comfort herself or the animal; she was simply grateful he had finally grown quiet.

Emelyn watched the darkness where she knew the doors to be. Soft yellow light streamed through the cracks while footsteps scuffled beyond the walls. Her eyes were drawn to the window as light flickered on the sill. A man came into view, his face shrouded by a dark grey hood. He held a lantern before him, his hand old and wizened. Eme-lyn shrank into the shadows as she clung to Ferrin's neck, silently willing the animal to remain quiet. Neither she nor the mule uttered a sound, yet the man remained, holding his lantern before him with a thin, outstretched arm. His head turned and he lumbered towards the window. He held the lantern high and close to his face. Light from the flame illuminated his darkened cowl, and Emelyn gasped at what she saw: the man had no eyes. His skin was ashen, his cheeks hollow, and where his eyes should have been was only pale, smooth skin. Yet even without eyes, Emelyn felt he was looking right at her, that no amount of shadows could hide her from him. Her heart thundered in her ears and she fought the urge to run. He couldn't see her, she told herself. Be silent and still and he would leave.

The gaunt man's ashen lips split into a wretched smile, and, as his eyeless gaze fixed on her, Emelyn knew she was wrong.

The stable doors rattled and the light shining through the cracks grew brighter. The doors swung open and another gaunt man shrouded in a grey cloak stepped inside. He held his lantern high, peering at Emelyn with an eyeless face. Behind him stood several other shrouded figures, each holding a lamp of his own.

Panic gripped Emelyn as the shrouded man lumbered towards her, his eyeless gaze unwavering. She fumbled along the ground, searching for a stone, anything she could use to defend herself. But there was nothing—only strands of hay and cold, hard earth. Driven by panic and fear, Emelyn dug her fingers into the ground, ignoring the pain of her nails breaking and the scraping of her skin. She was only vaguely aware of her actions, her mind preoccu-pied with a single thought: blind them.

The thought resonated within her, a mantra that kept her from losing her mind to fear. Blind them. Blind them.

She burrowed her fingers deep into the earth, gripping the cold soil with numb fingers. Emelyn closed her eyes, wishing herself away from there, wishing for shadows dark enough to hide her.

An icy wind gusted through stable that knocked the air from Emelyn's lungs. Her body seized, unable to breathe as though she had plunged into frigid water. All thoughts of the shrouded men were forgotten; her only concern was to draw a single breath.

The wind subsided and the air warmed. As Emelyn breathed, she remembered the cloaked men. She looked up, fearful of being surrounded by gaunt, ghastly figures. But there was only darkness. No light in the window; no sinewy hands holding flickering lanterns. She didn't know if the shrouded men had gone, or if they were still there, lurking in the darkness. Not wanting to find out, Emelyn threw herself onto Ferrin's back.

"Run," she whispered.

The mule ran. Emelyn hugged Ferrin's neck, struggling to keep herself from being thrown off. She could see nothing as they dashed through the darkness, and she hoped that Ferrin saw better than she. The mule ran on. Emelyn's fear and panic subsided and, along with it, her strength. Her arms and legs grew weak. Unable to hold on any longer, she slipped from the mule's back and fell to the frigid ground.

CHAPTER 7

EMELYN AWOKE to a pair of spectacles looming over her. She cringed into her pillow, startled.

"S . . . Sorry," Aldren said, stepping back. "We found you in the field, outside of town. You were unconscious, so we brought you back here."

Emelyn looked around. She was lying in a bed, surrounded by stone walls. Corran stood near the door, and a square window showed a grey, weeping sky. "Timmerfell."

Aldren nodded. "Yes."

Emelyn pushed herself upright, her hands throbbing with the effort. She looked down and found them bandaged in cloth. "What happened?"

Aldren studied her. "You do not remember?"

Emelyn fell silent, trying to recall the night's events. She remembered Ferrin's cries, shadows, and lanterns. "I'm . . . not sure."

"Do you remember the lamphyr?" Corran said.

"Lamphyr?"

"We found old cloaks and lanterns outside the stable, it had to be them."

"An old sea-folk superstition," Percival said as he walked into the room. "Which has very little bearing on the matter at hand, I assure you."

Corran crossed his arms and scowled at the Magister's back.

Emelyn glanced back and forth between the two men. "I don't understand."

Percival sat on the edge of the bed and patted Emelyn's bandaged hand. "What, exactly, do you remember, my dear?"

Emelyn thought a moment. "I woke up in the night and heard Ferrin braying. I went out to check on him." She paused, closing her eyes as she tried to remember. "I . . . there was something out there . . . I remember shadows and lanterns and pale hands . . ." And eyeless faces. Her eyes snapped open, the memory jarring. She didn't want to say it. She didn't know if she could. "That's all I remember."

Percival studied her with his pale blue eyes. "No matter."

"What happened?"

"Another disturbance."

"Disturbance? Like in Fallow?"

"Yes. I sensed it in my sleep and awoke." Percival gave a weak smile as he patted her hand. "A bit too late, I am afraid."

Emelyn looked down at her bandaged hands.

"But that is of minor consequence," he continued. "What is significant is how you seemingly handled the situation."

Emelyn frowned. "What do you mean?"

"When I woke I sought to investigate the matter. Yet all I found were old lanterns and rags, and you were gone. We found you later, along with the mule, on the outskirts of town. You were unconscious, your hands caked with dirt and blood."

"You found Ferrin? Is he all right?"

Percival's lips stretched into a thin smile. "He is quite well, not to worry." The smile faded. "Tell me, is there nothing more you remember from the night?"

Emelyn tried to remember, but it was all a blur of shadows tinged with the acidic taste of fear. She shook her head.

Percival nodded, patting her hand one last time. "Very well. You may remember, in time. Until then, we will let you rest." He rose from the bedside. "Come, Aldren. Let us make preparations for our journey while our little friend rests."

Corran remained behind, his arms still folded across his chest. Once the Magi left, he relaxed. He smiled at Emelyn as he approached the edge of her bed. "How are you feeling?"

"Well enough, I suppose." She lifted up her bandaged hands and gave a crooked smile. "To be honest, I'm mostly confused. My mind feels muddled. It's like I can see the memory of last night in the corner of my eye, but when I try to look at it, it fades away."

"You've had a trying night. I'm sure you'll sort it out, given some time."

Emelyn nodded, trying to feel reassured, when she remembered something Corran had said. "What's a lamphyr?"

Corran sat down on the floor and rested against the wall. "Fairy tales. Superstition. The Magi was right in that regard."

"Tell me. Please?"

Corran gathered his thoughts. "I've told you that where I'm from people hold to old beliefs, old superstitions. Well, among these is the belief that there are spirits that walk the world with us."

"Spirits?"

Corran nodded. "Otherworldly beings that aren't like you or me yet walk among us all the same. The lamphyr are such spirits. It is said that the lamphyr were once sailors, charged with lighting the fires on the cliffs along the sea so that ships would not wreck upon the rocky shores in foul weather.

"But these men, being sailors, did not like being left ashore while their brethren sought adventure upon the waves. So they shirked their duties and let their fires grow cold, causing the ships at sea to crash upon the jagged cliffs and killing those they once called brothers. For their crime they were cursed, struck blind so that they, too, would know the perils of darkness.

"And so they wander the earth, carrying with them a lantern and lighting their way with its fell light. For, even though they are blind, it is said that the lanterns glow with the light of the Otherworld, giving them sight beyond that of mortal men. It is said the lamphyr must never let their light go out, or their spirits will be swept away to the Void, lost forever."

Silence hung between them as Emelyn considered Corran's story. It chilled her to hear these shadowy men described so aptly. Yet it also gave her a measure of comfort to hear them named, knowing that others also knew of them. As frightening as the night had been, it wasn't a nightmare reserved solely for her.

"It's all nonsense, of course," Corran said. "It's just a story mothers tell their children so they won't misbehave. 'You best mind yourself, Corran,' my mother would tell me, 'for the lamphyr know when little boys have been naughty and will come and snatch them from their beds whilst they sleep.'"

Corran chuckled, shaking his head. "Yet no one in living memory has ever seen a lamphyr, or any of the other spirits we so frequently speak of. It is mere superstition, and I shouldn't have spoken of it. I'm afraid I got caught up in the moment. When I saw those ratty grey cloaks and the lanterns on the ground . . . well . . . it was like I was a boy again, and I could hear my mother shrilling at me to behave." He smiled again, though his eyes were distant, looking at a memory Emelyn couldn't see.

"But it was them," she said. "Dark cloaks and lanterns and . . . no eyes. I thought they were blind, that they couldn't see me. But they could." Emelyn recalled the memory as she spoke of it, her clouded mind clearing with every word.

"You remember, then?"

Emelyn nodded.

Aldren stood outside the inn, clinging to the edge of the building as he tried to keep out of the rain. The roof had meager eaves, and icy drops of water still dripped onto his bald head. He shivered. He didn't have to be cold and wet—he could use the Art to keep the rain off. But he was supposed to be focusing his power towards other tasks.

"Find out what she knows," Percival had whispered to him as they left Emelyn's room. "Find out if she truly cannot remember what happened. She is withholding something, and I mean to know what it is."

Aldren had nodded even as his heart sank. Spying. The idea sat poorly with him; it always did. This wasn't the first time his lord had asked him to gather information through secretive means, nor would it be the last. Aldren was, of course, honored to assist the Grand Magister in his duties. Having been appointed to the office of High Magister, second to the Grand Magister, was a point of great pride for him, and he took his responsibilities seriously. Still, the Art was a gift, one granted only to the noblest of men. It saddened him to have to use it in such a base manner.

Aldren gripped his staff, using the tip to draw the runes that would help him focus. Around and around he traced the intricate lines in the mud until they encircled him. He looked up at Emelyn's window. Raindrops spattered his spectacles, blurring his vision. It didn't matter; he didn't need to see to accomplish his task.

Aldren focused his attention and listened. He could hear the rain pattering on the ground around him, on the rooftops of the buildings; he could hear the drip-drops of water as they fell into puddles and gathered in barrels. He focused. He could hear the wind blowing, rattling the windows and shutters, whistling as it rushed through cracks in the door. He focused. The rattling faded, replaced by a girl's hushed and hurried voice. Having found the thread of sound, Aldren latched onto it with his mind. He lowered his head and listened.

Corran said, "What happened? Where did they come from? Where did they go?"

"I don't know," Emelyn said. "I just saw flickering lamplight. I thought it was you at first, until I saw there were several of them. I was afraid; I didn't know who it was. Then they were there, at the stable and I saw . . . They had no eyes, but they could see me. The one in the window, he lifted his lantern and *saw* me."

"What happened to them?"

Emelyn closed her eyes and shook her head. "I'm not sure. I was so afraid. It was different this time, not like before."

"Before?"

"In Fallow, the other disturbance, as the Magisters call it. The little men, the boggans. I was afraid then, too. But this was different. It was . . . sharper . . . somehow. The fear. I don't know . . ." Emelyn trailed off, hearing how she rambled. He must think she was crazy. She glanced at Corran, but the man sat patiently waiting for her to resume.

"I don't really know what happened," she said when she had calmed again. "I remember looking on the ground for a stone or something to throw at them. But there was nothing. So . . . I wished." Emelyn stopped, realizing how ridiculous she sounded. She glanced at Corran again, expecting him to laugh or accuse her of lying. Miss Cook would have boxed her ear and told her that wishes are for wells and moon-calf ninnies without two bits of sense to rub together.

But Corran didn't laugh. "You wished?"

Emelyn nodded. "I . . . wished that they were gone, that they couldn't see me. That's all I remember thinking, that they couldn't see me. Then it grew cold and dark and I fled with Ferrin. That's all I remember."

Corran was quiet a moment. "What of your hands? How did they get bloodied?"

Emelyn looked at her bandaged hands and shook her head. "I don't know. Maybe I hurt them, somehow, looking for a rock. I don't remember." She glanced at Corran. "Do you believe me?"

Corran scratched his head and nodded. "Yes, I do. We have already seen strange things in Fallow. And now, with this town deserted for reasons unknown . . . Well, there is no reason not to believe you."

Emelyn relaxed, feeling relieved.

"It's strange, though," Corran said. "First boggans, now lamphyr. I only ever heard stories of them. I never knew anyone who had seen them and yet here they are. Two of my boyhood stories come to life, one right after the other." He shook his head.

Rain pattered against the windowpane.

"Ah, well," Corran said as he stood. "My mother would be pleased to know they did not steal me in my sleep, so I must have been a good boy after all." He smiled as he brushed off his trousers. "You try and get some rest. I wager we'll stay another night. No point in setting off in this weather. If you need anything, let me know, and I'll have Aldren fetch it."

Emelyn grinned and nodded. Corran left and she lay back, her mind restless, roiling over the events of the night as she tried to make sense of them.

Aldren heard Corran walk from the room. He released the thread, finding himself back in the mud, his robes soaked with rain.

The inn door opened and Corran stepped outside. He stopped when he saw Aldren and glanced to the runes in the mud. Corran's eyes narrowed. Aldren said nothing, leaning upon his staff as he watched the other man. They stared at each other for a moment before Corran turned and walked away.

Aldren exhaled. He knew his unease around Corran was foolish and unwarranted, yet he couldn't help it. He should not be here. Why did the Grand Magister allow it? The thought of his lord brought Aldren's mind back to his duties. With the tip of his staff, he smoothed away the runes in the mud as best as he could before turning and walking further into town.

Although the Grand Magister had insisted they all sleep at the inn at night, Percival had chosen to spend his waking hours in a different house within Timmerfell. It was the largest house in town and, judging by the quality furnishings, likely belonged to the owner of the mill. For a town like Timmerfell, the house was undoubtedly a haven of luxury of which most would be envious. Yet for the Magisters, accustomed to the lavishness of the Towers, it was a cozy, country abode. "Quaint," the Grand Magister had called it.

Aldren approached the door to the house, pushed it open and walked inside. The entry hall was dark and gloomy, with only a single meager window to let in light. Timmerfell folk, it seemed, were fond of their stone walls.

Aldren walked through the dim hall to a door on the far side and swung it open.

A fire crackled in a spacious stone hearth, casting flickering light on the tapestried walls. A few bookshelves lined the room—a modest library for so small a town. Carpets covered the cold stone floors, while plush pillows padded the sofas and chairs. It was a comfortable room, one in which Aldren would prefer to stay.

Percival stood near the fire, leafing through a book. "Yes?"

"I have done as you requested, my lord. The girl has indeed remembered the events of the night. Though, she may not have been withholding from us. It is possible she came to remember while talking with . . . him."

Percival closed the book and turned to Aldren. "It makes little difference, either way. What have you discovered?"

"The girl seems to be in agreement with the other that it was these 'lamphyr' she saw. She said they were eyeless but that they could see her with the aid of their lamps. When they came towards her, she became frightened and . . . um . . . *wished* for them to go away, as she put it."

Percival looked into the fire. "And does she remember how, exactly, they came to depart?"

"No, my lord. She said only that it grew dark and cold before she fled."

Percival studied the flames. "Interesting. So she is not yet aware of her capability in the Art, yet capable she is. Our suspicions have been correct." Percival turned back towards Aldren, catching him in a stern gaze. "You will not be able to procrastinate further. You will need to speak to her on matters of the Art. She will need to understand such things if she is to allow her power to manifest consciously."

Aldren lowered his head. The Grand Magister had encouraged him to speak with the girl so that they might be better acquainted in order to facilitate any future discussions of the Art, should they be required. But he had put the matter off, citing his shyness as a reason. While it was true that Aldren was uncomfortable around people he did not know, particularly if they did not belong to any of the Towers, he had other reasons for avoiding the girl. Some things were better left alone. The girl was a reminder of an unhappy time, of something that should not have happened. They should have left her in Fallow and tended to this matter in the north themselves.

"It will be done, my lord," Aldren said.

CHAPTER 8

ALDREN AND EMELYN SAT in the common room as he unraveled the bandages from her hands.

"How do they feel?" he asked.

Emelyn wiggled her fingers. Her nails had broken to the quick and the skin was torn around her fingertips. They throbbed dully, but not enough to warrant any additional fussing. "They feel all right."

"Are you hungry? I have made some porridge, I can fetch you a bowl if you like."

Emelyn nodded.

Aldren rose, leaving her alone by the fire.

She watched as the fire crackled in the hearth. It still felt strange to be waited on and fussed over so, especially by a Magister. She had been appalled that morning when she found him rummaging around in the kitchen as he prepared breakfast. He had refused to let her help, insisting that she sit by the fire and wait until he removed her bandages. Given that she hadn't been allowed to leave her bed the previous day, Emelyn yielded and went to sit in the common room without further protest.

Aldren returned from the kitchen, carrying in his hands two bowls. "A simple breakfast this morning," he said, handing a bowl to Emelyn. "To help in your recovery."

Emelyn looked at the bowl of grey, lumpy porridge and forced a smile. "Thank you."

Aldren fidgeted with his spoon. "The past two days have been trying for you. Are you feeling well?"

"Yes, thank you."

Aldren nodded, though he seemed dissatisfied with the answer. After a few moments of silence, he spoke again. "Tell me, do you know anything of Magisters or of the Art?"

Emelyn raised her eyebrows. "Magisters? No, of you I know very little, and I know nothing of . . . 'the Art'?"

Aldren nodded, staring at his porridge. "That is what we call it. You called it magic, but we call it the Art, for it is an ability that requires skill, focus, dedication—just as any other art form. And it is, at times, capable of creating just as much beauty."

The Magister looked at the fire and whispered a few foreign words. The flames within the hearth flickered golden, green, and violet. Emelyn's spoon froze at her lips as she stared.

"Just so," Aldren said. "Beautiful. He whispered more words and the flames returned to normal.

"How . . . ?"

"The Art is a force of nature, much like a rainstorm or the warming rays of the sun. Like the sun, the Art is ever present, and those with the aptitude can tap into its power to accomplish extraordinary things. It is a gift bestowed upon only a few and forms the foundation of my Order."

"The Magisters."

Aldren nodded. "Yes. The Order of Magisters is dedicated to teaching those with the aptitude how to harness and wield the power of the Art. We also strive to further our understanding of it through study."

He caught Emelyn's eyes in a fixed gaze. "Do you understand? The Art is like a pool of which the waters comprise pure power. The ways in which that power can be harnessed is nearly limitless if one has the proper knowledge. The Magisters are dedicated to the pursuit of that knowledge."

Emelyn remained silent, caught in Aldren's intent gaze as she tried to make sense of what he was telling her. "I think so." She hesitated. "But is 'the Art' the ability to wield this power or the power itself?"

Aldren smiled, pointing a finger at her. "That is the very question our new apprentices most often ask. It is both the power and the ability. It is a little confusing at first, but you will soon understand as we do."

"I will?"

"Yes, for I will teach you."

Emelyn dropped her spoon in her bowl. "About the Art or how to wield it?"

"About it. For now, at least."

Emelyn looked askance at the Magi. "Do you mean to say I have the aptitude?"

Aldren paused. "That is a decision for the Grand Magister to make."

Emelyn poked at her porridge with her spoon. Why was he telling her this?

After a lengthy silence, the Magister continued. "It is, in most cases, impossible to tell if one has the aptitude or not. We can never be completely sure until an apprentice makes the attempt to wield the Art. Of all the novices that come to the Towers, only a fraction of them will have the aptitude, and of those fewer still will go on to become Magisters. It is a . . . rigorous . . . training process."

"What happens to those who don't make it?"

"Those without the aptitude sometimes choose to stay within the Tower, performing vital duties such as cooking, cleaning, and caring for the grounds. Others choose to leave and start families, living their lives elsewhere. The choice is theirs." Aldren paused. "Those with the aptitude who do not become Magisters . . . are not so fortunate."

"What do you mean?"

Aldren spread his hands open. "It is difficult to explain to one who does not understand. To one outside of the Tower."

He fell silent again and for a while Emelyn thought he might not continue, but he did.

"To become a Magister, one who is capable with the Art must undergo a . . . test, a trial of a sort, to determine whether he has the will and focus to wield the Art at the more complex levels required of a Magister. The test itself is quite difficult . . . and dangerous." He paused, glancing at her before looking away again. "We call it the Threshing."

Threshing. Each winter in Fallow, farmhands would toil away in barns and basements as they threshed the grain gathered from the autumn harvest. Though Emelyn had never partaken in such a task, she knew it to be tiresome work in which the grain was beaten with wooden flails in order to separate it from the chaff. The idea of such a task being applied in some way as a test for aspiring Magisters gave her chills.

"Only the strongest are able to complete the test," Aldren continued. "Those weaker in their abilities with the Art . . . well . . . it is regrettable. Yet even passing the test comes at a price." He passed a hand over his head.

"What kind of price?"

Aldren shifted in his chair. "All who are able to withstand the Threshing are scarred in some manner. It is different for each Magister. I was fortunate and lost only the hair on my body. Others have fared much worse, suffering blindness . . . burns . . ." He fell silent.

"Yet not all scars are visible. The strongest among us come out of the Threshing managing to evade all forms of physical deformation; yet the emotional toll is . . . untold."

Aldren paused, lowering his head. "The Threshing exacts its price upon us all, no matter how strong the individual, and some pay a greater price than others, whether visible or not."

"How terrible," Emelyn whispered.

"Indeed, yet necessary. The Art is a powerful gift, one that is not to be squandered on the unworthy. To undergo the Threshing is a voluntary choice, to force one to endure it would be little more than cutting one's throat with a knife." Aldren raised a hand. "I apologize for my crudeness, but such is the case, for one must possess sufficient will to survive. For that, it is imperative one undergo the trial of one's own volition."

"What happens if one chooses not to do the trial?"

"Those who choose to forego the trial are considered failed apprentices, little more than those who showed no aptitude with the Art at all. They remain in the Tower, contributing through other means than study in the Art."

"You mean they can't leave?"

Aldren hesitated. "They lead a comfortable life. Those that live in the Tower want for nothing. As it is, very few refuse to undergo the Threshing. Once one has had a taste of the Art, it is very difficult not to long for more."

Or maybe they felt they had nothing to lose when their only other option was imprisonment. Emelyn reminded herself to breathe. She didn't understand why he was telling her all of this. Did the Magi truly know anything about her parents? They hadn't said anything about it since leaving Fallow and Emelyn's refusal to speak up was dissolving.

"The Grand Magister said he knew of my parents. Was that true?"

Aldren blanched. "Y . . . yes. Of course."

"Then why have you said nothing to me of them? Who are they? *Where* are they? Why did they leave me?"

Aldren looked as though he wanted to run. "I am sorry,

but I cannot be the one to speak of them to you. The Grand Magister will do so when the time is right."

Emelyn frowned. What was that supposed to mean? Why couldn't they tell her now? She was tired of not having any answers.

Aldren rose from his chair.

"What of the people who lived here?" Emelyn asked. "What happened to them? Where did they go?"

Aldren sat back down. "We do not know."

When Emelyn said nothing, he continued. "We cannot know for sure, but we think that whatever happened was caused by the same thing that caused the disturbances in Fallow and the strange creatures you encountered."

Emelyn looked down at her battered hands. "The creature of magic."

Aldren said nothing.

"Will they be all right? The people who lived here, will they return?"

Aldren shook his head. "I do not know."

"What of Fallow? Is everyone there gone as well?"

"No, there were others of my Order seeing to the town's safety, as the Grand Magister said. Unfortunately, there was no one here capable of warding against such incidences, and I fear we are now seeing the outcome."

Emelyn felt numb. Everything was changing too much, too quickly. "Why is this happening? Why is this 'creature' doing all of this?"

Aldren gave a pallid smile as he stood. "Try not to worry, all will be well." He turned and walked from the room.

Try not to worry? He had just told her that something terrible had happened to the people of this town—that the same thing very nearly happened to the people of Fallow—and then told her not to worry. What else could she possibly do?

Emelyn did her best to keep busy, mostly tending to Ferrin in the stables. She tried not to think too much on what Aldren had said about the Art, or about the people of Timmerfell.

It was all too much to take in at once, so she focused on Ferrin instead. She enjoyed brushing his shaggy coat and feeding him hay from her hand. She was still there later in the day when Corran found her, holding in his hands two wooden staves.

"That's for you," he said, handing her the shorter of the two. "I found a carpentry shop and was able to make these. When your hands are better, I'll teach you to use it."

"Use it? How?"

Corran smiled. "It's a weapon for defense. Traveling can be dangerous, and I prefer not to leave our protection in the hands of the Magi."

Emelyn ran her sore hands over the staff. Could she really learn how to wield such a thing? The idea seemed ludicrous, yet she was eager to try, all the same. "Where did you learn to use a staff?"

Corran shrugged. "Not sure I can say I ever learned. Really only ever played with sticks with friends. My father, seeing us, taught me more disciplined moves. He thought it prudent, for a stick or cudgel is something easily obtained, unlike other weapons such as a sword. I might not be a master at fighting with a staff, but I know enough to hold my own and enough to teach you a thing or two so that you can defend yourself if needed."

Emelyn studied the wood of the staff, but her mind went elsewhere. "Do you miss them? Your parents, I mean."

Corran blinked. "My mother took ill after I left to apprentice in Fallow and died shortly after. My father . . . well, we haven't seen each other since I was a boy."

He hadn't answered the question, but Emelyn remained silent.

"We have a fair amount in common, you know," Corran said. "Life as a young apprentice is not glamorous. Lots of cleaning, fetching things, and running deliveries. I used think that my parents had sold me off into slavery, that my master had no intention of ever teaching me any woodcraft." He chuckled.

"Why did you stay?"

He shrugged. "I had little choice. It was the path chosen for me by my parents, one they had paid a good sum of money for. I couldn't leave, not without betraying them and sullying my father's name. I wouldn't do that."

Emelyn nodded, wondering why she had stayed in Fallow for so long. But where could she have gone? "Do you regret staying? I mean, if you could have left, would you?"

He tilted his head. "No. I'd not have left for anything."

It wasn't the answer Emelyn wanted to hear.

"Is something bothering you?"

Emelyn ran a sore finger along the grain of the wood. "The Magi . . . they want to teach me. About this Art of theirs."

"And that bothers you?"

Emelyn shrugged. "I don't know. I don't know what to think." She looked at Corran. "They said they knew of my parents, yet they won't speak of them to me. I don't understand why, and that bothers me. I feel like . . ."

"What?"

Emelyn took a deep breath. "I feel like they're planning something, that they have this idea about me that I don't understand. It makes me wonder if I was wrong to follow them. That maybe I should have stayed in Fallow."

"Maybe. But had you stayed, would you have been happy?"

Emelyn frowned at him—happiness wasn't the point.

"Did you have friends in Fallow? Loved ones? Someone who you wouldn't want to leave?"

Emelyn considered the question. "My friend Tilly . . . and Mr. Hibberly was always nice."

"And would you be willing to give up on finding about your parents in order to stay with them? Are they that important to you?"

She knew the answer immediately, and that pained her. "No."

"Then you made the choice you needed to make."

"I thought you would agree with me, tell me I should have stayed. It's what you said on that first night."

"I know. But we each have our own path in life. It's easy to forget that sometimes, especially when someone's path is very different from your own."

"But you're still here. Maybe your path isn't all that different."

Corran smiled. "Maybe not."

Chapter 9

The days passed as they traveled northwards. Aldren, despite his claim to teach Emelyn of the Art, kept his distance. He stayed close to the Grand Magister, speaking only a few polite words to Emelyn at mealtimes. She did not ask him again of her parents, feeling as though nothing could be gained by repeating that conversation.

Almost two weeks passed before they again cleared the dense forests, coming to a wide valley that marked the outskirts of Roelith. Small cottages dotted the low rolling hills, while golden grass rippled in the wind like waves. Roelith lay in the distance and, beyond that, the spiraling shadow of a Tower. It looked just like the one in Fallow, and Emelyn wondered if all Magister Towers looked the same and how many of them there were in the world.

They left the cover of the trees and Emelyn marveled over the beauty of the valley. She gazed at the cottages upon the hills, imagining herself in one of them. She wagered Roelith had a need for housemaids or cooks. In time, she might be able to save enough money to buy a small patch of land where she could spend her wintering years. Her doubts about following the Magi remained strong. Her conversation with Corran had helped allay some of her fears, allowing her to realize that, had she been given the choice again, she would still have chosen to follow the

Magisters. But that didn't mean she was willing to follow them indefinitely, especially if they wouldn't answer her questions. Now they were in a well-populated area and a better opportunity to part ways might not come again.

"Did you know the name 'Roelith' is quite old?" Aldren said, breaking the silence. "It is derived from a dialect that predates the time of colonization and carries the meaning 'northern gate' or something to that effect. The name is quite appropriate, as Roelith is truly the last bastion of civilization in the north. Beyond the city lies predominately wild lands with very few towns to speak of, and none of civilized worth."

Emelyn glanced at Corran, remembering the story he had told her of times prior to the Magisters. But his gaze remained fixed ahead, and Emelyn wasn't sure if he was even listening.

Despite her tenuous relationship with the Magi—and Miss Cook's voice telling her to remain silent—Emelyn spoke. "'The time of colonization'? Is that when the Magisters came?"

Aldren glanced back and smiled. He slowed his pace and, for the first time since leaving Fallow, walked alongside her. "Yes. Do you know much of this time?"

Emelyn shook her head.

"Well, long ago this land was wild and largely uninhabited save for a few rustic settlements and a number of barbaric tribes. To the south, in Solmere, civilization thrived and the people there accomplished many wondrous things, the most remarkable being the establishment of the Order of Magisters. Through the Order, the land and people achieved an unrivaled prosperity. As life in Solmere grew easier, people began searching for new challenges, and sights were soon set upon the unknown lands in the north.

"Explorers ventured forth, crossing the waters of the Randen Sound and founded an outpost that would, in time, grow into the city of Sunbridge. These explorers journeyed into the wilds of the north, mapping what was, at that time, uncharted territory. In time, the Order of Magisters followed suit, building new Towers in the northern lands that allowed the light of the culture and civilization of the south to spread throughout the region. It is in this light that the people of the North Reaches have thrived."

Emelyn had many questions, yet she was surprised by the one that passed her lips. "What of the forest people? Were they the 'barbaric tribes' you mentioned?"

Aldren glanced at Emelyn out of the corner of his eye. "Yes, an uncivilized people prone to wandering across the land as they saw fit. Very little is known of them."

"Do you know what happened to them?" Emelyn had always been intrigued by stories of the forest people and had wondered why they had disappeared.

"They are a people with a propensity to wander. They likely moved on to other, unexplored regions."

She was disappointed, though unsurprised. If he knew, others would know too, and then it wouldn't be a mystery at all.

They walked in silence for a while. Emelyn expected Aldren to return to walk alongside the Grand Magister as he had done for their entire journey. She was surprised, therefore, when he remained at her side, his staff tap-tapping on the hard-packed earthen road.

She gathered up the courage to ask another question. "What is the town like? Roelith, I mean?"

"It is quite an extraordinary town, to be sure. Despite the substantial distance between Roelith and Sunbridge, the inhabitants of the old 'northern gate' have fully embraced the culture of the south and enjoy the quality of life that such civilization brings. Nowhere else in the North Reaches has a township come close to the grandeur of

Sunbridge. And while the fine town of Roelith might fall short in some aspects, it is still a shining example of how civilization and culture can thrive even in the shadow of the northern wilds. It is fortunate we are passing through. For, if one cannot make the journey to Sunbridge, Roelith is a worthy destination and I think you will see many wondrous things here."

They arrived at the city wall later that afternoon to find a pair of rigid guards at the gates, standing watch. They were dressed in well-tailored black coats with wide, white cuffs and high collars. Emelyn glanced up at one of them as they passed, glimpsing ruddy cheeks and hard, flinty eyes. She quickly looked away.

They passed through the gate and into the town proper on a wide, cobbled street. Men in long black coats and tall hats strolled along the road, tapping the cobblestones with the silvery tips of their canes. Beautiful ladies in fur-trimmed cloaks and plumed hats swept alongside them, resting dainty gloved hands on proffered arms. Such couples kept to the side of the street, making way for the carriages and horses that rattled and clopped down the thoroughfare.

There were manicured gardens marbled by cobbled walkways, while mazes of trimmed hedges partially obscured the drab city wall. Water bubbled from carved stone fountains, adding a delightful note to the noise of the bustling city. Many of the gardens were brown and barren, but Emelyn could see in her mind the beauty they would bring come spring.

All around rose the grand houses of Roelith, with their tall arched windows and curtains of ivy that hung from wrought iron balconies. Emelyn, having lived all her life in Fallow, had not expected such grandeur. She gazed around in wide-eyed awe, realizing that Aldren's praise had not been idle.

Percival led them down the road. Emelyn trailed behind while craning her neck to look at the buildings. Many were built from plain grey stone, while others were golden, flecked with crystals that gleamed in the sunlight.

"Sunstone," Aldren said, apparently seeing her curiosity. "Imported from the south. Those with the means often choose to construct their houses with it. A status symbol of sorts."

Emelyn realized her mouth was hanging open and she snapped her jaw shut. She had thought many in Fallow to be wealthy, her employer among them. Yet no one had ever constructed any houses out of this sunstone. Emelyn was beginning to suspect that what was considered wealthy in Fallow was not necessarily the same in Roelith.

Percival slowed as he neared an inn. Fire-colored ivy clung to the brick walls, nearly eclipsing diamond-latticed windows before disappearing into the eaves of the roof. The sign was painted with "The Hillock Roe" and showed a spotted red fawn upon a green field. A boy appeared from the nearby stables and offered to take the mule. Emelyn hesitated but then relinquished the reins at a nod from Aldren. They walked inside and were soon greeted by a stout innkeeper.

"Greetings, my lords," the innkeeper said, smoothing wispy strands of hair combed over his balding pate. "What can I do for you?"

"We will be needing accommodations," Aldren said, "if you have rooms to spare."

"Of course, my lord, of course." His beady eyes darted to Emelyn and Corran. "Will my lords require separate lodgings for their servants?"

Emelyn heard a sharp exhale of breath as Corran scoffed.

"Yes. A room each, if you can manage it."

"Yes, yes, of course. Please, allow me." He led them upstairs, smoothing his hair as he showed them to each of their rooms. Emelyn had only been in her room a short while when she heard a soft knocking at the door. She opened it to find Corran. He walked in without waiting to be invited. Emelyn frowned.

"So, it seems we've been reduced to servants."

"I am a servant," Emelyn said, much more curtly than she had intended.

Corran frowned, looking puzzled. "No, you're not."

Emelyn looked at him askance—she couldn't tell whether or not he was joking.

"Anyway, that's not why I've come," he said. "I was wondering if you'd like to go out and look around. I've never been to a city like this before; I reckon you haven't, either. Could be fun."

Emelyn, still annoyed with Corran's lapse in manners, said nothing.

"Come on," Corran said, smiling. "I'll buy you a tall hat. Except I don't have any money, so . . . I'll steal one instead. For you."

"I don't want a tall hat."

"Oh?" Corran's eyebrows arched upward. "Why not? They're tall . . . and . . . fancy . . . I'll get a plumed one and we can gallivant about the town, just like all the other fine ladies and gentlemen."

Emelyn giggled at the thought of Corran in a feathered hat.

Corran's smile widened as he offered Emelyn his arm.

Emelyn, feeling as though she should still be angry, pursed her lips. But it was no use—the anger was gone. Shaking her head, she took Corran's arm and together they left the inn.

"Where should we go?" Corran said when they reached the road.

Emelyn looked up and down the thoroughfare. "One way is as good as the next, I suppose." She picked a direction and started walking.

They passed numerous shops, and Emelyn slowed as she peeked through the windows. There were hat shops and haberdasheries, toy shops, trinket shops, and shops displaying freshly cut flowers. There were butchery shops with rows of sausages hanging in the windows, and shops with tea that smelled sharp and pungent. There were alehouses and pie shops, soup shops, and cheese shops, all with enticing aromas that made Emelyn's stomach growl.

But the shop that made her stop in her tracks was the confectionary. Dainty chocolates shaped into balls and squares decorated with sugar flowers and golden flakes sat in the window, plump and enticing. Emelyn had never tried chocolate.

"Those look tasty," Corran said.

Emelyn said nothing.

"You should get one."

"I haven't any money." Emelyn mourned her money pouch, left in her chest in the basement at home. She wondered if it was still there, or if some grim and grisly creature had taken it. She turned away. "Let's go."

"Wait."

Emelyn turned to find Corran tousling his hair before approaching a passing gentleman with an outstretched hand.

"Please, sir," Corran said, "a little something to help ward the cold."

The man gave Corran a chilling look before hastening past.

"Corran!" Emelyn hissed, afraid of saying his name too loudly lest people know they were together.

Corran either didn't hear her or was ignoring her. "Please, sir," he said, limping towards a genteel couple. "Take pity on a poor wretch. My leg is wooden and there's no work to be had for the lame."

The woman at the man's arm gasped in horror while the man glowered at Corran under bushy eyebrows.

Corran was unfazed. He continued his shameless antics, approaching numerous passersby with pathetic stories of lost luck and hard times until a plump woman in a grand feathered hat shook her head and clicked her tongue.

"Poor thing," she said as she pulled a coin from her purse. She tossed it towards Corran—apparently her pity did not extend to putting herself in too close a proximity to beggars.

Corran picked up the coin and, grinning, sauntered back to Emelyn. "There," he said, placing the coin into her hands.

Emelyn gaped at him. "You shouldn't have done that!"

"Why not? These people have more than enough to spare, I'm doing them a favor reminding them of their charitable duties. I bet you the lady who gave that coin will tell all her lady friends about it at tea, and they'll all be aflutter with how kind and good she is. Trust me, it will be the highlight of her day."

Speechless, Emelyn could only stare.

He smiled. "Come on." Corran pushed open the door walked inside. Emelyn followed.

The aroma of cinnamon and vanilla hung in the air, sharp and sweet and pleasantly cloying. A narrow-faced man with a pencil-thin mustache stood behind the counter.

"Yes?" he said, eyeing Emelyn and Corran up and down. "May I help you?"

"My friend here would like a piece of chocolate," Corran said.

The man's eyebrows twitched upwards, but he said nothing.

Emelyn cleared her throat and walked to the counter. She placed the coin on the glass.

The man brightened. "Of course. Which kind would the young miss like?"

Emelyn peered at the numerous chocolates through the glass. There were so many and they all looked wonderful. "That one," she said, pointing to one with golden flakes.

"An excellent choice." The man fetched the chocolate from under the glass and gave it to Emelyn. He took the coin and gave her a smaller one in return.

Emelyn placed the coin in her pocket before heading back outside, chocolate in hand. She lingered a moment, admiring the candy, wondering how it had been formed into such a shape. She lifted it to her nose and breathed in its aroma.

Corran hovered near her shoulder. "Aren't you going to eat it?"

"It's just so lovely. It almost seems a shame to eat it." Though the smell of the chocolate had sent her mouth watering.

Corran chuckled.

Deciding she had looked long enough, Emelyn bit into the candy. Chocolate snapped under her teeth as dried fruit steeped in a spiced liqueur warmed her tongue. It was delicious.

"Well? How is it?"

Emelyn nodded, too busy chewing to answer.

He grinned.

Emelyn glanced at him. She was still feeling a little awkward over all the fuss Corran made about the chocolate. But she was also touched. Never before had anyone done such a thing for her, and the gesture of it meant more to her than the candy itself.

"Thank you," she said, wanting to say more, but not knowing what else to say.

Corran nodded.

They continued walking. Emelyn, content with the taste of chocolate lingering in her mouth, no longer paid so much attention to the shops and looked more closely at the town. The city was, in some respects, similar to Fallow. The way the different shops lined the streets, the way the streets themselves all seemed to lead towards the center of town. One difference was that Roelith was remarkably clean. Fallow, although a fairly clean town, still had muddy streets and gutters, along with the occasional scraps of trash that blew around in the wind. Emelyn would have thought that such a big town would have even muddier streets and even more trash littering the place. But if anything, Roelith seemed less dirty than Fallow. Maybe it was just this part of the city that was exceptionally clean.

If the town did have separate districts, then she and Corran were most decidedly in the wealthy area. From the fancy shops to the people in their fine clothing, everything about them exuded an air of wealth and opulence. Emelyn felt quite out of place in her worn breeches and rumpled coat. As she looked at the people around her, she noticed her attire had not escaped their attention, either. She felt a twinge of embarrassment as others glanced and gaped at her, sometimes with looks of shock or disdain. She wondered if it was because she was a girl in breeches or if it was the state of her dingy clothing. Perhaps it was both. Aside from the slight heat she felt in her cheeks, Emelyn was surprised to find she otherwise didn't much care. Granted, she would have preferred to go unnoticed, but the unwarranted attention did not make her want to run and hide as she would have in Fallow. She ignored the people as best she could, keeping her gaze to the shop windows or straight ahead. That was when she saw the park — an island of greenery in sea of stone. Emelyn quickened her pace.

She reached the park, her booted feet leaving the hard cobblestone road for soft grass and soil. Pebbled pathways wound through the grass and leaves, their stones grinding under Emelyn's boots. A pond glinted golden in the fading sunlight, while ducks and swans glided over the water. Away from the path was a grove of barren trees. Emelyn stepped from the pebbled walkway and rustled through fallen leaves. She breathed deeply, smelling the earthen autumnal air. It was quieter here, and Emelyn could almost forget she was in a city.

They walked in silence for a time. The shadows from the trees grew longer as the sky darkened, and Corran suggested they return to the inn. Emelyn reluctantly agreed, saddened to leave the peaceful park. They retraced their steps, heading back towards the pebbled path. They were about to leave the grove when a rustling from the leaves nearby made Emelyn stop. She walked towards the sound.

Emelyn knew she was drawing closer as the rustling grew louder; yet she couldn't see what was causing it. She scanned the ground, searching among the fallen leaves for the source of the noise, but saw nothing. Then, from the corner of her eye, a pile of leaves cavorted about. Emelyn blinked, thinking she must be confused. But the heap of leaves continued to flap and flutter until it looked at her with a small, black eye. That was when she saw a yellow hooked beak; a mottled, feathered head; and long wings that beat against the air yet were not able to take flight. Of course it was a bird, and not leaves, thrashing on the ground; Emelyn felt silly for not seeing it sooner.

She crouched down to get a better look, as did Corran. The bird grew still, the black eye darting back and forth as it kept them within view. The bird was much larger than the songbirds Emelyn normally saw perched in trees. It looked closer to a duck in size, though that was where all similarities ended.

"Do you know what it is?" Emelyn asked.

"It's a falcon. You can tell by the hooked beak," he pointed with a finger, "and the sharp talons."

The bird, agitated by his movement, snapped at his hand. Corran jerked back, managing to evade the bird's beak. He grinned.

"Why can't he fly? Is he injured?" Emelyn thought the bird must be hurt, but its wings appeared intact as they flapped against the ground.

"I'm not sure." Corran looked closer. "There." He pointed at the bird again, this time keeping his finger at a safe distance. "Around the leg. Do you see it?"

There was a thin cord tied around the falcon's leg, tethering it to the ground. "What is that? How could such a thing get around his leg?"

Corran rubbed his chin. "I reckon it's a trap of some sort. Though I haven't a clue as to how it works. I haven't seen anything like it before."

"A trap? Do people eat falcons?" Emelyn didn't like the thought of such a regal bird caught in a snare. "We have to help him."

Corran shook his head. "It's considered poor form to tamper with another's traps. I don't think we should."

"We can't just leave him here. We're in the middle of a city! Hunting shouldn't even be allowed here. If someone wants to eat a bird, they can find themselves a chicken."

Corran frowned, hesitating. "What do you propose?"

"We need to cut that cord somehow. Do you have a knife?"

Corran looked at her as though she had lost her senses. Even so, he reached into his boot and pulled out a knife. He handed it to her. "That bird will rend your hand bloody if you get near it."

Emelyn ignored him as she crept towards the bird, watching the beady, black eye that peered back at her. The falcon was calm for the moment, for which Emelyn was grateful. She looked at the thin cord tied around the falcon's leg and tried to follow it to where it was anchored, but she could see nothing below the layer of leaves. She considered a moment, then figured the line couldn't be very long, given that the falcon wasn't able to fly very far from the ground, and that it must be anchored near the bird itself. Emelyn eyed the falcon's talons—long and black and looking as sharp as glass. She swallowed, hoping her hands would be steady. Inching forward, she watched the falcon as it watched her and slipped the knife behind its yellow leg to the tether.

In a flurry of feathers and deafening screeching, the falcon took flight, flapping its wings in Emelyn's face. She reeled backwards, covering her face as hot, searing pain tore at her hands. Then, as quickly as it had begun, it stopped—the falcon was gone. Shaking, Emelyn lowered her hands, looking at rivulets of blood covering her fingers.

A hand took hers, warm and dry against her cold, clammy skin. Emelyn looked up to see Corran's hazel eyes glowering at her under a furrowed brow.

"You are mad," he said, though his voice was gentle. He blotted at the blood on her hands with the sleeve of his shirt. Emelyn watched with detached interest. He would ruin his shirt.

A faint screeching rang in Emelyn's ears. She looked up, wondering if the falcon had returned, but the sky was clear. Corran released her hands and rose to his feet. She looked at him and, consequently, saw a little man running towards them. Emelyn hurried to her feet as the man hollered and shook his fist.

"Stealers!" he shrieked, showing crooked brown teeth as he pointed a filthy finger at Emelyn. "Stealers steal feathery dinner! Now high-hats frown at Cobbe and chase her away with prickly broom! No more shiny circles for Cobbe to hide in pouches!"

"What?" Emelyn said, trying to understand the man's furious chattering. He was short, about half of her own size. He had a mane of brown hair, long and unruly that had, rather unsuccessfully, been tied back in a tail. Dark eyes peered from a muddy face as though he had wallowed in a puddle for his morning wash. His clothes, just as filthy, hung on him like they were two sizes too large. Yet even so, Emelyn could discern a slight curvature in the hips and chest, indicating that the little man was, in fact, a little woman.

The woman scrunched up her face at Emelyn's question. She stormed past, picking up the severed cord that lay on the ground. She held it up for Emelyn to see, as if that would resolve all questions on the matter.

Emelyn said, "Did you trap the falcon?"

The woman drew herself up and nodded. "High-hats want hunter-bird for dinner. Say it make them stronger than walking round bird. Cobbe very clever, leave to prepare stewpot while waiting for hunter-bird to land. But now Silver-eyes wrecks dinner and Cobbe soon feels broom prickles on backside." She frowned.

"Silver-eyes?"

The woman sighed, exasperated. She pointed at Emelyn. "Silver-eyes." Pointing at herself she added, "Cobbe."

"That's your name!" Emelyn was happy to have finally understood something clearly amongst all the nonsensical chatter.

Cobbe scrunched up her face again, looking at Emelyn as though a tree were sprouting from her head. She pointed another grubby finger at her. "Silver-eyes make good on stealing. Cobbe follow until she have shiny circles hidden in pouch." She gave a curt, single nod.

Emelyn looked to Corran for help.

He shook his head and put up his hands. "I told you not to tamper with someone else's trap."

Emelyn shot him a sharp glare before turning her attention back to Cobbe. "You want to follow us . . . for letting the bird go?"

Cobbe nodded. "Yes."

"For 'shiny circles'?" Emelyn still wasn't sure what that meant.

"Yes."

She considered a moment before reaching into her pocket and pulling out the coin given to her by the confectioner. "Do you mean this?"

Cobbe's eyes widened as she hopped up and snatched the coin from Emelyn's fingers. Before Emelyn knew what was happening, the coin disappeared into a hidden pocket.

"Not enough, but is good start," Cobbe said.

Emelyn stood dumbfounded, gaping at the little creature that had just stolen her coin. She glanced at Corran. The man seemed to be enjoying the confrontation and offered no assistance.

Cobbe grinned, showing her crooked, filthy teeth. She poked Emelyn in the thigh, prodding her to lead the way. Not knowing what else to do, Emelyn headed back to the inn.

CHAPTER 10

EMELYN STOOD IN the common room of the inn, trying to have a conversation with Corran, but failing. Cobbe had vanished into the kitchen upon their arrival, and all Emelyn could do was watch the door, wondering what the woman was up to.

A clamor of crashing pots shattered the calm and Emelyn flinched. Patrons chatting over mugs of ale ceased their conversations and looked towards the commotion. Corran shook his head and grinned, giving Emelyn a look that seemed to say, "Now look what you've done." He turned and walked outside. Emelyn was tempted to follow.

A woman screamed, and soon Cobbe came bolting through the door, her arms filled with onions, a loaf of bread, and a whole, freshly plucked chicken. A portly woman crashed through the door after her, her tousled hair covered with a kerchief and her round cheeks thoroughly flushed. She brandished a wooden spoon like a weapon, shaking it at Cobbe.

"Get back here, you foul creature!" the woman said before swinging at Cobbe with her spoon.

Cobbe dodged the attack, dropping a few onions on the floor. She grimaced, showing her weathered teeth that, together with her filthy face, gave her a frightful appearance.

The cook, taken aback, paused and licked her lips. "Come now," the woman said, reaching out with her spoonless hand. "Be a dear, and give me the food."

Cobbe twisted her face and spat on the floor. "Cobbe more clever than doughy Spoon-wench! Spoon-wench not know how to make good dinner. Cobbe can teach, but Spoon-wench have only dough between ears and won't listen."

The cook growled and lunged at Cobbe. Cobbe spun out of the way, rounded a corner and disappeared from sight. The woman was about to give chase when the stairs overhead creaked as the Magisters walked down. Upon seeing their robes, the woman quieted and lowered her head, her cheeks flushing an even deeper shade of red.

Percival surveyed the scene, his gaze darting from Emelyn, to the cook, and even to Cobbe who was now peeking around the corner. "It seems there is a disagreement," he said as his gaze settled once again on the portly cook. He arched an eyebrow, indicating that he expected an answer even though he hadn't posed a question.

"N . . . no, my lord," the cook mumbled, her cheeks flushing so deeply that she looked to be on the verge of choking. "A minor misunderstanding is all. Nothing to warrant the attention of one such as yourself." She wrung the corner of her apron as she studied the floor.

Expressionless, Percival looked at her. "Indeed."

His gaze shifted to Cobbe, visible only for the shock of brown hair shooting from around the corner. Percival beckoned her forward with a wave of his hand. To Emelyn's surprise, Cobbe complied, though the little woman glowered at the Magister in defiance as she tightened her grip on her procured goods. Aldren emitted a startled gasp when he saw her, but otherwise remained silent.

Percival studied the woman before turning to Emelyn. "I trust you had good reason for bringing this . . . person . . .

here." He indicated Cobbe with an outstretched hand. "Though such creatures are, in truth, little more than vermin. I fear you may have doomed our generous host to an infestation just as surely had you released a crate of rats within his pantry."

Emelyn was shocked to hear the Grand Magister speak of Cobbe in such a manner, especially while in her presence. Cobbe remained silent, though she scrunched up her face into a vicious scowl at the Magister's back.

"She requires payment, I think. I released a bird she had trapped and now she wants compensation for it." Emelyn could feel her cheeks redden at her blunder. Not for releasing the bird—she had no regrets about that—but rather for her inability to resolve the matter herself.

"Oh?" Percival turned back to Cobbe. "Aldren, see to it that . . . it . . . is fairly compensated." Having resolved the problem, Percival disappeared up the stairs.

If Aldren had heard the Grand Magister, he gave no indication of it. He remained fixed in place, staring at Cobbe with a wide, wondrous grin.

Cobbe narrowed her eyes as she watched him. "Cobbe take shiny circles and leave. Cobbe not vermin—much too clever to be vermin. Cobbe try to be nice and teach Spoon-wench new things, but Spoon-wench too daft, so Cobbe take shiny circles and go."

The words washed over Aldren with no perceivable effect as the Magister sidled over to Emelyn and whispered to her, "Do you know what that is?"

"*She* is a person," Emelyn said, annoyed at the Magister's low regard for the woman.

Aldren sobered as though splashed with cold water. "Yes, of course." Then the smile returned, his voice excited once again. "That is a Wylkin—a small people of the forest. I have never seen one, but they are renowned for their cookery skills. All the nobility in Sunbridge vie to employ one in their kitchens, hoping to be the envy of society. Elaborate dinner parties are held for no other reason than to boast over one's employed Wylkin's capabilities. The Wylkin themselves are never allowed to be seen, of course. They are notoriously ill-tempered and their, ah, unkempt habits would make even the most slovenly of housekeepers blush. No person of good breeding would ever deign to be seen with one. But tucked away in a sooty kitchen where the gentry never wander, they can forget the little folk's presence easily enough. I had always hoped to see one or, better yet, be invited to such a dinner party only a Wylkin can provide. But I know of no one who has one employed and they are rarely seen outside their forest homes. It is often said that, in the forest, the little folk are near impossible to find to outsiders should they not wish to be found." Aldren grinned at Cobbe, who was sitting on the floor eating an onion as though it were an apple.

Emelyn marveled at Aldren, wondering how a powerful Magister could be reduced to a giddy schoolboy over the sight of a remarkably filthy woman no larger than a child. Then something the Magister had said resonated with her. "Are they the forest people? The ones that used to live around Fallow?"

"Hmm?" Aldren floated out of whatever reverie he had been caught in. "Forest people? No, they are not the same. Though it has been put forth that they might, in some respects, be related. So little is known about either people that we cannot know for sure." He resumed his study of Cobbe before approaching her and crouching down to where she sat.

Cobbe looked up at him and offered an onion that Aldren politely accepted.

"Tell me," Aldren said while rolling the onion around on the palm of his hand. "How would you attempt to lessen the bitterness of leechwood bark?"

Cobbe paused her munching as she pondered the question. "Cobbe boil for three hours then soak in milk and vinegar." She snatched the onion out of Aldren's hand and returned the bulb to her stash.

Aldren seemed not to notice the loss of the vegetable and beamed at Emelyn. "Remarkable! So few even know what leechwood is, let alone how to prepare it!"

Emelyn stood mute, unsure how to answer.

Aldren returned his attention to Cobbe. "I wonder, little one, if you might have anything to teach me. I am no novice in matters of cookery, but there is still much for me to learn."

Cobbe studied him with narrowed eyes before her face split into a wide, toothy grin. She handed him her stash of onions and bread and, keeping the chicken for herself, led him towards the kitchen.

Emelyn watched them go, finding the whole exchange odd yet feeling strangely excluded at the same time. What should she do, now? She thought about venturing into the kitchen to see what Aldren and Cobbe were doing, but the woman seemed to be in a good humor and Emelyn feared her presence might spoil it.

The innkeeper walked through a door, wheeling a cart laden with a barrel of ale. He surveyed the room and, apparently finding nothing amiss, resumed his business. Emelyn watched him as he worked. She considered walking up to him, excusing herself for the intrusion, and enquiring if he knew of any opportunities of which a young servant might avail herself. In her mind, she imagined he would tell her of a position at a nice estate home with expansive gardens and horses and geese that had need of a young woman. The work would be difficult, she had no illusions about that, but her strife and toil might be lessened in such grand surroundings. She sat down at an empty table as she pondered the possibilities.

Possibilities? What possibilities could there be other than putting herself in the exact same position she had been in before? The idea of returning to such a life filled Emelyn with dread. It was a feeling that perplexed her, for it was the only life she had ever known. Until the Magisters, that was. Then everything had changed. Part of her wished she had never encountered them. That she was still in Fallow, oblivious to the workings of the outside world, toiling within her bubble, for it was the only world she would ever know and might, in time, find contentment in it.

She continued to watch the innkeeper bustling about. She knew she ought to enquire after some kind of employment, that she ought to part ways with the Magisters. Yet she couldn't bring herself to do it. Emelyn had been telling herself that she had followed the Magi for information about her parents. And it was true, in the beginning, at least. But much had changed during her time with them. She was no longer a servant, no longer scraping and bowing to those deemed to be her betters. She recalled the altercation between the cook and Cobbe, of how the cook had flushed and worried her apron, staring at the floor as Percival spoke to her. Emelyn saw herself in that woman, and she felt saddened and ashamed. She didn't wish to grow old living under the bootheel of another, scraping together a menial existence only to die forgotten as though she had never existed at all.

She found herself hungering for more, for something that might give her life some meaning. Finding her parents, though still important, somehow seemed less vital. It was strange. Part of Emelyn felt that she would never be complete until she discovered what had become of her parents, that her heart would always be punctured with an emptiness that could not be filled as long as her heritage remained a mystery. Yet, important as it was, she realized it was no longer the driving force in her actions. That, once knowledge of them was obtained, she might not go back to Fallow as she had thought. For the first time, the idea of never seeing Fallow again didn't frighten her.

Emelyn's thoughts were interrupted as the innkeeper placed a tankard of ale in front of her. He walked away before Emelyn had a chance to thank him. She sipped her ale, ignoring the bitter taste as her mind roiled with turbulent thoughts.

Percival descended the stairs and sat down in the chair opposite her. The innkeeper hustled over with another tankard of ale.

"Two plates of your finest dinner," Percival said.

The innkeeper bobbed his head and left.

The Grand Magister studied Emelyn for a moment and said, "You have the look of one who is weighed down by heavy thoughts. You may unburden some of them upon me, should you so wish."

Emelyn considered the Magister, hearing his kind words yet wondering what was meant behind them. What should she say to him? That she no longer wished to return to Fallow? That she wished to find a way to occupy her time beyond that of service? What would he say to that? Would he say anything? Or would he simply sit there, smugly sipping his ale as she played into some unseen plan of his?

The silence lengthened, and then Emelyn said, "What do you want with me?"

Percival, clearly unfazed by her bluntness, gazed at her. Emelyn fought the urge to look down, and she met his gaze, though not with the same level of confidence.

Percival smiled. "My dear, you have a gift, though I am not sure you yet realize it."

"What do you mean?"

"Surely your conversation with Aldren has shed some light on that matter. He told you much, did he not?"

Emelyn thought back on her talks with the Magister, as few as they had been. One among them stood out. "You mean the Art?"

"Indeed."

"What has that to do with me?"

Percival paused, sipping some ale. "I have reason to believe you are gifted with the ability to wield the Art."

It was the answer Emelyn had expected. Aldren had hinted as much, as had Percival before Emelyn made him utter the words. Yet now that they were uttered, the words sounded strange and came as a shock all the same. "That's not possible."

"I assure you it is."

"Two weeks ago I hadn't even heard of this 'Art.' I've never been taught anything of it. Magister Keller said that it was impossible to know if one had the ability until one actually tried. I've never tried, so how can you know?"

"Oh? What of your incident in Timmerfell? With the 'lamphyr' as our rustic friend so charmingly called them. How did you manage to escape that situation?"

Emelyn flinched. The recollection of that night was unsettling. "I don't know. I ran."

"Indeed you did run, but not before dispelling those apparitions. No mean feat, I assure you. There are robed Magisters within the Towers that would not have been capable, yet somehow you managed."

"That's not possible."

Percival smiled, his stern eyes softening. "My dear, you have much to learn of what is possible in this world."

Silence hung between them as the innkeeper brought them their dinner: roasted quail stuffed with leeks, fruit, and nuts, swimming in a rich, dark sauce. Any other day Emelyn would have been delighted with such fare. Now all she could manage was to poke at it with her fork. Percival had no such difficulties. He carved his quail with quick and deft strokes, eating in silence as he left Emelyn with her thoughts.

"Suppose you're right," Emelyn said as Percival finished the last of his meal. "Suppose I do have the ability, as you say. What will happen then? What does it mean?"

Percival dabbed at the corners of his mouth with a napkin before pushing his plate away. "Aldren shall teach you the ways of the Art so that you might better harness your capabilities."

"And then what? Will I be carted off to one of your Towers? Locked away until I undergo the Threshing?"

Percival folded his hands as he held her in a stern gaze. Emelyn wondered if her bluntness had finally landed her in trouble.

"It is difficult to say. Your case is an exceptional one. I have not yet decided how to resolve it."

"What do you mean? Exceptional in what way?"

"As you yourself noted, you have not received instruction of any kind in the ways of the Art. For our young apprentices, even those who later prove capable, it would be quite impossible for them to apply it without the proper training. To wield the Art as Magisters do requires training in runes—how to speak their names and how to inscribe them. It is these acts that allow Magisters to tap into the Art and wield its power. It is a learned ability that requires only the strength of mind to master. A lowly stable boy could, in theory, become a powerful Magister if he exhibited the proper mental acuity.

"Yet you, who have had no training whatsoever, can wield the Art with substantial power." Percival grew silent and watched Emelyn, making her feel like an insect trapped in a glass.

She rubbed her forehead. "What does that mean?"

"It means you have an inherent ability to wield the Art; an ability you have acquired through nature alone, just as you acquired the color of your hair and eyes. Very few individuals have had such a capability, and none of them were ever Magisters. How one such as you would find a place within the Towers is not yet known."

Emelyn tried to understand what Percival had told her, but it was too much, too unbelievable. She stared at her cold quail as she sought to make sense of it all.

"What of my parents?" she said, looking up to meet the Magister's eyes. "Did you ever know anything about them or did you only bring me along because you suspected I had this . . . 'gift'?"

"Both are true, though I will admit I acted more upon my suspicions than of my knowledge of your parents. I knew you would not likely follow without a reason you found to be important. So I gave you one, though it was not a lie."

"Why won't you tell me about them? When I asked Magister Keller, he said he couldn't tell me. Why?"

Percival smiled. Emelyn suspected it was to be kind, but in her rising anger she found the smile condescending.

"My dear, there are some things in this world that you are simply not ready to understand. To explain them to you would likely do more harm than good. But I promise you, when you are ready, I will tell you all you wish to know." Percival rose and left the table.

Emelyn looked down at her dinner. The sauce had congealed, looking like a pool of blood around the cold quail. Her stomach lurched and she ran upstairs to her room where she emptied the contents of her stomach into the chamber pot. Footsteps approached the door, then Corran's voice expressed concern. Emelyn wiped her mouth and locked the door, leaving him unanswered.

Proficient in the Art. Exceptional. Percival's words stabbed at her like pin pricks. How could she possibly begin to believe what he was telling her? She was a simple housemaid, how could she have done what he said happened?

Over the next few days, Corran's visits to her door increased at first, as did his gentle rapping and pleas for her to come out. Emelyn ignored him and, in time, his visits ceased and she was left in silence. She sat in a chair near the window, watching people bustle in the street below. She felt strange watching them. Distant. Like an animal watching people pass by her cage.

The innkeeper came to her room at regular intervals. Emelyn could hear the clinking of plates and cups as he set a tray of food outside her door, along with a clean pot for her room. His knock was always quiet, tentative. Sometimes, after the innkeeper's footsteps had receded down the stairs, Emelyn would crack the door open and bring in the supplies. Other times she would leave them there, untouched. The tray was always removed, though Emelyn couldn't recall ever hearing the innkeeper take it.

The days wore on, passing like a dream as Emelyn watched from her chair. The sun wheeled through the sky, throwing shadows across the cobbled road until the shadows themselves were all that remained. Emelyn knew that the Magisters were still there, sleeping under the same roof as her. They had not come knocking at her door, for which she was grateful. Yet their presence still troubled her. Memories of her conversation with Percival floated about her, sparking in her mind turbulence and unease.

She knew a decision was required of her; that she would need to leave the confines of her room and face the outside world.

Would she follow the Magisters and learn of the Art as Percival had decreed? Would they let her stay, should she decide to remain behind? The idea that she no longer had a choice in the matter frequently surfaced, turning her stomach to ice. What would happen to her if she did follow? Would she be swept into the world of Magisters and Towers? Of runes and the Art? Emelyn couldn't begin to comprehend what such a life would be like. As unremarkable as her life had been, it had, at least, been simple. Safe. Although she had no desire to return to service, she had just as little desire to become a plaything of the Magisters. What should she do? The question echoed within her, yet no answer came. So Emelyn continued to sit and watch out the window.

Time crept by, quiet and unassuming. The tentative knocks at her door faded into the beating of her heart, the brilliant light of the sun ebbed to the pale glow of the moon. A quiet descended, and Emelyn wondered if that were all the peace she would find.

A lone girl stood upon the cobblestones, looking up at Emelyn's window. At first Emelyn didn't recognize her; she was only something Emelyn happened to be looking at. The girl was, at first, insignificant. But as Emelyn looked, the girl's features sparked distant memories. She was young, perhaps around eight or nine. She had long, dark hair, wore a dress of rough leather and her feet were bare. The girl from Fallow. Any other time Emelyn would have been surprised, shocked even, to see the same strange little girl so far from home. She would have sought an explanation, wondering how the girl came to be on the busy streets of Roelith and looking up at her window. But somehow none of that seemed important and Emelyn's heart leapt to see a familiar face—one not tied to her problems.

Emelyn rose from her chair to get a better view, worrying that the girl might disappear into the crowd. But she remained, staring up at Emelyn's window as though expecting her to come down. Emelyn watched a few moments longer.

When she had assured herself of the girl's location, Emelyn unlocked her door and hurried downstairs. She felt a brief pang of fear as she hurried through the common room, worried she might see Corran or, worse still, the Magisters. But the common room was empty and Emelyn stepped outside.

A smile bloomed across the little girl's face as she watched Emelyn approach. Just as Emelyn drew near, the girl laughed before turning and running away. Emelyn felt a pang of helplessness. She hadn't the energy or desire to run; yet she didn't want to lose sight of the girl. Gathering what energy she could muster, Emelyn gave chase as best as her legs would carry her.

Emelyn's pace was painfully slow, and on more than one occasion she lost sight of the girl. But just when she was about to give up, she would see a trail of dark hair or hear a faint clicking of beads, and she would plod on, wondering when the chase would end. Sometimes the girl came back for her, drawing close before darting away again in a peal of laughter.

The game seemed to carry on for hours, though Emelyn knew it couldn't have been so long. In time they came to the great park in the center of town and the girl, once among the trees, slowed to a walk.

Emelyn followed in silence as the girl wound her way through the trees and shrubs. They came to a circle of rosebushes—a tangle of barren, thorny branches. The girl ducked through bushes without so much a snag on her dress. Emelyn followed, though her passage was much more difficult. After a short struggle, Emelyn managed to make it through, though not before tearing a hole in her shirt.

The girl was sitting on the ground, playing with a little black beetle. Emelyn hesitated, not wanting to sit on the cold, damp earth. The air was chilly enough, biting at

Emelyn's skin, and she wondered how the girl could be running around in so few clothes without so much as a shiver. Yet, after several minutes of being ignored by the girl in favor of the beetle crawling over her hands, Emelyn decided to sit.

As soon as Emelyn had settled among the leaves and twigs, the girl set the beetle free and turned her eyes on her. Emelyn blinked. She recalled that the girl had grey eyes in Fallow, similar in color to her own. Yet now she peered at her with bright blue eyes—as clear and luminous as the sky. Emelyn had never seen eyes such a color, made all the more striking against the girl's dark skin and hair.

"You are sad," the girl said.

Emelyn nodded, fighting the lump rising in her throat. "Why?"

"Because I'm alone and frightened."

"Why?"

Emelyn looked at the little girl, unsure how to answer such a question. "You wouldn't understand."

The girl looked down, fiddling with the dead leaves on the ground. "I get sad sometimes, too," she said, more to the leaves than to Emelyn. "And afraid."

"Oh?"

The girl nodded. She picked up a leaf and placed it in Emelyn's hand. "Sometimes when I'm sad I like to make things new and pretty." She picked up a leaf of her own, holding it between her fingers. Emelyn gasped as the brown, wizened leaf grew green and glossy as though it had just been plucked from the summery branches of a verdant tree.

The girl giggled. "Now you try."

Emelyn dropped the leaf as if it had burned her. "I can't . . ."

The girl smiled, dimples creasing her cheeks. She picked up the leaf and put it back in Emelyn's hand. "I understand. I don't usually show other people either, but you're different. You can do it later, if you want."

Emelyn opened her mouth to protest, but words escaped her. It was all she could do to simply humor the girl and nod her head.

The girl seemed pleased and she stood up, brushing the dirt off her dress. Then her smile faded as she looked Emelyn in the eyes. "Don't be afraid," she whispered. "It makes them stronger and you'll need to be strong, too, when the snow comes."

Emelyn frowned. "Who . . . ? And why?"

The girl said nothing. She placed the fresh green leaf into Emelyn's hand before resting her own hand upon Emelyn's shoulder. Emelyn looked into the girl's brilliantly blue eyes and felt an inexplicable sadness and longing.

"What is your name?" she whispered.

The girl smiled, the dimples returning. "Iyen," she said before turning and disappearing through the thorny bushes.

Emelyn thought to call after her, to get up and follow her and ask her more questions. But her energy was drained, and she knew that by the time she had fumbled her way through the brambles the girl would have long been gone. Instead, she remained sitting on the ground, running her fingers over the smooth, glossy leaf the girl had given her. She ran in her mind all Iyen had told her, revisiting all that she had seen. Emelyn knew little of the Art, but she felt certain that this girl was proficient in it, given what she had just done with the leaf. And that girl was no Magister.

Emelyn looked at the desiccated leaf resting in the palm of her hand. How could she possibly change it? The idea seemed ludicrous. Yet, with Iyen's green leaf lying beside it, Emelyn started to truly believe Percival's words—that she had no idea of what was possible anymore. Looking at the leaf, she wanted to believe it was possible, that she could make it alive and green again, that she could make something beautiful in the world.

Emelyn closed her eyes. What if she could change it? What if she did have the ability and could learn to use it as Iyen did and make things beautiful and bright? Would she still be afraid? Would she still feel alone?

She looked down at her hand and found resting in her palm two perfect green leaves. Emelyn choked back a gasp of emotion—something between a sob and laughter— as she tucked the leaves into her pocket. She turned her face towards the sky, allowing the cold wind to caress her fevered cheeks. A smile crossed her lips and, for the first time in many days, Emelyn could feel the warmth of hope blossoming within her.

She got to her feet and dusted off her breeches. The once clear sky had clouded over, grey and steely and foreboding ill weather. She wove her way through the tangle of rose bushes. Passing was easier this time and she managed to spare her clothes any further snags. Once out of the bramble, Emelyn looked around for the girl, but she was nowhere to be seen.

She turned and headed back towards the inn just as the first feathery flakes of snow started to fall.

CHAPTER 11

THE FIRE CRACKLED, illuminating the darkened camp with flickering light.

Aldren drew another rune in the snow with the tip of a stick. *"Caelum,"* he said. "Air."

Emelyn looked at the row of runes, a line of scrolling swirls and angular strokes. They looked like little more than scribbles of an aimless mind. She pointed to the first rune Aldren had drawn. *"Ignis,"* she said, then pointed to the other runes. *"Aqua, Terra, Caelum.* Fire, Water, Earth, Air."

Aldren nodded, his eyes sparkling with approval. "Yes, correct."

He lifted the stick he had used to draw the runes. "Now, focus the word to the object you wish to alter. Visualize the meaning of the word, the *power* of the word, bend it to your will so that it may manifest. Like so." Aldren spoke the rune, *Ignis,* his face illuminating when the tip of the stick blossomed into flame. Then he spoke another rune, *Caelum,* and the flamed flickered and died as though extinguished by a hidden wind.

It was a display Emelyn had witnessed several times. This was the fourth lesson Aldren had undertaken with her since leaving Roelith in order to teach her the ways of the Art. Each lesson involved Aldren performing some feat—such as lighting a stick on fire, or making a stone weep water—in order to illustrate the application of the Art. Such exercises were, Aldren had assured her, the most rudimentary means of testing young novices. Should a novice fail such a simple task, it was concluded that he had no aptitude with the Art and was put to other tasks or out of the Tower entirely. It was, quite obviously, a point of consternation for Aldren that Emelyn had not been able to succeed in a task he deemed suitable for children.

After each demonstration provided by the Magister, Emelyn would make her own attempt. She would speak the words, just as Aldren had done, yet only ever achieved a blinding headache. When she told him of the pain that flashed behind her eyes, his puzzled expression told her that it was not a usual occurrence among new students of the Art. He tried not to let her see his concern, however, and dismissed her failures as "no matter."

Yet it mattered to Emelyn, she was surprised to discover. As distressing as her conversation with Percival had been regarding her abilities in the Art, Emelyn had begun to come to terms with the idea. Her encounter with Iyen had helped ease her fears, giving her comfort in the knowledge that she was not alone. Emelyn had kept the two leaves from that day and would sometimes stroke them with her fingers to help reassure herself that it had not been a dream, that she really could do remarkable things, even if she didn't know how, exactly, to do them.

Aldren watched her as he handed her the singed stick. Emelyn's heart sank. She could already feel the sting of failure, the shame of disappointing both her teacher as well as herself. She took the stick with trembling fingers, giving a silent plea to succeed so that she might not see the look of disappointment in Aldren's eyes. She focused on the stick as Aldren had instructed and whispered the rune, *"Ignis."* Pain flashed behind her eyes and she winced, lowering the stick that she knew, without looking, she had failed to ignite.

"No matter," Aldren murmured.

Emelyn ground her teeth, reminding herself that he was only trying to be kind. She rubbed her eyes until the pain subsided.

"You are tired. We will try again tomorrow."

Emelyn nodded as Aldren rose and left.

As soon as the Magister had gone, Cobbe toddled over and thrust a bowl of stew into Emelyn's hands. "Eat."

Emelyn lifted the bowl to her nose, smelling the savory spices. "Thank you."

A broad smile stretched across Cobbe's face.

Emelyn had been surprised that morning when they left Roelith and Cobbe had come trailing after them, riding a great brown pig as though it were a horse. Emelyn had spent that morning trying to figure out which was the greater surprise: the pig as a beast of burden or the fact that Percival gave no objection to Cobbe accompanying them. Emelyn had later discovered that Aldren and Cobbe had come to some kind of agreement that Cobbe would follow them and supply her services as camp cook. How Percival was made to agree to such an arrangement, however, Emelyn never knew.

A sharp poke in the shoulder startled Emelyn from her reverie.

"Eat," Cobbe said, pointing at the bowl of stew as though Emelyn needed reminding of what, exactly, she was supposed to be eating. Cobbe stood and watched as Emelyn lifted a spoonful of stew to her mouth. Satisfied that her directions were being followed, Cobbe settled herself down on the ground and watched Emelyn eat.

After a few moments of silence, Cobbe said, "Silver-eyes tense. Frowns even though eating dinner Cobbe make. This not natural."

Emelyn stopped eating as Cobbe spoke, though she snapped the spoon back up to her mouth again lest she suffer another sharp poke in the shoulder. "I'm just tired."

Cobbe shook her head as she scowled at Emelyn. "Cobbe not fooled. Cobbe very clever and knows when Silver-eyes speaks falsehoods." Cobbe narrowed her large eyes to further show her displeasure.

Emelyn felt a pang of guilt. "I'm sorry, Cobbe. It's just my lessons with Magister Keller aren't going well and I'm frustrated. It's making my head hurt."

Cobbe's scowl faded as she nodded with the gravity of a sage. "Cobbe understands. Red-robes very demanding. Think they know all, but Cobbe knows better."

She nodded at Aldren, who was eating his dinner with the Grand Magister. "Though Glass-eyes more clever than most red-robes. Cobbe might be able to teach him some things."

Emelyn hid her smile behind a spoonful of stew. She was never sure what might offend Cobbe, so she usually tried to keep her amusement to herself.

"Lessons with Hollow-man, these go better for Silver-eyes?"

Emelyn glanced at Corran, who was busy brushing down Ferrin. She didn't know why Cobbe insisted on calling him "Hollow-man." Emelyn had asked once but the only reply she received was a quizzical look from Cobbe, who then stated, "Because he is."

"The lessons are going well," Emelyn said. Corran had begun teaching her how to use the staff as he had promised back in Timmerfell. Emelyn had been worried that Corran would be upset with her for refusing to speak with him while in Roelith. But if the man was upset, he showed no sign of it. He was as friendly as ever, though he did seem to spend more time alone than he used to. Emelyn suspected this might be due to Cobbe, as the two didn't get along very well. It was little wonder for Cobbe, more often than not, would act and speak as if Corran wasn't there.

"Let Cobbe see." Cobbe grabbed Emelyn's hand. She peered at Emelyn's palm in the light of the fire, scrutinizing the newly formed calluses. She nodded.

"Good," she said, releasing Emelyn's hand. "Silver-eyes also clever. In time, maybe almost as clever as Cobbe. This is great honor."

Emelyn couldn't help but smile at Cobbe's compliment and the woman shared her delight with a wide smile of her own. She continued to prattle on about cooking, traveling, and the weather—whatever seemed to enter her head—as Emelyn ate her stew. Once the bowl was empty, Cobbe scooped it up and disappeared.

Left alone at the fire, Emelyn's thoughts wandered back to her lessons with Aldren. She had never thought herself a proud or ambitious girl, but her stark failure bothered her so much that, upon reflection, she realized that never before had she failed an appointed task. Any instruction given to her by Miss Cook—whether cooking, cleaning or running errands—Emelyn had always been able to execute without error. When learning something new, she required only a single demonstration of the proper way of doing it before being able to replicate the task perfectly. Failure, she began to realize, was not something she had been acquainted with. Not that they were difficult tasks. Aldren would likely split his sides laughing if he knew she was comparing the Art with menial housework. Thinking about her struggles only served to put her in a foul mood, so she rose from her spot by the fire and wandered over to Corran and Ferrin.

Corran had finished brushing the mule and was whittling a stick with a knife. Ferrin, tethered to a nearby tree, rooted along the ground as he grazed for whatever grass he could find. Now that winter had arrived, grass was becoming increasingly sparse. The snow was not yet so deep as to prevent stray tufts from poking through, but Emelyn suspected that it wouldn't be long until Ferrin could no longer graze and would rely entirely upon the provisions on his back to sustain him. This worried her, for the further north they traveled, the more scarce supplies would become, and Emelyn feared their supplies would not last.

She rummaged through the packs. Ferrin's apples had long since run out, but Aldren had found some roots that, he had said, "Those of an equine nature are quite fond of." Having found them, she waved one in front of Ferrin's nose. The mule stopped rooting in the snow and nibbled on the proffered fare. Emelyn smiled.

"It's a good thing that mule has such heavy packs, else he'd surely grow fat with all the extra food you give him," Corran said as he whittled.

"It's *because* his packs are so heavy that I give him the little extras. He works hard and deserves them."

Corran chuckled. "How is your training with the Magi progressing?"

Emelyn's smile faded as she studied the velvety hair on Ferrin's nose. It was strange to be discussing her training in the Art with Corran. She knew how he felt about the Magi, even though he usually tried to hide it.

"It's not going well, truth be told."

Corran stopped whittling and looked up, his eyebrows raised. Emelyn searched his face for any sign of smugness or judgment, of some look or glance that said, "I told you so." But there was none.

"Why do you say that?" he asked.

Emelyn gave Ferrin a final pat on the nose. "Because it's not," she said, turning to face Corran. "I've not been able to complete a single task Magister Keller has given me. I'm starting to think they're wrong about me. That I can't do the things they say I can."

Corran was silent. "The Magi may be many things," he said after a while, "but they are not fools. I doubt they have made a mistake."

Emelyn was surprised by Corran's answer. She had expected him to object to her lessons with the Magister, that he would take the opportunity to try and talk her out of it. "Then why do I keep failing? Magister Keller says he is giving me the simplest tasks. If they're right about me, then why can't I do them?"

Corran smiled and shrugged. "I don't know. All I know is that you are not one of them. Despite what they say, you are different. Perhaps their way is not your way."

Emelyn fell silent, remembering that day with Iyen and the two green leaves she still kept in her pocket. It was then Emelyn remembered something she had meant to ask Corran. "I never told you that I met a girl back in Roelith before we left. She said her name was Iyen. Wasn't that also your wife's name?"

Corran's knife froze over the piece of wood. "Yes," he said, his voice hoarse.

"I wouldn't have thought it a very common name," Emelyn said. "She was strange, that girl. She wore leather clothes I've never seen before, with pretty little beads dangling from the hem. But most strange of all is that I saw her in Fallow, the morning of the festival. And yet there she was in Roelith, the same clothes, the same beads, though her eyes were a different color from what I remembered. Isn't that odd?"

Corran's knife trembled in his hand. He laid it on the ground, his face so twisted with confusion and pain that Emelyn felt as though she had just stabbed him in the heart.

"What's the matter?"

Corran's brow furrowed, his eyes distant. Rising to his feet, he wandered off into the darkened forest.

Emelyn watched him go, surprised and upset that she had caused him so much pain. Stupid girl, of course mentioning his wife upset him. She should have left well enough alone. She turned back to Ferrin and was petting the mule's long nose in order to comfort her own troubled mind when a shadow among the trees caught her eye.

Heart racing, she turned. Out from the trees soared a bird that alighted upon a supply sack.

"Hello," she said, watching the bird from a safe distance. In the firelight, it looked remarkably similar to the falcon in Roelith.

The falcon fixed a single black eye on her, put its beak to its feathers, and began preening.

Emelyn leaned in for a closer look. Its head and wings were mottled brown while its breast was white, studded with darts of black. Long, glossy black talons curved from yellow toes, digging into the canvas sack like it was paper. Around one leg dangled a thin piece of cord. She gasped, realizing the falcon was, in fact, the same one she had freed in Roelith.

"Have you been following me?"

The falcon shook its wings as it continued its grooming.

A wretched howling broke the calm evening and sent Emelyn staggering backwards. The falcon took flight just as Cobbe charged forward, swinging a spoon as she tried to strike the bird.

Emelyn watched in stunned silence as Cobbe shouted—quite possibly profanities—in an unknown language at the bird as it perched in a nearby tree.

After a few minutes Cobbe calmed down, though her brow remained furrowed and her expression grim. "Silver-eyes loses hunter-bird again!" she said, leveling her spoon at Emelyn. "Cobbe thinks Silver-eyes likes eating roots and herbs for dinner and purposefully chases away any tasties that fly by!"

Emelyn backed away from the threat of the spoon, holding no doubt that Cobbe would strike her with it should she take to the notion. "Did you see the falcon? It was the same one as in Roelith!"

Cobbe grimaced and shook her spoon. "Of course is same. Hunter-bird has been following for many days. Cobbe sees it soaring in sky and flitting from tree to tree as all walk by. Cobbe wait for hunter-bird to come into reach, but when it does, Silver-eyes chases it off again." Her scowl deepened.

It was Emelyn's turn to frown. "I didn't chase the bird away, Cobbe, *you* did with that horrible screeching. I imagine you must have frightened off any poor bird within five leagues with your hollering, so don't blame *me* if you can't catch a bird for dinner."

Cobbe narrowed her eyes while hunkering down, and Emelyn feared the woman would pounce on her. But after a moment she straightened, looking forlorn, like a child that had lost her sweet.

"Cobbe sometimes forgets to be clever," she mumbled. "Cobbe very hungry for tasty hunter-bird and . . . sometimes gets too excited."

Emelyn hid a smile behind her hand.

Cobbe shuffled her feet, kicking at the snow. Her sulking was short-lived, however, when she saw Corran's knife lying on the ground. Perking up, she hustled over to the knife, swooped it up and tucked it into her belt in one fluid motion. Cobbe's mood was so improved that Emelyn didn't have the heart to tell her the knife was Corran's. He would have to sort it out himself.

Cobbe sauntered back to Emelyn. She drew herself up as tall as her little frame would allow and pointed at the falcon in the tree. "Hunter-bird follows Silver-eyes. Cobbe sees this. Cobbe can make new trap, catch hunter-bird and cook tasty dinner for Silver-eyes." Cobbe patted the knife tucked in her belt as though assuring Emelyn she was up for the task. "Maybe hunter-bird make Silver-eyes strong, like high-hats say."

Emelyn put on a smile so as not to offend Cobbe. "That's very kind of you, Cobbe, but wouldn't it be nicer if we let the falcon be? He's such a beautiful bird, I'd hate to see any harm come to him. I certainly don't want to eat him."

Cobbe scrunched up her face as Emelyn spoke. Saying nothing, she turned and walked off, patting the knife at her belt. Emelyn wondered if Cobbe would truly leave the bird alone, and wondered even more over the likelihood of Corran ever retrieving his knife.

Later that evening, the weather turned harsh and virulent. The snow flurried in violent torrents, whipped by a fierce and icy wind. Emelyn crouched near Ferrin, trying to avoid the biting wind and blinding snow. She drew her coat around her as she gave silent thanks to Beryl for the gift, though the protection it provided was meager in such cruel weather. The fire had been extinguished under a blanket of snow, and Emelyn feared the long and cold night.

Ferrin whinnied and stamped his hooves. Emelyn reached up and patted his haunch. His skin was cold and coated with snow, and Emelyn's worry deepened. The wind wailed through trees that shivered and bowed under the force of the gale. Emelyn hid her face in her arms, trying to find some sort of shelter.

"We must leave," Aldren said, his voice urgent. "We must find shelter."

Emelyn looked up and found the Magister gazing down at her, snow wreathing his bald head. He was no longer wearing his spectacles.

"We must leave," he repeated, extending a hand.

Emelyn took his hand and the Magister pulled her up, bringing her into the full force of the wind.

"Bring the mule and follow me," he said. "Leave the supplies, we will come back for them later."

Emelyn obeyed, untying Ferrin's tethered reins as fast as her frozen hands would allow. "What about Corran?" she said as she worked. "He left earlier, I've not seen him since. We can't leave without him."

Aldren grimaced. "We have no choice in the matter. We cannot tarry here too long. He will have to find us later." He hesitated, then added, "I am sure he will be all right."

Emelyn frowned at the Magister's poorly veiled indifference, but she knew he was right—they could not stay there. Having managed to untie Ferrin's reins, Emelyn followed the Magister as he led the way to Percival and Cobbe.

"There is a stone cliff not too far from here," Percival said when they arrived. "It will provide us with a means for shelter." The Grand Magister turned and led the way through the snowy night as the others filed after him. Emelyn glanced behind her to see if she could catch a glimpse of Corran, but all she saw was Cobbe atop her faithful pig. Beyond, the snow fell like a grey, murky wall.

Shivering, Emelyn pulled herself atop Ferrin's back, hoping to share his warmth. She kept low, resting her head against his neck. His skin was cold at first, and coated in snow. Then he grew warmer and the rhythm of his walking was almost calming. But Emelyn couldn't relax. She glanced back from time to time, both to see if Corran might be following as well as to check on Cobbe. Though there was no sign of Corran, Cobbe managed to keep up splendidly. She had donned an ample cloak that covered both her and the pig. Her small face peered out from the vast hood while the pig's bristled snout peeked out from below. It was an unusual sight and Emelyn might have laughed had she not been so cold and worried.

They pressed on through the wind and snow. Emelyn, despite Ferrin's warmth, grew numb in body and in mind, and she no longer had the energy to look for Corran. In time, they came to a sheer stone wall, looming high above the trees as it disappeared into the darkness.

The Magi severed branches from the nearby pines with the help of their staves and spoken runes. Emelyn didn't know what the words meant, but she knew enough of the Art to know what they were doing. Green boughs heavy with snow crashed to the ground and Cobbe ran to gather them up. Emelyn hurried to help her, even though she didn't know what purpose the branches would serve.

"Take the branches to the cliff face, there," Aldren said, pointing to the stone wall. "Place the branches in the ground and create a perimeter. Like so." Aldren took a branch from Emelyn and pushed it into the snow so that it stood upright, like a small sapling growing up out of the ice.

Emelyn and Cobbe busied themselves with setting the branches in the snow as best they could. The snow was deep enough in most places to hold the branches upright. If a branch proved problematic, Cobbe dug a small hole with the help her newly acquired knife. In little time they had created a boundary extending out from the side of the cliff.

Once they had finished, Percival and Aldren scribbled runes in the snow around the newly placed branches. They worked swiftly, stopping only when the entire perimeter was adorned with enigmatic shapes and scrawls. The patterns in the snow were beautiful, but Emelyn still felt the stirrings of fear, for the Magi were engaging in something she didn't understand.

Percival spoke a rune, igniting one end of his staff before snuffing the flame in the snow. Using the charred wood, he then drew another rune on the cliff face—a black, angular design that gazed at them like a great eye. Both Percival and Aldren stood in the center of the perimeter, waving their staves in the air as they spoke more runes. The branches glowed yellow and bright as though infused with the sun, as did the great rune on the wall. Above, the air glimmered like a curtain of gossamer threads sparkling in sunlight. The wind and snow that had torn at Emelyn's face and clothes stopped, causing her skin to tingle in its absence. Snow flurried beyond the branches but did not fall within the boundary. Emelyn looked up to the sky and watched as the snowflakes fell before evaporating upon the sparkling threads as if they had fallen upon a flame. Within the branches all was calm, a pale haven of gentle light that soothed Emelyn's nerves and fears.

She turned towards the Magisters. Aldren was arranging a few spare branches into a pile in the middle of their sanctuary while Percival sat on a stone near the wall. The Grand Magister gazed into the darkness with weary eyes.

"This is remarkable," Emelyn said. "Truly wondrous."

Aldren smiled, though he looked tired. Once he had finished piling the branches, he spoke a rune, and the boughs glowed red and orange. Snow melted and steamed as the branches became as warm as any fire—yet they weren't burning.

"Why don't you do this every night?" Emelyn said. She had spent more nights than she could count freezing upon the cold earth while trying to sleep. She had no idea the Magisters had been capable of creating such a warm and cozy haven.

Aldren pulled out his spectacles from a pocket in his robe and polished them with his sleeve. "It is quite a demanding task, creating such a space protected from the elements. It requires much concentration to erect as well as maintain. I fear if this storm persists for too long, our efforts may be for naught." He placed the spectacles upon his nose and blinked.

"What do you mean?"

Aldren warmed his hands near the glowing branches. "In the Art, there are what we call Natural and Constructed runes. Natural pertains to using runes in compliance with nature. I can, for example, use a rune to light a piece of wood on fire. The amount of concentration I would need would be only that which is necessary to ignite the wood. I could then forget about the wood entirely and it would continue to burn, as is consistent with nature." He looked at Emelyn. "Do you understand?"

Emelyn nodded.

"Good. Now, Constructed runes are those that are *not* in compliance with nature. It involves bringing about something that cannot occur within the natural world. The lightstones we use are one such example; as are these branches, here, that are emitting heat without burning. Constructed runes require constant concentration to maintain. The amount of concentration required depends on the task in question. The lightstones require very little concentration and an accomplished Magister can keep one lit while having seemingly forgotten about it. This fire here requires more, yet not so much that I cannot hold a conversation while maintaining it."

"And this?" Emelyn asked, waving her hands towards the walls of the haven.

"Significantly more still." Aldren glanced back at Percival sitting upon the rock, his shoulders sagging as if under some unseen burden.

"This," Aldren said, indicating their sanctuary, "is beyond my means. It is the Grand Magister who is maintaining it. I can muster enough concentration to maintain the perimeter for a time. But that," Aldren pointed to the gossamer ceiling, "*that* is beyond my means, entirely."

"Why?"

Aldren grew quiet, gazing into the fiery pine boughs before he said, "To understand, you must first understand the way in which the Art works." He paused. "As you now know, Constructed runes require more concentration than Natural runes. Depending upon one's goal, the concentration cost can be substantial. One way to mitigate this cost is to always use natural objects as a means of conducting the power of the Art. These branches, for instance, serve as an object from which the heat I've conjured can emanate. The same principal applies to our lightstones. It is, for all intents and purposes, a simple stone, yet one that we command to emanate light when the need arises. The rule guiding this is that it is always easier to change the nature of an existing object than to conjure something out of nothing. It is easier to draw warmth from branches or light from a stone than it is to bring forth fire and light out of thin air. Do you understand?" Aldren looked at Emelyn as though he suspected she had not, in fact, understood at all.

Emelyn considered the Magister's words. She looked at the glowing branches surrounding them, and at the sky, glittering with glowing threads. "What about that?" she asked, pointing above.

Aldren smiled and nodded. "Indeed. So you do, perhaps, understand. The Grand Magister has, in our time of need, conjured that portion of our shelter from nothing." He pointed to the sooty rune that Percival had drawn upon the wall. "That rune there serves as a focus, but it is the Grand Magister's own will that has drawn that power over our heads and it is his will alone that keeps it there."

Emelyn pursed her lips. She pointed to the runes drawn in the snow. "And those, there. Do they also serve as a focus?"

Aldren nodded, his eyes sparkling with excitement. "Yes! They help conduct the power of the Art up into the branches, keeping out the wind and snow. It is why we could not have those branches emanate heat, for then the snow would melt and the concentration required to maintain our shelter would become too great. Even for our Grand Magister."

"How long will he be able to keep his concentration?" Emelyn asked as she watched the storm rage out in the night.

Aldren spread open his hands. "It is impossible to say. I will be able to help him maintain the outer perimeter for a time, but that is all. The rest, as I have said, is beyond my capabilities. There are few in the Towers who can command the Art thus; the fact that our Grand Magister can do so speaks much of his own mental discipline and acuity. We are fortunate."

Emelyn had more questions she wanted to ask—about all that Aldren had just told her, about her own misgivings of her capability with the Art, but Aldren interrupted her before she could speak.

"I am afraid I cannot tell you more at this moment. I must assist the Grand Magister in his efforts. You should try and get some rest." Aldren rose and walked over to Percival's side.

Emelyn remained by the warm, ember-like branches, deep in thought. How could she possibly sleep now, after all that had happened? She looked up at the magical threads, sparkling like strings of stars. She wondered if she really did have capability with the Art and, if so, if she would ever be able to do something so remarkable. Not likely. Given that she couldn't even light a stick, she doubted she could ever accomplish anything so grand.

She made a simple bed with some of the leftover boughs before wrapping her coat around her and lying down. She gazed upwards, watching the threads glitter as the snow flurried beyond. Emelyn had never seen anything so beautiful, and she soon forgot the cold in her limbs, the pain in her muscles, and the fear in her heart. All that existed for her was silent, sparkling snow.

CHAPTER 12

EMELYN AWOKE COLD and stiff. The storm had passed, leaving behind only a sprinkling of snow to drift through the gloaming. The shelter that the Magisters had constructed was gone; the branches that had glowed with light were now only shadows. Nearby, the figures of the Magi lay heaped on the ground as they slept. Emelyn wondered how long they had maintained the structure before fatigue took them. Given that she had not woken under a thick blanket of snow, she reckoned they must have lasted through the entire storm before allowing themselves to sleep. She was grateful, for without them it would have been a terrible night, indeed.

She rose to her feet, tiptoeing about the camp as she looked for the others. One shadowed heap proved to be Cobbe, snoring next to her massive pig. Ferrin was still tethered near the cliff face where Emelyn had left him, but she found no one else. Corran was still gone. She looked out towards the forest. All was still, the snow undisturbed. Where was he? Worry for her friend deepened. What would she do if he didn't return? Corran had left because of her, upset when she had mentioned his wife. If something happened to him, how would she be able to live with herself?

She remained near the pine boughs and watched as the sky lightened. Nearby, the branches of a tree shivered, sending snow cascading down as a large bird perched among the frosted needles. Emelyn smiled, glad to see the falcon had survived the storm.

She slipped past the hedge of branches and walked to the tree where the falcon roosted. As soon as she arrived, the falcon took flight. Emelyn watched as the bird disappeared, the soft flapping of its wings fading into silence. She lingered, enjoying the quiet solitude of the morning. She did not wish to return to camp, so she turned and walked deeper into the forest.

Snow crunched under Emelyn's boots as her breath plumed in the cold air. Ice crystals floated on the wind, glittering in the first rays of sunlight. A soft flapping announced the falcon's return and Emelyn stopped to watch the bird alight on a nearby branch. That was when she heard the muffled sobs of someone crying. The cry was faint, delicate. A single, soft footstep was enough to drown it. Emelyn paused, unsure of what to do. They had not seen anyone else since leaving Roelith. It was as though all travelers had stopped at the "northern gate." But even as she hesitated, the mournful sobbing tugged at her heart and she knew she couldn't ignore it.

Passage through the snowy terrain proved slow and laborious. The ground was uneven and the snow hid hollows that Emelyn found only after she sank to her thighs. Yet even over her ragged breathing, Emelyn could hear the sobbing, and she knew she was drawing closer. When she saw a figure on the snow, she stopped to peek from behind a tree.

A lone woman sat on a rock. Her back was turned, showing only a cascade of long, dark hair tumbling over a pair of slender shoulders. Again, Emelyn hesitated. Part of her wanted to approach the woman, to see why she was crying. Another part of her said she had no business being there, that her presence would be viewed as an unwelcome intrusion. The falcon fluttered by, landing on a branch above Emelyn's head. She cast an inquisitive look to the bird, as if asking what she should do, but the falcon gave no answer.

When Emelyn looked back, the woman was no longer alone. Three young men had emerged from the trees and were walking towards her, their eyes sneering, their grins twisted. The young woman ceased her weeping. She stood and turned to walk in the opposite direction. The boys followed after her, casting sharp remarks and leering glares.

Emelyn watched the girl as she tried to flee; for a girl she was, Emelyn could see that now. Under the long leather dress that the girl wore, her body was slim and slight, having not yet attained the curves of womanhood. Emelyn thought of Iyen, thinking that the dress this older girl wore was quite similar to the dress of the little girl.

"Savage!" one of the boys said, his voice rising in his excitement.

"Treehopper!" said another.

The third boy, having drawn close to the girl, grabbed her by the arm. The girl spun around and crushed the palm of her hand into the boy's nose. He staggered backwards, cradling his face as the other boys fell silent. The girl stepped back. Whatever courage she might have had now seemingly dwindled as she watched the boys with wide eyes, looking like a trapped animal. The boys, who had been mirthful in their cruel taunting, grew serious. The injured boy balled his hands into fists while blood streamed down his face. He hissed at the girl, causing her to flinch as though struck.

Emelyn tensed and regretted leaving her staff back at the other camp. She was still not proficient in using it, but it would have been better than nothing. She didn't know what she could do, but she couldn't just sit there and watch them harass the girl. Emelyn took a deep breath and stepped out from behind the tree. But before she could take another step, another young man appeared. He ran through the snow, passing the girl before arriving at the group of boys. He grabbed the nearest boy by the collar and crashed his fist into the other's face. The remaining boys, stunned by the sudden attack, regained their senses and threw punches of their own. The young man fought hard and fierce. But the odds were not in his favor, and he was soon receiving far more blows than he dealt. He buckled under the onslaught, collapsing to the ground.

"Stop!" the girl screamed.

The boys kicked the crumpled form on the ground, ignoring the girl's plea. She ran to them and placed her hand on one of the boys' shoulder. The boy barely noticed, shrugging off her hand as if she were an annoying insect. Pursing her lips, the girl grabbed his arm and forced him to face her. The boy narrowed his eyes and he tried to turn away, but before he could, the girl wrapped her hands around his face, holding him still. At first he looked puzzled, then his eyes grew wide, fearful. His flushed cheeks grew pallid underneath her fingers. His hair, once brown and curly, faded into waxen, straw-like strands. The boy struggled, but the girl held fast. Only when tears of blood oozed from the boy's terrified eyes did she loosen her grip, letting him fall to the ground.

The other boys stopped kicking to stare slack-jawed at their friend. A boy narrowed his eyes and clenched his hands. "Witch!"

The girl hunkered down close to the ground. "Leave!" she said, her voice piercing the air with a strange sharpness.

The boy flinched but did not move.

The girl dug her hands into the forest floor as easily as if the soil had been freshly tilled. The boys shifted their feet, glancing about liked they wished to leave, but refused to be run off by a girl.

The air grew still. In the distance, a groaning broke the silence, like the creaking of floorboards or the bending of branches during a storm. Suddenly the ground shifted and Emelyn lost her footing. Cold snow dashed against her cheek when she fell, knocking the air from her lungs. She tried to push herself up. As she moved, the earth below her hands and knees shivered as though the soil roiled beneath the ice and snow.

Emelyn staggered to her feet and ran to a nearby tree, clinging to it in fear of being pitched to the ground again. Nearby, the two remaining boys stared at their feet. One of them cried out, his eyes wild as he swatted at his legs.

"Get them off me!"

The other boy stood frozen, his mouth hanging open as he stared at his friend's legs.

Emelyn crept forward, trying to get a better look. She kept to the trees as closely as possible, both for support as well as for cover. She came to an outcropping of stones covered in a layer of snow and climbed atop them.

The earth at the boys' feet had been disturbed. The white snow was mottled with black, upturned soil, within which dark, sinuous strands twisted and writhed. At first, Emelyn thought they were snakes, then she saw the way the tendrils twined around the boy's legs, reminding her of the climbing rosebush they had in Fallow. Black vines from the ground? Were they roots?

The other boy continued to watch as the vines crept up his friend's legs. Soon, his courage failed him and he turned and ran, leaving his friend behind. The remaining boy, seeing that he was alone, screamed.

The girl stirred, removing her hands from the snow. As she stood, the roots fell away from the boy's legs, limp and lifeless. She raised her chin, looking at the boy as if challenging him. He turned and ran.

With the last of the boys gone, the girl relaxed and walked over to the young man that lay bleeding in the snow. She bent down, placing her hands upon his chest. She remained still, her head lowered, until he groaned and stirred. She helped him sit up. When he tried to get to his feet, she stopped him

"I'm fine," he said, managing a weak smile.

The girl looked at him askance a moment before helping him up. The two stood together in silence, their heads bowed. The young man took the girl's hands and held them. He spoke something to her, too quietly for Emelyn to hear. The girl laughed, a short ring of merriment, though there was a strain in her voice that hinted at tears.

The young man lifted his face, looking at the girl with open adoration. Emelyn's breath caught as she watched them, for the young man, through all the blood and bruises, bore a striking resemblance to Corran. Yet they were not the same. This man was noticeably younger, his frame more slight. But he had the same sandy brown hair and eyes that were quick to smile. If Emelyn hadn't known better, she would have sworn he was Corran's younger brother.

The young man leaned down, and his lips lingered on the girl's cheek. She clung to him, and the two remained in each other's arms. Emelyn, feeling like an intruder, turned to leave. She climbed down from the outcropping, careful not to disturb the couple in their affections. But the forest was silent, and the slightest of noises carried far. The girl's eyes snapped open, fixing directly upon Emelyn.

Emelyn froze, her heart thumping in her chest. She felt like she had been caught committing some foul deed. But she had done nothing wrong. She watched the girl, wondering what she would do. But the girl did nothing other than glare at her. The young man seemed to be unaware, his face buried in the girl's long, black hair. Deciding it would be best to leave, Emelyn turned and headed back towards the camp.

She hurried as best she could through the snow, resisting the urge to turn and see if the girl was still watching. Around her the snow crunched with the sound of footfalls while shadows flickered among the trees. She stopped, but the footfalls continued. She turned just as a figure stepped from the pines. It was a man, tall—nearly twice as tall as Emelyn—and broad in the shoulders. His arms were long and sinewy, his fingertips reaching his knees. His skin, dusky and pale, glinted in the morning light as if slick with oil. Yet it was his black, vacant eyes that filled Emelyn with fear.

The man lumbered towards her. His skin gleamed, not from oil, but from tiny crystals embedded in his skin. Emelyn might have thought him beautiful were it not for those terrible eyes. The vacant stare that he fixed upon her made Emelyn feel transparent, as though he could stare right through her, straight to her heart beating within her chest. Emelyn's stomach turned leaden as a scream escaped her lips and pierced the air.

The giant flinched. Emelyn tried to turn and run, but the giant reached out and gripped her neck in a frigid grasp. She kicked and struggled as he squeezed her neck and lifted her feet off the ground. Emelyn scratched and tore at his hand, but to no avail. Stars sparkled in the corner of her vision as the giant's broad face watched her struggle with calm indifference. Fire burned in Emelyn's lungs, and the world blurred and fell into darkness.

A piercing shriek resonated from above and the darkness receded. A cloud of feathers flurried around the giant's head, distracting him and allowing Emelyn a brief gasp of air. The grip tightened and the stars returned; then it was gone and Emelyn was vaguely aware that she was falling.

Cold hit her like a wall, and she writhed upon the ground, gasping and coughing. Tears streamed from her eyes, blurring the world beyond recognition. The giant loomed over her, though his attention was fixed upon a nearby shadow. He lunged at it, but the darkened figure danced away.

Emelyn got her coughing under control, but her head throbbed and her vision, already blurred from tears, throbbed with it. She tried pulling herself up to see what was happening, to try and get away. But her arms were like jelly, her throat like fire, and her teeth jolted with pain in time with the pounding of her head. She curled up on the ground, willing herself to be small and unnoticed.

Another screech overhead pulled Emelyn's gaze upward to the vague shape of a bird soaring high above. Nearby, the giant flailed as he swiped at the shadow next to him. The figure dodged the attack, spinning around to jab at the giant with a long staff. The two carried on for a time, the shadowy figure evading every attack, striking blows with his staff when the opportunity arose. Emelyn watched the battle as she lay on the ground, fear slowly draining from her body and replaced by fatigue. Her eyes grew heavy as the cold snow soothed her fevered body. She blinked, watching with detached interest as the giant grew sluggish before crumpling under the final blow of a strange shadowed staff. At that moment, Emelyn knew she was safe, and she succumbed to the darkness.

CHAPTER 13

ALDREN AWOKE TO a damp, bristled snout nudging his face. He bolted upright, wiping his cheek as he stifled his annoyance. Cobbe stood next to the pig, smirking as she held a steaming bowl in her hands.

"Glass-eyes lazy. Sleep late in the morning, leaving all work for Cobbe alone." She thrust the bowl at Aldren before stalking away, her pig waddling after her.

Aldren blinked at the food he found in his hand. Sleeping late? He looked up at the sky. The sun was well up, shining upon a world turned white. Memories of the previous night's turmoil came back to him and he dismissed Cobbe's complaints. She could not possibly understand. The night had been long and difficult, and Aldren had stayed up with the Grand Magister, assisting in maintaining their structure. It was exhausting work, and Aldren felt that a late morning was well deserved.

He returned his attention to the bowl of food. It was stew, left over from last night, and topped with a piece of freshly made flatbread. Aldren used the bread to spoon the stew into his mouth. He was about halfway through his meal when a thought occurred to him.

"Cobbe."

Cobbe left her place by the fire and walked over to the Magister, raising her chin as she looked down her dingy nose.

"Where did you get the food? We left the provisions at the old camp. We brought nothing with us."

Cobbe drew herself up, her chin still raised. "Cobbe very clever, leave early in morning to old camp and fetch food." She pointed a grubby finger at him. "Without Cobbe, red-robes go hungry and cold."

Aldren smiled at the Wylkin in amazement. "You mean to tell me you traveled all the way to the other camp alone? How did you find your way? The snow would have covered all tracks."

Cobbe furrowed her brow as she looked at him, the confusion plain on her face.

"Never mind. Very well done, Cobbe."

Cobbe beamed at the compliment, the sourness from her early-morning toils seemingly forgotten.

Aldren looked around as he ate. "Where is Emelyn? Did she go with you to the other camp?"

"No, Silver-eyes gone when Cobbe wake up."

Aldren stopped eating. "Gone? Where?"

Cobbe raised her chin again. "Cobbe not Silver-eyes' mother. Glass-eyes should ask Silver-eyes such questions." She turned and left, returning to her duties near the fire.

Aldren set down his bowl and rose to his feet, gazing out at the surrounding forest. Fresh snow blanketed the ground, sparkling like a crystalline quilt. Tearing through the snow from one end of the camp was a wide trail, trampled by both feet and hooves. From the other end a narrower trail led into the forest, made by a single set of footprints. Aldren's gaze followed the trail into the trees. He whispered runes, trying to sense if anything was wrong, but there was nothing. Where had she gone?

He considered going out to look for her, following the trail and tracking Emelyn down. Yet a nagging reluctance gave him pause. Perhaps the girl had decided to part ways. After everything that had happened, after everything that she had learned, it was understandable if it were too much to cope with. Aldren was surprised the girl had followed them for as long as she had. That she was allowed to accompany them at all was the Grand Magister's doing, a decision with which Aldren did not agree. If she wished to leave, it was, perhaps, for the best. Yet Aldren was still troubled. Fallow would have been the appropriate place for them to part ways, or the Meadowlark Inn, or Roelith. Not alone in a wintery forest where the girl likely couldn't tell up from down in regards to the direction in which she should travel. What if she didn't want to leave at all? What if she was hurt? Aldren sighed, unsure of what he should do.

He glanced at the Grand Magister, still curled up on the ground, asleep. Waking him was not an option—Percival had expended much energy the previous night sustaining their shelter throughout the storm. Aldren would have to decide about the girl on his own. It was still morning, no cause for worry just yet. If she did not return soon, he would go out to look for her. Yet Aldren's disquiet still nagged at him. His persistent concern for the girl surprised him, given his previous reluctance for her joining them.

Pushing his unease aside, Aldren walked over to Cobbe to offer assistance with anything she might need. Cobbe put him to work sorting through the reacquired goods to check what had been damaged in the storm. Most of the goods were in satisfactory condition—no doubt in large part to Cobbe's careful attendance to their provisions and the pains she took to ensure that everything was properly bundled and stored. Keeping his hands busy and listening to Cobbe's cheerful chatter helped Aldren to forget his worry, yet not so much that he forgot the passing of time.

By the time Aldren had finished assessing their supplies, the sun had risen well up in the sky, indicating the end of morning. He glanced out into the woods, looking for a sign of the girl, but she was nowhere to be seen. It was time, then. Aldren fetched his staff. Nearby, the Grand Magister still lay sleeping. Aldren considered leaving a message with Cobbe should Percival wake while he was away, but decided against it. If he should wake, the Grand Magister would not likely ask Cobbe of his whereabouts. However, as a courtesy for the Wylkin, he notified Cobbe that he was going to look for Emelyn. Cobbe seemed unconcerned, giving Aldren a cursory wave before resuming her task of feeding the pig ruined provisions from their supply store.

Aldren followed the narrow trail left by Emelyn into the woods. He hurried, telling himself that it was simply a matter of getting on with the task at hand. Yet, deep down, he had a nagging fear that he shouldn't have waited, that he should have gone to look for Emelyn as soon as he realized she had left. Relief bubbled within him, therefore, when he saw a slight figure ahead.

Emelyn plodded through the snow as though it took great effort to put one foot in front of the other. Her clothes were caked with snow and mud and Aldren's relief faded into concern. He quickened his pace and, upon reaching her, his breath caught in his throat. Her neck was red and raw.

"What happened?" Aldren said, surprised to hear the tremor in his voice.

Emelyn looked at him with bleary, blood-shot eyes. Aldren wasn't sure if she even recognized him.

He gently took her arm and helped her along the snowy path. When they arrived at the camp, Aldren barked to Cobbe for some tea. Cobbe hesitated, scowling at the harsh command. But her frown faded upon seeing the dazed girl and she hurried to put on a kettle of water over the fire.

Aldren led Emelyn to the fire and helped her sit on a pile of sacks thrown together by Cobbe. He spoke a rune, sending the small, smoky fire into a blaze. He stood nearby, wanting to do more, but there was little more to be done. Aldren eyed the mottled bruise on Emelyn's neck as she sat staring into the fire. The Magisters were gifted with great power, the envy of all men. Yet the power to heal was one outside their capabilities—something Aldren had not regretted until now.

He sat down next to Emelyn, watching the flames flicker as Cobbe prepared the tea. She poured the brew into a cup and placed it in Emelyn's hands. Emelyn stared at the liquid as if she didn't know what to do with it. Aldren helped her put the cup to her mouth, tipping it back until the warm liquid met her lips. Emelyn drank, wincing as she swallowed. The tea helped revive her somewhat—her eyes lost some of their glassiness and she was able to sip the liquid on her own.

Aldren remained silent, waiting until the color came back into Emelyn's cheeks before quietly asking, "What happened?"

Emelyn turned and looked at him. The whites of her eyes were still red with blood, eerily contrasting the silver-grey of her irises. It gave her a frightful appearance, and Aldren felt unsettled under her gaze.

"I'm . . . not sure," Emelyn said, her voice raspy and weak. She winced as she spoke and sipped more of her tea.

"You left early this morning, perhaps on a walk?"

Emelyn thought for a moment. "Yes. I had woken up early, everyone else was still asleep. I saw the falcon in the tree and I walked to it. But not far . . . I didn't go far . . ." Emelyn broke into a fit of coughing. She sipped the rest of her tea.

Falcon? Aldren looked up and scanned the nearby trees and, sure enough, there was a large bird perched high up on a branch. He frowned, unsure of what it meant.

Cobbe pushed a fresh cup of tea in Emelyn's hands as she took away the empty one.

"It was a lovely morning," Emelyn said when her coughing had subsided. "I wanted to go out for a walk, just for a little bit. I hadn't gone far, at least I don't think I had, when I heard someone crying." She continued to tell Aldren all that had happened, of the girl and the boys that had been taunting her, of the young man that had come to her rescue.

"They beat him," she whispered, tears filling her red eyes. "The boys . . . there were too many of them and they beat him . . . horribly. The girl . . . the young woman, she told them to stop and they wouldn't. So she . . . she made them."

"Made them? How?"

Emelyn stared into the fire. "Magic."

Aldren stiffened, the realization of what had happened dawning upon him at last. "Tell me everything."

Emelyn told him how the girl had seemingly healed the young man, of the giant that came out of the trees as she tried to leave. Her voice grew shaky and she trailed off, tears rolling down her cheeks.

Aldren coughed, clearing the lump rising in his throat. "Never mind," he said, glad that his voice was even. "You are safe now."

Emelyn's lips trembled as she nodded, staring at the tea in her cup.

Aldren knew he should ask how she managed to escape—Percival would require the information when he learned of the events—but he was reluctant to do so. The girl had been through much, and he knew well enough how she had escaped, even if the details were unknown to him. The Art.

"Has Corran come back?" Emelyn asked. "Has he found us?"

Aldren frowned, puzzled. "No, he . . . has not."

Emelyn's own brow furrowed. "Oh."

"Why do you ask?"

"I thought I saw him. Someone was there . . . they had a staff. They saved me. I . . . thought it might be Corran."

"You didn't see him?"

Emelyn shook her head. "It was all so blurry. All I remember is shadows. I don't know who else it would have been, though."

Aldren watched her as she drank her tea. "You have been through much. Try and rest."

Emelyn nodded as Aldren rose to his feet. He walked to the rear of the camp where the Grand Magister still lay sleeping and sat down. He watched Emelyn as she lingered by the fire, refusing food offered by Cobbe, though she accepted more tea. In time, she wrapped her coat around her and lay down by the fire. Aldren hoped that she slept.

He sat alone for some time, turning troubling thoughts over in his mind. He glanced up at the falcon still perched in the tree. The girl had a way with animals as well as the Art. Yet her ability with the Art seemed to manifest only while under duress. Much like her mother, in a way. Aldren sagged under the sadness that always filled his heart when he thought of that young woman from so long ago—a girl with long, dark hair, not much older than Emelyn was now. The past could not be allowed reoccur. Aldren had few regrets in his life, but the hand he had played in that girl's fate was one of them. He would not make the same mistake again.

Nearby, the Grand Magister stirred from his slumber, and Aldren's thoughts were pulled out of the past. Percival sat up and looked at the sky.

"It is late," he grumbled.

"Yes, my lord. You needed your rest."

Percival scoffed, though he did not argue. "We should depart at once. We can still manage half a day of traveling."

Aldren hesitated. "There has been an incident, my lord."

"Oh?"

Aldren told the Grand Magister all that Emelyn had told him. When Aldren had finished, Percival remained silent, his expression distant and thoughtful.

"How have your lessons with the girl been progressing?" Percival said at length. "Has she been able to manipulate the Art in any fashion through the means you have shown her?"

Aldren straightened his back. His failure in this particular instance was a sore point with him. "No."

Percival nodded. "Then we must proceed differently. I trust you have come to the conclusion that she can only harness the Art while under stress?"

Aldren nodded.

"Then we must see to it that she is properly challenged. Thus far, we have been avoiding all anomalous projections of the Art whenever possible. We shall instead alter our course so that we encounter them more frequently."

Aldren's jaw tightened. "I would not see her come to harm."

"Nor would I. But it is a dangerous world, now more than ever, and we all risk harm. You do her a disservice by trying to prevent her from developing her own means of protection."

"Is that what this is? Helping her protect herself? If that was the case we should have left her in Fallow." Aldren's cheeks burned—he had never spoken to the Grand Magister in such a manner.

Percival narrowed his eyes. "We all have our places within the world, as well as obligations. You would do well to remember yours. We will not speak of this again." He brushed past Aldren and picked up his staff before walking over to Emelyn.

Aldren exhaled as he ran a hand over his head. He was an old fool. He walked over to Cobbe and asked her if there was any work to be done. He thought it best to stay clear of the Grand Magister for a while. Cooking would be a welcome distraction from his blunder as well as provide a small beam of light in what looked to be an ever-darkening day.

Chapter 14

Emelyn bounded across a field of ice with the long-legged gracefulness of a hind. Snow-encrusted trees flew past her in a blur as the wind sang in her long ears. Her heart soared as her body flew across the snow. She was free. If she willed it, she could grow wings and soar up to the sky, dancing among the wind, clouds, and sparkling sun. Joy filled her heart so completely that it bubbled forth, escaping her lips in a mirthful laugh.

Then her voice cracked and withered into a raspy wail. Her heart fluttered, and, from the corner of her eye, movement shadowed her among the trees. Fear hissed in her ears, drowning out the song of the wind, and her long slender legs slipped on the ice. She fell . . .

Emelyn jolted awake in a fit of coughing. Percival handed her a cup of tea that had been perched on a stone near the fire. The cup was warm from the flames, though the tea itself was tepid. Emelyn didn't mind and was grateful for the soothing liquid on her coarse throat.

Percival watched her drink, saying nothing. Once Emelyn's coughing had subsided, she glanced up at the Magister, unsettled by his scrutiny. He studied her face before his gaze flicked down to her neck. Emelyn stiffened.

"What do you want?" she croaked, and then drank more tea to keep herself from coughing.

"Aldren told me what happened. I came to see if you were all right."

No, she wasn't all right. Emelyn remained silent, however, fearful that speaking would bring tears; she didn't want to cry in front of the Grand Magister.

Percival nodded as though she had answered. "We will need to leave soon, it will not do to tarry here. But we will wait until you are strong enough to travel."

Emelyn nodded. The Grand Magister remained, still studying her face. She raised her eyebrows.

"I wonder," Percival said, "how you got out of the situation? Can you answer me that?"

Emelyn frowned. "Didn't Magister Keller tell you?"

"I would like to hear it from you."

"Someone saved me."

"Who?"

Emelyn hesitated. "I don't know."

Percival continued studying her face. "I see." He gave a feeble smile before rising to his feet. "And yet," he added, "I wonder why you do not yet realize that you are saving yourself." He turned and left.

Emelyn's frown deepened. The Magisters kept telling her what she was capable of, but Emelyn didn't understand how they could know. They weren't there; they didn't know what happened. It seemed to Emelyn that they kept telling her what they wanted to be true. Whether or not it was true for her remained to be seen.

She spent the rest of the day near the fire, sipping the tea that Cobbe brought to her at regular intervals. The Wylkin was not her usual, talkative self, and brought the tea to Emelyn in silence before disappearing again. Emelyn didn't mind; she didn't feel much for conversation.

Later in the day, Aldren and Cobbe left with Ferrin to fetch the rest of the supplies that remained in the other camp, leaving Emelyn alone with Percival. Though the

Grand Magister showed no indication that he wished to speak further with her, Emelyn still wrapped herself in her coat and pretended to sleep. The pretense didn't last long, however, and she soon drifted off into a dreamless slumber.

She awoke early the next morning, but the fire was already blazing, tended by an industrious Cobbe.

"No tea for Silver-eyes. Cobbe make thin soup instead. Silver-eyes must eat this."

Emelyn smiled. She had not eaten anything the previous day, and the idea of food set her stomach rumbling, even if it was only a thin soup. She gave no protests when Cobbe brought her a bowl of the steaming, cloudy broth.

Cobbe eyed Emelyn as the she sipped her soup. "Silver-eyes careless. Get into bad scrapes and nearly killed. Silver-eyes must be more careful, find better protection." Cobbe patted the knife hanging from her belt, suggesting she was well prepared for any danger that might come her way.

Emelyn's gaze lingered on the knife. "Has Corran returned yet? Have you seen him?"

Cobbe frowned, looking puzzled. "Hollow-man gone. This is good."

Emelyn was shocked by Cobbe's bluntness. "What? How is that good?"

Cobbe's puzzlement deepened. "Silver-eyes tired. Not understand simple things. Cobbe leave, let Silver-eyes rest."

Emelyn finished her soup amidst her troubled thoughts. It had been two days since Corran left. That he had not returned did not bode well. Even more troubling was that nobody seemed to care. Putting down her empty bowl, Emelyn got to her feet and walked over to the Magisters.

The Magi had already woken and were sitting and talking. As Emelyn approached they quieted, turning to face her. Emelyn stiffened. She would have preferred to talk to Aldren alone, but she knew the Grand Magister would not willingly give up his seat, nor did Emelyn feel she had the right to ask.

She steeled her nerves, clasping her hands behind her back. "Corran has been gone for two days and has not returned. We need to go look for him."

The Magisters gazed at her, saying nothing. Emelyn began to waver and lose her resolve. It was Percival who broke the silence.

"You care for him, I see."

Emelyn blinked, frowning. "Yes, but I don't see how that matters. He's gone missing; we ought to look for him. It's the right thing to do." Emelyn couldn't believe that she had to explain this.

Aldren fidgeted. He looked as though he wished to leave, but he remained sitting. The Grand Magister continued to gaze at Emelyn, seemingly considering her words with great care.

"Of course it is the right thing to do, and of course we shall look for him," he said.

Aldren shot Percival a startled look. He quickly recovered, his face calm and placid once more. Yet Emelyn had seen the brief break in his composure and was troubled by it.

"How would you suggest we proceed?" Percival said. "He has not returned to our old camp and the snow has covered any tracks left behind."

Emelyn frowned, confused as to why the Grand Magister was asking for her advice. He ought to know better than all of them how to proceed. "We should branch out, each searching in a different direction."

Percival nodded. "That is one way to go about it, yes. But these woods are dangerous, as you, unfortunately, are well aware. I would not have anyone else come to harm.

If we are to search for the young man, then we must do it together."

Despite her concern for Corran, Emelyn was relieved. She had no desire to head back out into the woods alone, and she was glad to have the option removed. Yet she didn't know of a better way to find Corran. "What would you suggest?"

Percival held Emelyn in an intense gaze before answering. "You must understand that we cannot go wandering about aimlessly through the forest looking for the young man. It would accomplish nothing other than draining our energy and resources, neither of which we can afford to squander at this point."

Emelyn nodded, seeing the truth in his words. "But how will we find him?"

"I suggest that we continue on as before. Since we do not know in which direction he has gone, one direction is as good as the next, so we may as well continue north as we have been. Yet, as we travel I will use the Art to try and sense if anything is amiss. Should I detect something, we will alter our course and investigate.

Emelyn frowned. "Can you do that? Will it work?"

"Such a feat is well within my capabilities, I assure you. Whether or not it will work depends on whether or not anything is amiss. It is possible that the young man is quite well and simply decided to leave for reasons of his own. We cannot be sure. But I assure you I will do my best to find him for you."

Find him for her. Emelyn didn't like the way the Grand Magister seemed to be humoring her, as though he had only agreed to look for Corran to keep her happy and quiet. Emelyn suspected he didn't care in the least if they found Corran, leading her to doubt the validity of his promise to do everything possible to find him. Yet Emelyn didn't know of any other options. She was not prepared to head out on her own to find him, and their supplies *were* limited and would not sustain them indefinitely in a winter-wrought forest. With a sinking stomach, she agreed. "Very well."

Percival smiled, though his eyes remained cold. "Good. It is settled. We will leave as soon as you feel strong enough."

"I'm strong enough now."

"Are you, now? Very good, then; we will leave at once."

With the matter decided, Emelyn turned and left. The truth was she didn't feel strong enough. She would have liked another day or so to rest before resuming the harshness of traveling. But she didn't want to give a reason for delay when Corran was missing. She would have to be stronger, for his sake. *You will need to be strong, too, when the snow comes.* Iyen's words surfaced in Emelyn's mind, and she wondered if this was what the girl had meant.

They spent the rest of the morning packing up their supplies and getting ready for the journey. Cobbe, when told they would soon be departing, howled in protest.

"Silver-eyes too weak to travel," she said, slapping at Aldren's and Emelyn's hands as they tried to pack the supplies. "Silver-eyes must rest and eat food Cobbe make before traveling again!" But the woman's protests were ignored and Cobbe, seeing that she was outmatched, relented.

They filed out of the camp later that afternoon, heading north under a clear blue sky. Emelyn turned her face upwards, watching the sunlight sparkle from behind the lush pine boughs. Above the treetops, the falcon soared on the wind and Emelyn smiled, wishing she had wings of her own. She tried not to think about the pain in her throat or the fatigue in her legs. She pushed the dark memory of the previous day to the corner of her mind, where it lurked like a bruise on her thoughts. Emelyn feared to think of it, to look directly at it. She was afraid that if she did, she would lose her resolve, choosing instead to curl up into a ball and hide.

Traveling was difficult, and Emelyn grew tired much more quickly than usual. Even though they walked at a slower pace, by the time they stopped to make camp she was exhausted. She slumped down against a fallen, snow-laden tree as the others prepared the camp. Guilt tugged at her mind almost as prominently as the fatigue that tugged at her eyelids. But in the end, fatigue won and she drifted off into sleep.

Emelyn awoke to a bowl of warm food thrust under her nose. She opened her eyes to a filthy face looming close to her own. The face creased as a toothy grinned appeared and Emelyn felt the bowl placed into her hands.

"Good, Silver-eyes awake. Must eat first, then sleep." Cobbe pointed at the bowl, encouraging Emelyn to eat.

Emelyn blinked the sleep from her eyes as she peered at the food in her hands. She had expected more soup and was surprised, therefore, when she found a nice, glistening chunk of freshly grilled meat sitting atop a pile of mashed roots. Emelyn blinked again. "Is that meat?"

Cobbe puffed up, her face radiating from behind all the grime. "Cobbe find fine tree-rat, cook it up nice. Silver-eyes will get strong again now." She gave a curt nod.

Emelyn smiled, glad for the change in fare. "You found it? Do you mean you caught it?" She picked up the meat with her fingers and took a bite.

"No, Cobbe find it there." She pointed to the ground near Emelyn's feet.

Emelyn stopped chewing. "It was already dead?"

Cobbe looked puzzled. "Of course was dead. Not nice to cook living beasties." She gave the matter some thought before adding, "Is possible, though, in a pinch."

Emelyn dropped the meat back into the bowl as if it had bitten her. "You cooked up a dead squirrel? How long was it there? It could be rotten . . . or worse!"

Cobbe lifted her chin. "Is not rotten. Is very fresh. Hunter-bird dropped tree-rat at Silver-eyes' feet while Silver-eyes sleeping. Cobbe sees this, fetches tree-rat to cook up properly." She crossed her arms, glaring at Emelyn with large, defiant eyes.

Hunter-bird? Emelyn looked up at the trees and there he was, the falcon that had been following her since Roelith. "The falcon caught the squirrel?"

Cobbe deflated. "Yes . . . but Cobbe just as good as hunter-bird at catching things. Cobbe much too busy now to set out traps, and red-robes refuse to wait for traps to fill." She scowled. "If not for busybody red-robes, Silver-eyes would have nice meat to eat more often."

"Of . . . course," Emelyn said as her sleep-addled mind tried to make sense of their conversation. She picked up the piece of meat and nibbled at it. It didn't taste rotten. In fact, it tasted quite good. "Thank you, Cobbe."

Cobbe gave a sharp nod before turning and walking away.

As Emelyn ate, her hunger grew and, along with it, her strength. She was still very tired and her limbs still felt heavy, but she also felt more alert and able to think more clearly. She eyed the Magisters as she ate, wondering what they were talking about and, more importantly, if Percival had kept his word in regards to finding Corran. During their journey, Emelyn had tried to be vigilant of their surroundings, looking for any sign of footprints and listening for any sound that might lead them to Corran. But she had seen and heard nothing unusual, and she knew that with her fatigue much went unnoticed.

Sadness weighed heavy on her as she thought about Corran, wandering alone in the frozen woods. Was he all right? Was he warm and fed? Emelyn wished she could do more to help find him. She hated having to trust the Magisters to keep their word, especially since they didn't seem to care about finding Corran at all. She wished that she could use the Art as they said they could to find her friend on her own.

At that moment the falcon flew from the trees, swooping down to land at Emelyn's feet. She froze, afraid to move for fear of scaring away the bird. The falcon gazed at her with a single black eye and Emelyn felt like it was purposefully watching her.

"Was it really you who left the squirrel?" She smiled to herself, feeling a little silly for talking to a bird. She bet the falcon could find Corran. He could just soar up over the trees, the forest spread out before him like a map. If anyone could find Corran, it would be him.

The falcon continued to watch Emelyn. Then it took flight, leaving her alone once more. She sighed, feeling a little sad that the bird had gone, though she knew it was more than the falcon's departure that had caused her sadness.

Emelyn settled herself against the fallen tree, trying to find a reasonably comfortable position on the cold, hard ground. She reached into her pocket and pulled out the two leaves she had been saving since Roelith.

The leaves showed no signs of decay and were still bright and glossy. Emelyn ran her fingertips over the smooth surfaces, trying to remind herself that it was she who had transformed one of the leaves to its current beauty.

"Where did you find those?"

Emelyn started, surprised to see Aldren standing over her. "R . . . Roelith," she said, her face growing hot. Why did she suddenly feel ashamed as if he had found out a hidden, dark secret?

"I see." He watched her a moment, then said, "I wanted to see how you were feeling. We walked for several hours today and I wanted to make sure you were well."

Emelyn tucked the leaves back into her pocket, grateful he hadn't asked about them. "I'm tired, but well. I feel stronger, though, having eaten some proper food."

Aldren nodded, but his eyes looked distant.

He was quiet for so long that Emelyn grew concerned. "Are we to resume our lessons?" she said, hoping to stir up the conversation in some form. Anything was better than having him looming over her in silence.

Aldren focused on Emelyn. "No. I . . . we will not be having lessons anymore."

Emelyn felt as though he had struck her. "I see." She tried to sound nonchalant but only managed to sound cold.

Aldren's eyes softened, turning sad. "I know what you are thinking, and you are wrong. As your teacher, the lack of success in our exercises can be laid at my feet, not yours. You are not to blame."

"Yet I am the one failing what you call 'simple' exercises." Emelyn hesitated. "I think you might be wrong about me, about what I can do."

"I am not wrong. You and I both know that." Aldren pointed at her hip. "Those leaves you have hidden away. Trees only have leaves that green in the spring. Yet here we are, in the grasp of winter and you with two vibrant, living leaves. Quite remarkable, if you ask me."

When Emelyn said nothing, Aldren continued. "The time for doubting yourself is long past, I fear. You must learn to use this ability of yours and you must learn it on your own. I will not be able to help you."

Aldren's stern voice startled Emelyn, and confused her. "Why not? Why can't you help me?"

"Because you are too different. Your gift is not that of a Magister. I thought it might be the same, but I was wrong."

Their way is not your way. Corran's words came back to Emelyn, a sharp stab that reminded her how alone she was. As Aldren turned his back and left, she wished, now more than ever, that her friend was there.

CHAPTER 15

EMELYN FOLLOWED COBBE as they foraged through the forest. When they came to a young pine she stopped while Cobbe sidled her mount near the tree. The Wylkin climbed atop her stout brown pig and, standing on her tiptoes, hacked at the lower branches with a hatchet. Snow and needles cascaded down upon Cobbe's head while Emelyn half-hid her eyes, expecting the woman to fall and hurt herself.

Cobbe glanced at her and scowled. "Silver-eyes helpful like lump of rock. Stands there hiding while Cobbe does all the work."

Emelyn caught the hint and picked up the branches that had fallen to the ground. She was careful to give Cobbe and the pig a wide berth, not wanting to cause her to fall. But Emelyn's worries were for naught as Cobbe soon hopped down and put the hatchet away in a saddlebag.

Emelyn carried the branches over, unsure of what to do with them.

Cobbe grinned and pulled from a saddlebag a short length of rope. With it, she bundled the branches together before taking them and lashing them to her mount.

"What are the branches for?" Emelyn said.

"Green winter-trees very tasty, can be used in many different ways—as spice, as teas, many ways. Smoke gives nice flavor when burned, and woody bits can be chewed to keep tooths clean." Cobbe gave Emelyn a big smile, showing her darkened teeth in the process.

Emelyn did not doubt Cobbe in matters of cookery, but she was skeptical that the woman knew anything of personal hygiene.

Once Cobbe had finished securing the branches, they headed back toward the camp with Cobbe leading her pig as Emelyn walked alongside her with her staff. Several days had passed since the incident with the giant, and Emelyn had decided it best to keep her staff close to hand. Her lessons with Corran had been few, and Emelyn wasn't sure she would be able to defend herself with it, but it was better than nothing. She did not want to be caught defenseless again.

"Silver-eyes not being clever," Cobbe said, breaking the silence. "Silver-eyes must listen to Cobbe, learn many things about food in the wilds. When Silver-eyes hungry, Silver-eyes will want to know such things."

Emelyn glanced at Cobbe but said nothing. Percival had declared that Cobbe and Aldren would increase their efforts with foraging to help supplement their supplies. Today, however, Percival had needed Aldren for some matter, so Emelyn had accompanied Cobbe into the woods despite her own lack of knowledge in such things.

"Much food to be had in the wilds," Cobbe said, stretching her arms wide. "But only clever ones will find it. Especially in wintertime. Less food then, must be extra clever to find it." She tapped the pig on the haunch, sending the animal into a brisk trot. The pig surveyed the ground as he went, snuffling in the snow with his long snout. Cobbe smirked at Emelyn as the pig carried on, though Emelyn didn't know what was so special about his behavior.

The pig came to a halt and scratched at the ground with his hooves. Cobbe patted the pig on the neck while nudging him out of the way. She fetched the hatchet from her saddlebag and hacked at the frozen ground. Sweat beaded on her dirty brow as she worked. Soon she put down the hatchet and rooted in the soil with her hands. Emelyn felt as though she ought to help, but she didn't know how. She wasn't even sure what Cobbe was doing.

With a shriek of victory Cobbe pulled up from the ground a handful of filthy, stringy roots. Judging by Cobbe's wide grin, Emelyn took the roots to be a good thing, though she had difficulty in sharing the woman's enthusiasm.

Cobbe walked over to Emelyn and dropped the bundle of cold, damp roots into her hands. Emelyn held them at arm's length, wondering what she was supposed to do with them.

"These very tasty," Cobbe said, seemingly oblivious to Emelyn's unease. "Strong flavor, peppery, nice in soups and stews. Very difficult to find such roots, even for Cobbe. But bristle-snouts very clever at finding them. Bristle-snouts very clever at finding many things, but in wintertime, only thing left to find is roots."

"That's . . . nice, Cobbe," Emelyn said, still not quite understanding the significance of finding roots.

Cobbe nodded. "Not any bristle-snout will do, though. Bristle-snouts not always very clever, must be taught to find roots when wanted and not to dig them all up and eat them. Very difficult. Many bristle-snouts not learn. This bristle-snout very clever, like Cobbe." She smiled, patting the pig on the snout. "Learns very fast and only eats *some* roots when ground not frozen."

Emelyn smiled.

"Silver-eyes also clever. Trains hunter-bird to find tree-rats. Cobbe sees this and approves. Not as difficult as training bristle-snouts, but still very clever." Cobbe nodded her head, smiling at Emelyn with the approval and pride of a mentor.

"I didn't train the falcon, Cobbe."

Cobbe scowled and waved her hands as if refusing to accept whatever Emelyn had to say. She grabbed the roots from Emelyn's hands and stuffed them into her saddlebag. She continued leading her pig back towards the camp. Emelyn followed.

Emelyn had nearly recovered from the giant's attack. Her voice had returned, as had her strength. The only reminder she had of that day was a sore neck and her memories, but she tried not to dwell upon those. Traveling through the woods no longer fatigued her as it had when they first set out, and Emelyn was able to watch their surroundings much more closely. She watched the Magisters as they walked as much as she watched the trees, looking for an indication that they were keeping their word. But it was difficult to tell one way or the other. She had no idea in which direction they were supposed to be traveling and therefore could not tell if the Magisters diverged from it.

As Emelyn followed Cobbe, a flickering of shadows flitted in the corner of her eye. She looked towards the movement, but there was only snow and trees. She had been seeing such shadows since earlier in the day, always a hint of something moving from the corner of her eye. But there was never anything there. She dismissed it as stray memories from her encounter with the giant, but it was unsettling, and Emelyn's eagerness to return to camp grew.

Cobbe had pulled away while she was distracted, and Emelyn hurried to catch up. Shadows once again darted on the borders of her vision, this time accompanied with a faint knocking sound.

Emelyn stopped and looked. Once again, there was nothing. It was maddening. Though she could see no movement, the knocking remained and Emelyn fixed her sight on the direction of the sound. Trees rustled in a light breeze, but all else was still.

She turned in time to see Cobbe walk behind a tree and felt a sharp stab of panic when she disappeared from sight. Emelyn didn't want to be left in the woods alone. Ignoring the strange sound, she ran to catch up. But when she rounded the tree, all she found was barren snow.

"Cobbe?" Emelyn called, but there was no reply.

She looked around. The snow was smooth, absent of any tracks showing where Cobbe had gone. "Impossible."

You have much to learn of what is possible in this world. Emelyn's frown deepened as she recalled Percival's words.

"Cobbe!" Emelyn called again, but was met only with silence and that same distant knocking. She was alone.

Acid filled Emelyn's mouth as her vision dimmed and her heart bolted. She squatted down, resting her forehead on her knees as she filled her hands with snow. Sifting the snow through her fingers, Emelyn imagined that she could feel each individual flake before it melted, seeing in her mind the textures and facets of the tiny crystals. In time, her breathing calmed and her fear subsided, though it still lurked in the shadows of her mind.

She straightened and looked around. With Cobbe gone, she'd need to find her own way back to camp. But without any tracks, she didn't know which direction to take. She hesitated, struggling to keep calm while she considered what to do.

The distant knocking persisted, the only sound to be heard in the forest other than her breathing. Emelyn turned towards the noise, wondering what could be causing it. Maybe it was the Magi, or maybe someone that could help. Or maybe it was danger, and Emelyn should walk as far away from it as possible. But what other did choice did she have? Not knowing what else to do, she followed the sound.

The knocking grew louder, more distinct. It sounded like hammering. This gave Emelyn a measure of hope— craftsmen were familiar. Even so, she was careful in her approach, not wanting to stumble upon whomever was in the forest until she was ready. When the walls of a cabin peeked through the trees, she stopped and hid behind a pine.

The cabin was newly built, the wood pale and fresh. Tools and tables lay strewn about, reminding Emelyn of old Mr. Wainwright's carpentry shop. The hammering rang through the air, drawing her gaze to the roof. There a man crawled along barren beams as he hammered, preparing the roof for the bundles of thatch that lay nearby.

He was barely clothed, wearing only trousers and boots, foregoing a shirt as though it were the height of summer. He didn't seem to notice that the ground was covered in ice or that the sun did not warm the skin. Emelyn remained behind the tree, unconvinced the man was trustworthy.

From behind the cabin came a woman, carrying in her hands a plate of food. She had long, dark hair and wore a dress of rough leather. Emelyn's mouth turned to ashes—it was the same woman she had seen in the forest only a few days before. At least, she thought it was her. Although this woman looked similar, she was older and in the full bloom of womanhood, her belly swollen and heavy with child. She called to the man on the roof, waving the plate of food to entice him down. The man obliged, climbing down a nearby ladder and beaming at the woman as he took the plate. Emelyn gasped, her heart leaping into her throat.

"Corran!" she said, stepping out from behind the tree.

Corran's gaze snapped to her, his smile dissolving. "Yes?"

Emelyn faltered. She hadn't expected such a cold reception. "It's me, Emelyn."

The man smiled, though his eyes remained cold and devoid of recognition. "I'm afraid I don't recall our acquaintance. Have we met?"

Emelyn floundered before managing a weak, "Yes."

The man's puzzled expression told her he remained unconvinced.

Emelyn looked at the woman standing behind Corran. She was still, watching Emelyn with cold, brilliantly blue eyes. Emelyn shrank inwardly under that gaze, beginning to regret having come here.

Corran said, "Are you all right? Are you lost, perhaps?"

Emelyn shook her head, vaguely aware that he had spoken at all. Something was terribly wrong, and Emelyn was trying to reconcile her own sudden, unsubstantiated fear.

The man took a step forward but stopped when Emelyn brought up her staff, warding him away. His eyes widened, startled, though he was not afraid. He looked more wounded at her unprovoked threat than anything else. Though startled and wounded he may have been, he did not take kindly to being threatened, and his eyes hardened.

"Perhaps you ought to leave," he said, his voice cold.

Emelyn wanted to leave. Every part of her was telling her to run, but where would she go? How would she find her way back to camp on her own? She felt frustrated, angry. What was wrong with him? Why didn't he know her? Emelyn glanced at the woman behind Corran's shoulder. Stark, blue eyes gazed back at her, unflinching, unsympathetic. Emelyn narrowed her own eyes in response.

"What have you done to him?" she said, her voice low.

A shadow passed over the woman's eyes, turning them grey, just as a veil of clouds drew over the sun and darkened the world below.

Emelyn gripped her staff as the wind picked up, howling through the trees with a severity that made her teeth ache. Tears streamed down her cheeks, the howling growing so intense that it felt like nails were being driven through her skull.

With bleary eyes she looked at Corran and the woman, but they didn't seem to be affected or hear the screaming wind at all. Placid, they watched her, either unaware or indifferent to her pain. Emelyn knew she needed to act, needed to do *something* before the pain in her head drove her to collapse. Not knowing what else to do, she swung her staff.

Emelyn felt the jolt in her arms as the staff came into to contact with something soft. Someone. A person. With the pain in her head and the tears in her eyes, Emelyn couldn't see who it had been, nor did she know if they were about to retaliate.

Her strike was impulsive, and she soon realized she was ill equipped for a fight. But before she had time for regret, the wind calmed and the howling subsided and she no longer felt the grating ache in her spine or the nails driving into her skull. The tears cleared from her eyes and Emelyn realized that she was alone.

She blinked, tightening her grip on her staff even as the tension in her body faded, leaving her feeling deflated and confused. Where were they? Both Corran and the woman were gone. The cabin was gone. There were no footprints, no tools, no piles of thatch. It was like they had never existed. Was she going mad?

Emelyn walked around, looking for Corran, for any evidence that she had not imagined the entire incident. At a crunching of snow, Emelyn turned to find Cobbe walking towards her in the company of her bough-laden pig.

Cobbe scowled. "Cobbe not understand Silver-eyes. Sometimes, Silver-eyes very clever. Understand many things. Cobbe approves of this. Other times, Silver-eyes so very un-clever that Cobbe can only shake head. Cobbe not understand why Silver-eyes must wander off into the wilds like bumbling baby and not listen."

Emelyn grinned, bending down to hug the little Wylkin.

Cobbe stiffened in Emelyn's embrace. "Squeezing Cobbe does not make Silver-eyes clever. Silver-eyes must listen, not squeeze."

When Emelyn released her, Cobbe grunted. "Come, we leave now." She tapped the pig on the haunches and walked away.

"Cobbe, wait!" Emelyn said as she trailed after her.

Cobbe cast back a cursory glance, but kept on walking.

"Corran is out here, somewhere. Cobbe, stop!" Emelyn put a hand on Cobbe's shoulder, but let go when she saw Cobbe's menacing glare.

"Corran is here," she repeated, refusing to be fully intimidated by Cobbe's foul mood. "I saw him. We can't leave without him."

Cobbe's face darkened as she showed her teeth in a grimace. Then her scowl faded, and she looked more tired than angry. "Silver-eyes make Cobbe feel much too old. Cobbe still young, not yet ready to be Den Mother. Sky grows dark. Silver-eyes must follow or else sleep in wilds alone." She continued walking, this time without looking back to see if Emelyn followed.

Emelyn, of course, did follow. She had been so happy to see Cobbe that she wasn't about to let her vanish again. Yet Emelyn's heart was heavy. Corran's disappearance had shaken her. His reappearance and failure to recognize her left her saddened and confused. Cobbe's indifference only made matters worse. The joy she had felt upon seeing the Wylkin was fading, and Emelyn followed after Cobbe in leaden silence.

Cobbe was also quiet. Her liveliness from earlier in the day had diminished, and she now plodded through the snow in silent determination. She no longer spoke to Emelyn about foraging, and the few times she did stop to look at some bush or plant she didn't share what she found, or hoped to find. Emelyn feared she had offended Cobbe beyond repair, losing the only friend she had left.

The sun had set by the time they reached the camp. A fire blazed in the darkness, a warm and pleasant welcome. Upon arriving, Cobbe made her way to the supplies and unloaded her pig of the newly procured goods. Normally, Emelyn would have helped her, but Cobbe's mood gave her pause. Instead, she lingered by the fire, warming her hands over the flames.

"You were gone longer than expected," Aldren said, joining Emelyn by the fire. "Did you have trouble?"

Emelyn watched the flickering flames, giving no answer.

After a moment, he asked, "Are you well?"

"I found Corran," Emelyn said, still staring at the fire.

Silence hung between them for what felt like ages.

"I see." Aldren's voice was calm, even. "And where is he now?"

Emelyn looked up, studying the Magister's face. What was he not telling her? "He didn't know me. Something's happened to him and we need to help."

Aldren fell silent again. When he spoke, his voice was quiet, strained. "I am afraid there is much you do not understand."

"That has been quite apparent." Emelyn could hear the bitterness in her voice.

"Has it occurred to you that he might not be what he seems?"

Emelyn frowned. "What's that supposed to mean?"

"What, exactly, do you know of him?"

Emelyn floundered, surprised by the question. "I . . . I know he had a family. He said that Magisters took them . . . before they died."

Aldren frowned, looking thoughtful.

"Is it true?"

He started, as though he had forgotten she was there. "No."

Emelyn looked at him askance. "Why would he say something like that if it wasn't true?"

Aldren rubbed his brow. "Because his existence is not rooted in logic."

"What?"

He shook his head, looking tired. "What else do you know of him?"

Emelyn eyed the Magister, wondering if she ought to pursue the matter. Instead, she said, "I know that he is a carpenter and that he is from the west, near the Myrwind sea. He . . ."

"Yes?"

Emelyn glanced at Aldren. "There was something he said, long ago in Fallow. I had always thought it strange."

When Aldren said nothing, she continued. "He said that he had apprenticed in Fallow with Mr. Wainwright. But that couldn't have been because he was too young, and Mr. Wainwright hasn't taken any apprentices for nearly twenty years. I asked him about it later, but he couldn't account for it. Said that he remembered working there and that everyone else must have been mistaken."

"And what do you think that means?"

Emelyn shrugged. "I don't know. I figured he must have been mistaken or confused. He had lost his family. I guess I thought that maybe that had something to do with it . . . that maybe his sorrow muddled his memories." Emelyn shook her head, clearing her mind of her own confused thoughts. "I don't see what this has to do with anything. What difference does it make how well I know him? Are you saying we should just leave him in the woods? Something has happened to him and you just want to abandon him?"

"Emelyn," Aldren's voice was gentle, kind. "The man you think of as Corran does not exist."

Emelyn stared at the Magi. The notion was so absurd that she didn't know how to respond.

"I know this might be difficult for you to accept or understand, but this young man that has been calling himself Corran is nothing more than a phantom, an anomalous creature just like those we encountered in Fallow and Timmerfell. He is not real, he is merely an illusion created by the creature of magic in the north."

Emelyn put a hand over her eyes; she suddenly felt very tired. "What?"

"Think about all you have seen recently. The young man in the woods that looked very much like Corran. A man you claim to be Corran elsewhere in the woods, yet he does not know you. The inaccuracies of his memory. Is it too much to believe that he is a projection, a mirage, a manifestation of 'magic' similar to all the other manifestations we have seen?"

"Yes! It is too much to believe. Those things were foul and dangerous. Those other 'manifestations' seemed only to wish for destruction. Corran is none of those things. He saved me in Fallow and has always been kind. He is nothing like those other creatures. I don't understand how you can say he is the same!"

"Not all such apparitions are violent. What of the young woman you have seen—long, dark hair and wearing a leather dress? Perhaps you have also seen a young girl of a similar description? Were they violent? Destructive?"

Emelyn gaped at the Magister. She had told him of the older girl she had seen in the forest, but never of the younger one from Fallow and Roelith. "How did you know . . . ?"

"Because I have seen her. More than that, I know who she is."

"Who is she?" Emelyn barely managed to speak the words above a whisper.

Aldren hesitated, his eyes sad. "She is the one creating

these apparitions; the creature of magic, as it were. The girl you have seen is a manifestation of herself, a memory of herself. Of what she used to be."

"She's . . . not real?" Emelyn's voice was flat, dubious. It was too much to believe.

"She is real, just not as the person you have seen. Those girls, though they existed once, exist no longer."

"And Corran?"

"Iyen—that is her name—and Corran knew each other from childhood. Corran was apprenticing in Fallow and Iyen lived in the surrounding woods with her people. She would often come to town to trade, and the two struck up a friendship."

"Her people? You mean the forest people?"

Aldren nodded, "Yes. In time, the friendship turned to romance and the two married. They moved to a cabin in the woods and had a baby girl."

"Corran told me this. How could he have told me if it wasn't him?"

"Because the man you have come to know as Corran is a memory of the man as Iyen recalls him. His memories are her memories. The real Corran, if he still lives, would be well into his forties, not the young man that you know."

Emelyn shook her head. "I don't understand. You are saying Corran is only the memory of Iyen, his wife. But Corran recalls his wife dying. How can that be?"

Aldren spread open his hands. "Iyen's mind, unfortunately, is broken, twisted with madness. It is possible she recalls things that did not happen. Perhaps her fears have manifested in this form. It is difficult to say."

Emelyn studied the Magister. "How do you know all of this? Why do you know so much of these people?"

Aldren's eyes turned sad once more. "Let us just say that we have known Iyen a long time and, as such, have come to know the people in her life as well."

"Why is all of this happening now? If she is who you say she is and she's causing all of these strange occurrences, why has none of this happened before?"

The Magister shifted his feet, looking uncomfortable. "The Magisters had taken . . . steps . . . to insure that Iyen, in her madness, would not be able to cause any disturbances. It would seem that some of those measures have recently failed."

Emelyn's mind felt tangled. How could she possibly make sense of any of this? Yet through the haze of confusion one thing became stunningly clear.

"She's like me, isn't she? The way Iyen uses the Art, it's the same as me."

Aldren looked at Emelyn almost apologetically with his tired, sad eyes. Yet through the sadness, Emelyn also thought she saw relief. "Yes," was all he said before he turned and walked away.

CHAPTER 16

THE JOURNEY NORTHWARD continued. One day passed into the next as quietly and monotonously as the falling snow. Respites were few and sunshine rare. So when they stopped one sunny day along a snowy road, Emelyn took advantage of both.

She turned her face to the sky, smiling as the sun shone down on her. It seemed like ages since she had enjoyed simple pleasures. Her conversation with Aldren had left her troubled. She had a difficult time believing what he had said about Corran, yet she couldn't deny that there were strange occurrences that she couldn't explain. But it wasn't just Corran—Emelyn kept dwelling upon the story of Iyen. Knowing that they both used the Art in the same manner stirred in her a mixture of emotions. On the one hand, she was glad to know she was not alone in her abilities, on the other she was terrified of what Iyen had become. Of what *she* might become. Was Iyen's fate one she would share? Would she also lose her mind and use her ability to torment others?

Aldren hadn't said what had caused Iyen's madness, but Emelyn felt the words didn't need to be spoken. The way he had looked at her with his saddened eyes said much, as did the interest the Magisters had in her and her ability. She hadn't been able to account for their interest before, but now she felt she understood. They must have sensed in her the ability to wield the Art during their encounter in Fallow and were likely duty-bound to investigate the matter, to see if they would soon have on their hands another woman driven mad by her inexplicable ability with the Art. Or so Emelyn feared.

She knew she shouldn't jump to conclusions, that she ought to ask Aldren what had happened to Iyen, but she was afraid. Afraid to ask and have her fears confirmed, afraid to find out something she had not yet learned. The world she had once known had been irrevocably shattered, and Emelyn felt she didn't have enough time to adjust before something else arose to shatter it anew.

After that day, she avoided Aldren as much as possible, which was very little, given their close proximity while traveling. But she no longer helped Cobbe as frequently with the cooking preparations, especially when Aldren was assisting her. Emelyn kept closest to Ferrin, tending to his meager needs at all hours of the day.

She looked over at the Magisters as they talked amongst themselves. They had been holding a private conference ever since Percival had brought their traveling to a halt. It was just as well; the day was fine and she was in no hurry to reach their destination.

Aldren waved a hand in the air, pointing at the sky to the northeast. At least she thought it was northeast. Emelyn still hadn't quite honed her sense of direction. Whatever direction it was, the Magi seemed to be in disagreement that it was the proper course to take.

Aldren gesticulated with his hands while Percival stood with his arms folded, still as a stock, pressing his lips into a fine line. It would seem that the Grand Magister was not used to others disagreeing with him. Emelyn smiled in spite of herself, feeling wicked over her pleasure at his discomfort.

Ferrin whinnied and stamped his hooves. Emelyn patted his nose. The break from traveling had been nice, but Emelyn always grew restless with too much idling—as did Ferrin, it seemed. Picking up the reins, she walked along the road. The fact that they had found a road was a small wonder. Ever since leaving Roelith, they had spent a large portion of their journey traveling along narrow paths or straight through the snowy brush. Emelyn hoped that the existence of this road meant there was a town nearby.

She strolled along, admiring the way the snow sparkled in the sunlight. When she came to a bend in the road, she stopped and looked back. The Magisters were still talking while Cobbe leaned against her pig as she sharpened her knife with a stone. Turning back around, Emelyn started when she saw a figure on the road ahead. She hurried back towards the others, not waiting to see who was coming.

The Magisters, seeing her haste, walked forward to meet her.

"Someone's coming," Emelyn said as she walked past them. She didn't wait for the Magisters to respond, nor did she look back until she was well behind the others. Coward. She flinched at her own accusation, but brushed it aside. She had her fill of meeting strangers in these woods. Someone else could see who it was and deal with him.

Cobbe put away her stone and walked over to Emelyn, her knife at the ready. "Silver-eyes not worry. Red-robes very clever at keeping nasties away. If red-robes fail, Cobbe also very clever."

Emelyn forced a smile; she doubted that Cobbe could protect them should the Magi fail. She turned back to the newcomer, trying to see who it was. But the day was bright and the glare cast upon the snow made it difficult to see.

Cobbe walked forward a few steps, shading her eyes with a hand. Then, crying out, she ran towards the stranger.

Emelyn started after her but stopped when Cobbe ran past the Magi. Cobbe's pig, not wanting to be left behind, waddled after her. The pig would do what she was too afraid to do. Emelyn peered through the glare as Cobbe met the newcomer. The two remained on the road for a time, talking, or so Emelyn assumed. Despite shading her eyes, she still couldn't see well enough to know what was happening. After a few minutes, the figures on the snow started towards them. Emelyn, feeling braver, stepped forward.

Her breath caught when she saw another Wylkin with the same unruly hair and filthy face walking alongside a stout pig of his own. Emelyn studied the newcomer, making sure that it was, in fact, a "he." Cobbe's brow was furrowed, her expression dark. Her knife, still drawn, was held in a white-knuckled grip. Emelyn thought Cobbe would have been happier meeting one of her kin on the road.

"Hello," Emelyn said.

Cobbe's face darkened further while the other's face brightened. He wore a rumpled cap that he now snatched off, crumpling it further in his dingy hands.

"Hello!" he said. His face split into a wide grin, showing rows of teeth that looked to be in better condition than Cobbe's.

Cobbe reached out and smacked him upside the head, causing his smile to dissolve. The man scowled at Cobbe, and he received an even darker scowl in return.

Emelyn cleared her throat, worried that the two might come to blows. "Do you two know each other, Cobbe?"

"Not from same den, but kin is kin." Cobbe continued to frown at the man, offering no further explanation.

Emelyn, still confused and growing increasingly uncomfortable with the tension, did the only thing she could think of. "I'm Emelyn," she said, turning to the newcomer.

The man's face split into a smile once again while the hat he was holding was crumpled anew. "Bog," he said, placing a hand on his chest.

Cobbe grunted. Bog's smile wavered as he glanced at the woman. Once he saw there were no more blows incoming, he continued to beam at Emelyn.

"Very nice to meet you, Bog," Emelyn said.

Bog's smile widened even further, and Emelyn thought his hat might be crumpled beyond repair.

Cobbe swatted him upside the head again, but Bog failed to notice, for the Magisters had come to stand alongside Emelyn. He stared wide-eyed at the newcomers, his smile so big that Emelyn thought the top of his head might fall off.

"What have we here?" Aldren said when he saw Bog, his own smile rivaling that of the little man.

"This is Bog," Emelyn said, seeing that Cobbe was not inclined to answer. "He is kin of Cobbe, so it seems."

"Kin? Remarkable!" Aldren turned to Bog. "Magister Aldren Keller, at your service," he said, giving a small bow. "Allow me to introduce my lord and master, Grand Magister Percival Lacreld."

Bog's smile managed to somehow grow wider still, his eyes bulging from his skull. Emelyn couldn't see his hat anymore, so crumpled it was in his grasp. Bog was so delighted that he didn't seem to notice Percival's distinct lack of enthusiasm at their meeting.

"What brings one of Cobbe's kin to these woods?" Aldren asked.

Bog said nothing as he grinned at Emelyn and the Magisters. A quick slap on the back of his head from Cobbe brought his attention back to the present.

He cleared his throat. "Bog traveling in woods, gathering many things, many tasty and useful things for the den. Then Bog sees hunter-bird, flying high up among tall trees. Hunter-birds very rare in winter-woods. Bog follows, thinking maybe hunter-bird leads Bog to tree-rats or other tasty things. But hunter-bird vanishes and Bog instead finds tall-folk in the wilds." He beamed at Emelyn.

Aldren looked thoughtful. "Gathering for the den? Do you mean you have a village nearby?"

Bog bobbed his head. "Oh yes, den nearby. Very close. Very cozy. Bog take you there. Come." With the matter seemingly decided, Bog turned to his pig and prepared to pull himself up when he noticed the ruins of his hat still in his hands. He stuffed it into one of his bags.

The others hesitated, including Cobbe. After several moments of silence, Aldren spoke. "Where, exactly, is this den of yours?"

Bog, now bouncing atop his pig, waved somewhat northwards.

Aldren smiled as he turned to Percival. "It is not out of our way. We were at a disagreement on which path to take. This, perhaps, can settle it for us."

Percival did not share Aldren's enthusiasm. With dark-ened eyes and a clenched jaw, he remained silent. Emelyn was curious what his answer would be.

"They might have supplies that they would be willing to sell or to trade," Aldren said.

"Yes, yes," Bog said. "Kin have many things. Tasty things. Useful things."

"Very well," Percival said. Undoubtedly the prospect of replenishing their supplies was too good to refuse, regard-less of who was supplying them.

Aldren's face brightened, causing him to look twenty years younger. He and Bog beamed at each other while Cobbe, with a furrowed brow, pulled herself atop her pig.

They traveled in silence for a time before Bog sidled his pig alongside Emelyn. He beamed up at her, but said nothing. He seemed happy just to share her company. In time, however, he spoke.

"The girl has lovely eyes; silver, like moon beams. Is this common among tall-folk?"

Emelyn glanced down at Bog. She had always thought her eyes grey, but both he and Cobbe seemed to think them silver. Other than the little girl in Fallow, she had never seen another person with eyes like hers, either silver or grey. Aside from a few strange glances she sometimes received, no one else seemed to find her eyes remarkable. But then, she was only a servant, so maybe no one ever noticed.

"I don't know," Emelyn said. "I don't think so."

Bog nodded. "Tall-folk very different, not only from kin, but from each other." He pointed at the Magisters. "White hair with blue eyes, pale. No hair with blue eyes, dark." He looked at Emelyn. "Black hair with silver eyes. All very different. All very nice. Among kin, all have dark hair, dark eyes. All are same. Always have been."

"Have you seen many tall-folk before?" Emelyn asked, curious about the man's enthusiasm over hair and eye color.

Bog shook his head. "No, no. Bog never seen any tall-folk before. Not many travelers come through the wilds. Bog is often out gathering, but still never sees anyone other than kin. Bog hears stories, though. Sometimes other gatherers meet tall-folk and come back to the den to tell story. This happens not often, though. No, most stories come from wildings."

"Wildings?"

Bog nodded. "Kin that leave the den, live among tall-folk for many years before returning." He looked at Cobbe.

Emelyn followed his gaze. "Is Cobbe a wilding?"

Bog raised his eyebrows. "Cobbe?"

Emelyn glanced between the two Wylkin. "I'm guessing Cobbe didn't introduce herself?"

Bog's perplexity deepened.

"Never mind." Emelyn pointed. "That's Cobbe."

The smile returned. "Oh. Yes. Wilding-kin. Yes."

Bog's smile was contagious and Emelyn found herself beaming down at him in return. "You two are very different. You're much more . . . nice."

Bog's cheeks reddened, visible even through all the grime.

"So why do wildings leave the den?"

Bog hesitated, his expression puzzled once more. Then he brightened. "Because they are wildings."

Emelyn laughed, shaking her head. Bog laughed with her.

Cobbe cast an annoyed glance back at them, her face dark as a storm.

Emelyn bit her lip but Bog, seemingly unaware of Cobbe's annoyance, continued in his mirth. Emelyn leaned towards him. "Why is Cobbe so cross with you?"

"Cobbe-kin is she-kin. Cross at everybody, not just Bog."

"She-kin? You mean female?"

Bog nodded. "Yes. Very few she-kin in the den. She-kin always wilding, out in the world before returning to den to become mother, sometimes Den Mother."

"Den Mother? Is that what Cobbe will be?" Emelyn recalled Cobbe having mentioned the words before but she hadn't known what they meant.

"Bog not know. Cobbe-kin not from same den."

They continued in silence for a time before Bog yelped and sent his pig into a gallop. Emelyn craned her neck, trying to see past the Magisters. Had they reached the den? Already? As far as she could see there was only snow and trees. Cobbe and the Magi stopped, and Emelyn was about to ask what was happening when she saw them—several Wylkin emerging from behind the trees, pointing and looking at the newcomers. Bog was with several of them, waving his arms as he talked.

Neither Emelyn nor the Magisters moved; only Cobbe advanced, sending her pig into a trot until she met the other Wylkin. Her hands flailed in the air, and Emelyn caught snippets of her voice sounding heated and angry. Whatever she said must have been sobering, for many that came to look at the newcomers shuffled away and disappeared among the trees.

Cobbe turned back to Emelyn and the Magi and waved them forward. Glancing at one another, Percival and Aldren continued along the road. Emelyn trailed closely behind them, wondering what had just happened. Although the Wylkin's enthusiasm had been dampened, their curiosity had not been completely subdued. Several dirty little faces peeked from behind the trees while the Wylkin that walked along the road with them ogled and whispered among themselves.

They had only walked a short while before stopping again. The Wylkin hiding behind the trees reappeared and rushed towards the visitors, ignoring all protests and complaints from Cobbe. She soon gave up, dismounting her pig as she moved out of the way of the ever-increasing throng of curious little-folk. Emelyn and the Magisters soon found themselves surrounded by a sea of sooty brown faces. Most were chattering in an unknown language, while others looked on with wide eyes and open mouths. The Wylkin were careful not to crowd them, however, keeping a respectable distance from the visitors so that they could move unhindered.

It was odd. Where were they all coming from? As far as Emelyn could tell, they had not yet reached their village. She looked around. There was only snow and . . . a thin trail of smoke rising from a fallen tree. How had she missed that?

She squinted her eyes, trying to see if it was a campfire or if the log itself was burning. As she looked, the landscape changed. What Emelyn had thought was a fallen tree turned out to be a long rectangular cottage. She could see the little windows and little door so clearly now that she wondered how she had ever missed it. A great tree stump turned out to be another quaint cottage, round like a pumpkin and capped with snow. The thick, leafless oak that towered nearby was still a thick and leafless oak, but one in which a home had been carved out of the base of the trunk, with smoke that trailed from a chimney pipe.

Emelyn gazed all around at the little village, now as plain to see as the sun in the sky, even though a few moments ago it had only been trees. Magic. She looked at the Wylkin with a newfound respect and awe. Who would have known they were capable of such extraordinary feats?

Bog reappeared, a new hat atop his head. "Come! Bog show tall-folk the den. Come!" He turned and disappeared within the crowd.

Emelyn hurried after him as he scuttled through the snow. When he came to a cottage, he stopped and beamed at her.

"Bog's home," he said, stretching his arms out towards the house. He opened the door, inviting her inside.

Emelyn crouched down and poked her head through the door. Given the man's personal appearance and that of all his kin, she was surprised at what she saw: the home was spotless. The wooden floors had been scrubbed and sanded, the plates and cups all neatly arranged on shelves. A child-sized table was in one corner, adorned with a potted holly branch that sat on a clean white cloth. There was not one dirty dish, not one speck of dust. Even the hearth was clean, with the ashes cleared and the stones scrubbed. Emelyn looked at Bog in amazement, wondering how such a filthy little man could keep a house so clean. Even Miss Cook would have been impressed.

Bog drew himself up as a wide smile split his face. "Come, come. Bog make tea." He ushered Emelyn inside, herding her over to the table and offering her a chair before hustling to the hearth to prepare the tea.

Emelyn looked at the chair and smiled. How was she supposed to fit in that? She eased herself into the seat, worried that it would break. The chair groaned and creaked under her weight, but it held, and Emelyn relaxed. She looked around, enchanted by the little home.

Everything was just so. The little cups and plates, the little chair, and little washing basin. Everything was in its place. Everything was as it should be. She found herself remembering a dollhouse she had seen long ago at Mr. Hibberly's store, how perfect that little home had been and how her heart had ached to live there.

Bog's home was just like that dollhouse, and sitting in his perfect little kitchen as he prepared her tea filled her with such an indescribable joy that she felt a little foolish. It was a silly childhood fancy. Yet, even so, sitting there at the table, looking out through the frosted windowpanes filled her with such joy that, for the first time in her life, Emelyn felt happy.

Bog seemed to share her delight as he whistled while measuring out tea into a clay pot. He rummaged in a cupboard, pulling out crocks of honey and jam. A plate of biscuits made their way to the table, as did a pitcher of cream, procured from a cubby beneath the floor. He set the table with plates and cups, and Emelyn almost cried out with glee when she saw the little spoons and knives, and the dainty flowers painted on the cups and saucers.

"You have a wonderful home, Bog."

Bog beamed at the compliment, his cheeks reddening once more.

The kettle over the fire whistled and Bog hustled over to take it off and poured the hot water into the teapot. He then poured some tea into their cups, and together they sat, sipping tea and nibbling biscuits topped with honey and jam.

Emelyn looked out the window as she ate. The Magisters towered over a throng of Wylkin that surrounded them. Their gazes were fixed downwards, and Emelyn supposed they were talking to someone, though she couldn't see whom. Then Percival's gaze flicked upwards and fixed upon Emelyn as she sat in Bog's kitchen. She froze, dropping her biscuit onto her plate.

The Magisters, together with a group of Wylkin, walked towards Bog's home. Emelyn expected the knock at the door, but it startled her all the same. Why was she so nervous? She hadn't done anything wrong.

Bog looked delighted, surprised, and a little confused. He stuffed the last of his biscuit into his mouth as he rose from his chair and walked to the door. He had only opened it a crack when someone on the other side pushed it wide open.

In stormed a woman that looked much like Cobbe, though she was older, with streaks of silver running through her wild hair. Emelyn felt a brief flash of satisfaction for being able to discern the woman's gender so quickly. Her satisfaction, however, withered under the woman's stern gaze.

"Den Mother," Bog mumbled, biscuit crumbs tumbling from his mouth. He clapped his hands to his head, reflexively trying to remove a hat that wasn't there.

The Den Mother took no notice of him. She walked over to Emelyn, her brow furrowed as she considered her. Emelyn thought perhaps she ought to introduce herself, but before she could the Den Mother grabbed her wrist and pulled her from the chair. Emelyn cried out, stumbling over her feet as she was hauled across the room, out the door and into the cold. Once outside, the Den Mother released her grip and turned towards Emelyn.

"Kneel," she said, pointing to the ground so that there was no mistake as to where Emelyn ought to place her knees.

Emelyn scowled, rubbing her sore wrist. "No."

The Den Mother narrowed her eyes. Pursing her lips together, she walked behind Emelyn and kicked her behind the knees.

As Emelyn fell, her chin was grasped in a firm grip and yanked upward, forcing her to look at the clear blue sky. From the corner of her vision, the Den Mother peered down at her, making Emelyn feel as small as an insect. Her breathing grew hoarse and ragged as anger and indignation rose up in her. But before she had a chance to react, the grip was released and Emelyn sat puffing and scowling in the snow.

The Den Mother watched as Emelyn rose to her feet.

Thoughts flew through Emelyn's mind—of what she should say to the Den Mother, of how poorly she treated her guests; that if she wanted something, asking politely would go much further. But Emelyn held her tongue. She knew from experience that it would likely do little good and she didn't want to risk landing Bog in trouble; he had shown her nothing but kindness.

Seeing that Emelyn would behave, the Den Mother spoke. "Forest-child travels with red-robes. Why?"

Forest child? "They are my companions."

"Forest-child will answer the question."

Emelyn faltered, feeling that she *had* answered the question. Wanting to leave, she searched the surrounding crowd, looking for a familiar face. Far in the back the Magisters watched, though they showed no interest in helping her.

Close by was Bog, worrying his hat in nervous hands. He seemed more upset than the Magisters, and he barely knew her. Emelyn felt like she should be angry at the Magisters' indifference, but she only felt sad.

"We're heading north," Emelyn said, wondering if that would appease the woman.

"Why?"

Emelyn glanced again at the Magisters. "There is a creature . . . a person of magic causing trouble that needs to be stopped. That's what they've told me, anyway."

The Den Mother's scowl softened. "Does Forest-child doubt the red-robes?"

Emelyn considered the question. "I have no reason to doubt them. I know little of such things."

The Den Mother's face fell, seemingly disappointed with the answer. "Why does Forest-child come here?"

Emelyn glanced at Bog. She wanted to answer truthfully, but she worried what she said might get her new friend in trouble. "We were invited here," she said, gauging the Den Mother's reaction.

The scowl returned. "Forest-child will answer the question."

"We thought it would be nice to visit your den," Emelyn said, unsure of what answer the Den Mother wanted. "We thought that maybe we could trade for some supplies as well."

The Den Mother was silent a long while as she watched Emelyn. "Yes."

Emelyn remained silent, unsure of what "yes" had meant.

It didn't matter. The Den Mother turned to Bog, barking what sounded like orders though Emelyn couldn't understand her words. It must have been good, for Bog's face soon lit up and he bobbed his head up and down while trying to put on his hat.

The Den Mother turned back to Emelyn. "Visitors may stay in den. Bog-kin show visitors proper sleeping place. Forest-child will go and rest, but later must have more words with Den Mother." She turned and left.

Once the excitement with the Den Mother had ended, most of the crowd dissipated with only a few curious onlookers remaining. Emelyn, feeling a tug at her sleeve, looked down to see Bog's beaming face.

"Bog show Forest-child sleeping place. Very nice. Very cozy. Come." He tottered off.

Forest child. Emelyn didn't know why the Den Mother had called her that, but Bog now seemed to take it for her name. She sighed, wondering if she could keep up with the multitude of names these curious folk had for everything.

Bog led Emelyn through the village to a clearing on the outskirts of town. Cobbe was already there, attempting to unload the supply sacks from Ferrin's back. She shot them a withering glare, undoubtedly unhappy over having to do all the work herself. Bog's excitement dampened when he saw her, but he still bubbled with enthusiasm as he turned towards Emelyn.

"Forest-child and visitors sleep here tonight. Very cozy, sheltered from wind and very close to den." He lingered, fiddling with his hat as he looked at Emelyn with wide, hopeful eyes.

Emelyn hesitated. "Would . . . you . . . like to stay and help us set up camp?"

Bog grinned, nodding his head. "Yes."

They helped Cobbe unload the supplies, but the woman's mood remained dark. Emelyn wanted to ask what was bothering her, but felt it wasn't the time or place, so she remained silent. Once the supplies were unloaded, she and Bog started on the fire. Just as the sun was dipping behind the trees, the Magisters wandered into the camp. Emelyn didn't know what they had been doing all this time, nor, she realized, did she care. Their affairs were their own, and the less they involved her, the better. With the fire burning and Cobbe preparing dinner, Emelyn turned her attention to Ferrin. As she brushed the mule down, Emelyn saw from the corner of her eye a short figure. She turned, expecting to see Bog, but found someone else.

The Wylkin grinned as he held out a covered pot.

Emelyn smiled back and took the pot from his hands. She lifted the lid and was met with a waft of savory spices. She closed the lid, grinning even wider. "Thank you very much."

The man smiled and nodded before wandering off to where Bog was working and struck up a conversation.

Emelyn took the pot over to Cobbe. "It looks like someone made us dinner," she said, thinking Cobbe might appreciate not having to cook for once.

Cobbe cast a cursory glance at the pot and grunted. She waved to where Emelyn could put the food and continued her preparations.

Emelyn didn't try to understand Cobbe's behavior and set the pot down as instructed. When she turned around she was faced with another Wylkin, who also smiled, handing her another covered pot. Emelyn accepted the gift and thanked the man as he skipped off to join the others. Before she had a chance to set the pot down, another Wylkin arrived, this time bearing a pie. Behind him several more little-folk were on their way, all of them carrying pots, baskets, and other parcels. Cobbe remained uninterested, continuing with the dinner preparations as if nothing were out of the ordinary.

The Wylkin continued to file into the camp, handing Emelyn bowls and pots of food as quickly as she could take them. Some didn't bother to wait and placed their contribution with the rest of the food before wandering off to find someone they knew. Before long, the camp was bustling with people from the village—Emelyn suspected that the entire den must be there. Somewhere, someone started playing music, and many of the Wylkin danced to the lively tune. Emelyn smiled, realizing that she stood in the midst of a party.

Cobbe finished preparing dinner. Instead of serving the food in bowls like she usually did, she simply placed the entire pot along with all the other dishes the village folk had brought. Some of the Wylkin were already helping themselves to the wide array of food, pulling spoons out of their pockets and eating directly from the pots and pans. Cobbe walked up to Emelyn and handed her a spoon of her own. Emelyn thanked her, but the woman merely gave a curt nod before wandering off again.

Emelyn joined the crowd loitering around the food and dipped her spoon into a pot. It was a casserole of grains laced with dried fruits and meat. A seemingly simple dish, yet when Emelyn tasted it, she was astounded by the complexity of flavor. It was both sweet and salty, with an undertone of richness that she partially attributed to the meat; though there was something else she couldn't put her finger on. Maybe she was simply tired of the multitude of stews that had become their regular fare, but at that moment it was quite conceivably the best food Emelyn had ever tasted.

She dipped her spoon in for more and was met with several nods of agreement as others did the same. The amount and variety of food was astounding—soups and stews, pies and cakes, platters of roasted meat, and baskets of bread. All so delicious that it would have brought tears to Miss Cook's eyes. Emelyn lost all sense of propriety. She forgot about eating only as much as she needed to not go hungry, forgot about not wanting to appear greedy or gluttonous. She ate until she felt like her sides would burst. No one seemed to mind. The beaming faces all around her indicated that they appreciated her appetite, and more than one little Wylkin stumbled away from the party stuffed so full that they could barely walk.

Emelyn also waddled away from the food as she looked around for a place to sit or, better yet, lie down. Her search ended when a Wylkin stepped in front of her.

"Hello," Emelyn said to the Den Mother, trying to sound pleasant but not entirely succeeding.

"Forest-child will speak now. Come." The Den Mother turned and walked into the woods.

Emelyn watched her go and felt a strong desire to hide among the partying crowd. The idea was ridiculous, of course. Not only was she twice as tall as everyone there, but she also suspected the Den Mother would have no qualms over having her dragged into the woods, if needed. Emelyn didn't know what more the Den Mother wanted to discuss, but she knew she couldn't avoid it.

When they had walked a fair distance and the party was little more than a flickering of firelight and faint music, the Den Mother stopped and faced Emelyn.

"Where is Forest-child's kin?"

Emelyn stiffened. "I don't have any," she said, her voice cold.

The Den Mother frowned. "All have kin."

"I never knew mine."

The frown deepened—clearly it wasn't the answer she had expected. "Why is this?"

Emelyn scowled at the woman; she hadn't expected such personal questions. "I was abandoned as a baby, left on the doorstep of a household in Fallow. They kept me and allowed me to be raised by their housekeeper."

The Den Mother's frown melted as she placed a hand against a tree as though to steady herself. She was silent, her eyes far away in thought.

Emelyn eyed the woman. No one had ever reacted in such a manner over her story. While she was grateful to not have to endure the usual pitying glances or empty platitudes, she couldn't help but wonder why the Den Mother seemed to care so much.

After a lengthy silence, the Den Mother's gaze sharpened. "This explains much," she said at last.

When Emelyn said nothing, the Den Mother continued. "Forest-child is just that: a child. A child needs kin to teach it right from wrong and to teach it of the many dangers. Without kin, a child will never grow. It will only stumble through life, blindly facing the dangers it doesn't understand. A child that does not understand danger puts not only itself in harm's reach, but also those around it. Forest-child has done this."

Emelyn blinked. "What?"

"Red-robes that travel with Forest-child very dangerous. Dangerous to kin, but more dangerous to Forest-child. Den Mother very surprised and very confused to see Forest-child in such company."

Emelyn gaped at her. "How could you know that? You don't know them or me."

The Den Mother waved her hand. "All red-robes the same, all dangerous. Forest-kin know this best. Forest-child would also know this if Forest-child knew own kin."

Emelyn was reminded of a similar conversation with Corran, back when their journey had first started. "Why are they dangerous?"

"Red-robes take what they want, hurt others to get it. Those that are special, much like Forest-child is special, red-robes hurt the most."

"How do you know I'm special?"

"Forest-child has the eyes of And'estar. Very rare, even among forest-kin. But Forest-child has not yet woken."

"And'estar?"

"Wise ones among forest-kin. Important ones. Much like Den Mother. But Forest-child still sleeps, eyes still cloudy. When Forest-child wakes, then eyes will reflect the sky and Forest-child will be able to defend herself against red-robes."

Emelyn closed her eyes, shaking her head. "How do you know all this?"

"Den Mother wilding once, traveled much, seen much. Met many forest-kin and learned some of their ways."

Emelyn wondered if the Den Mother was talking of the same people as she suspected. "Do you mean the forest people?"

The Den Mother hesitated a moment then nodded her head.

Emelyn stared at the woman, her heart pounding in her chest. "Are you saying I'm one of them?"

The Den Mother frowned, looking perplexed. "Yes," she said, as if it was something Emelyn should have known all along.

Emelyn wasn't sure if she should laugh or cry. She felt like doing both. "Do you know where they are?" she said, almost afraid of the Den Mother's answer.

The Den Mother shook her head. "Forest-kin travel much, very difficult to find. Safer from dangers this way, especially red-robes."

"What did the Magisters do? Why are they so dangerous?"

The Den Mother continued to shake her head. "Some things are not for Den Mother to explain. Forest-child will need to learn some things on her own."

"But—"

"Forest-child has brought danger to the den," the Den Mother continued, "and Forest-child will need to take the danger away. Red-robes may not stay more than one night. Tomorrow, Forest-child will leave and take red-robes with her."

Emelyn watched as the Den Mother turned and left,

leaving her alone in the cold, darkened wood. Music from the party drifted through the trees, but she no longer found joy in the melody.

CHAPTER 17

EMELYN RETURNED TO the camp and to the throng of singing and dancing Wylkin. She navigated the crowd, avoiding the erratic movements of twirling dancers as she looked for Cobbe. Someone grabbed her hand and Emelyn looked down at the dirty face beaming up at her. She tried to pull away, but the grasp was firm and Emelyn found herself twirling amidst a sea of Wylkin. She relented to the revelry until she escaped the grasp and resumed her search through the crowd.

Emelyn eventually found Cobbe sitting alone on the edge of camp. She was perched on a rock next to her pig, sharpening her knife with a stone. The woman ignored the party around her and, as such, didn't seem to notice Emelyn's approach.

"Cobbe!"

Cobbe turned, brandishing her knife until she saw Emelyn. Scowling, she turned back around and resumed her sharpening.

"Cobbe," Emelyn said as she kneeled next to her. "I need to talk to you."

"Silver-eyes knows how to talk," Cobbe said, her eyes on her knife. "Needs no permission from Cobbe."

"Why are the Magisters so dangerous?" Emelyn whispered, fearful of being overheard despite the noise around them. "Do you know?"

Cobbe glanced at her. "All can be dangerous. Silver-eyes, bristle-snout, Cobbe." She pointed the knife as she named each one.

"Yes. But the Magisters in particular. Have they . . . done something?"

Cobbe stopped sharpening her knife to look at Emelyn. "Red-robes think they are more clever than they are. Other than that, Cobbe doesn't know." She looked at Emelyn askance. "Why is Silver-eyes troubled about red-robes?"

"I was speaking with the Den Mother. She knows something about the Magisters, telling me they're dangerous, but she wouldn't tell me why or what they had done."

Cobbe paused. "Cobbe knows nothing about such dangers of red-robes, but if Den Mother says they are dangerous, then Cobbe would listen."

Emelyn's heart sank. "What should I do?"

Cobbe scowled. "Why must Silver-eyes do something? If red-robes dangerous, they have always been dangerous. Silver-eyes has done well so far, will continue to do well." She resumed sharpening her knife.

"I'm thinking maybe I should leave." Emelyn could hear how ridiculous she sounded.

Cobbe scoffed. "Silver-eyes knows better than to wander in cold wilds alone."

Emelyn did know better, but things had changed. "Cobbe," she said, placing a hand on the woman's arm. "The Den Mother . . . she said I'm one of the forest people . . ." Emelyn trailed off for fear of weeping.

Cobbe frowned and pursed her lips as she looked at the hand on her arm. "Cobbe wouldn't know anything about that."

"Do you know what that means?" Emelyn said, ignoring Cobbe's glances. "I might have family. People who knew my mother and father . . . Grandparents . . ." Emelyn removed her hand from Cobbe's arm and wiped her eyes.

Cobbe's gaze softened but she said nothing.

Silence hung between them until Emelyn, her voice heavy, continued. "I was thinking I would like to try and find them. But I wouldn't know where to look." She looked at Cobbe.

Cobbe's scowl returned as she tried to resume sharpening her knife, but Emelyn grabbed the stone from her hands.

"Please, Cobbe. I can't do it alone. You know your way among the wilds, you can survive out there. Please . . ."

Cobbe sheathed her knife and rubbed her eyes. "Silver-eyes makes foolish request. Asking Cobbe to run off into wilds." She fixed her gaze upon Emelyn. "It is better to stay with red-robes. Wilds dangerous, especially in wintertime. Cobbe very clever, can manage, but it is very hard. Very risky. Cobbe doesn't see need for such risk. Safer with red-robes. Silver-eyes should know this." She grabbed the whetstone from Emelyn's hand and continued sharpening her knife.

Emelyn remained kneeling, examining the possibilities, both good and bad. She hadn't really expected Cobbe to agree to go away with her; she hadn't planned on asking. It had just occurred to her, at that moment, that she could go off on her own to try and find them . . . her kin. The thought of it was seductive, a tantalizing reminder of a childhood dream that she couldn't resist. With Cobbe's refusal, Emelyn was snapped back into stark reality.

She let her conversation with the Den Mother fade as if it were little more than a dream. It was likely the Magisters were dangerous, but then a lot of people were, just as Cobbe had said. In the time that Emelyn had known them, they had never given her any indication that they meant her harm. That had to count for something, didn't it? As Emelyn knelt next to Cobbe, it became easier to dismiss all the Den Mother had told her about the Magisters as well as the forest people. It was all too good to be true, knowing where she came from, that she might have a family.

Cobbe stopped sharpening and studied the knife and stone in her hands.

"Why are you so upset, Cobbe?" Emelyn said. "You've been in a foul mood ever since we arrived here. Why?"

Cobbe grimaced. "Silver-eyes not understand."

"Then help me understand."

Cobbe shook her head, saying nothing.

"Does it have anything to do with becoming a Den Mother?"

Cobbe glared at Emelyn.

"Well?"

The glare withered and Cobbe deflated. "Someday Cobbe must be Den Mother," she mumbled.

"That's great . . . isn't it?"

Cobbe's renewed glare told Emelyn it wasn't.

"Why is it so bad?"

"Cobbe wilding, always been wilding. Cobbe happy traveling, exploring. Does not want to return to den and be mother to all. Bossing others not for Cobbe."

Emelyn hid a smile behind her hand—for someone who hated bossing others around, Cobbe was extraordinarily good at it. "It's still a long time away, isn't it?"

Cobbe grunted as she resumed sharpening her knife.

Emelyn stood and wandered over to a fire in a calmer area of the camp. There were a few Wylkin there, chatting and sipping steaming beverages from tall mugs. As Emelyn sat down, a Wylkin swaddled in a thick, brown cloak passed her a mug of her own. Emelyn breathed in the sharp aroma of wine and spices before taking a sip.

The party carried on through the night. The music and carousing grew quieter, just as the group of Wylkin huddled around the fire grew larger. Some of the little-folk eventually rose and tottered to their homes; others remained curled by the fire as they drifted off to sleep. Emelyn felt a pang of envy, wishing for sleep to come to her as well. But it never did, and after many cups of watered wine, she watched as the day broke behind the trees.

Emelyn rose and walked around the camp. The numerous fires that had burned through the night were now nothing more than piles of glowing embers. Groups of Wylkin huddled around the coals, snuggled together for warmth. No one stirred except for Emelyn. She picked up a nearby stick and poked at a fire, prompting the coals to glow brighter and warmer. She kept walking and soon left the trampled grounds of the camp. A trail of footprints marred the fresh snow, and Emelyn followed it back to the Wylkin village.

She wound through a neighborhood of cottages, each one unique, yet still part of the whole. Each house had an adjacent garden, and on every step were stone pots, currently filled with snow, but Emelyn imagined them overflowing with flowers and vines. It saddened her to know she wouldn't be there when the spring came and would miss all the beauty the season would bring to such a wonderful place.

She stopped and leaned against a low wooden fence as she took in the surroundings. All was still; the only sound to be heard was that of her breathing. Emelyn turned her face to the rising sun and closed her eyes, listening to the silence. That was when she heard a distant lilting melody, like someone was singing.

She opened her eyes and the melody faded, but she knew she had heard it. She looked around, but there was no one in sight. Maybe someone in one of the houses was singing. It was possible, yet Emelyn knew in her heart that it wasn't the case.

She felt a sudden desire to turn around and hasten back to camp and hide herself among a group of people so that whatever was out in the woods would not be able to find her. The Magisters would keep her safe. The thought rankled her, for she knew it to be true. But as much as she had tried, she had not completely forgotten the Den Mother's words, and Emelyn wondered if she depended too much upon the Magi.

The eyes of And'estar. Wise one. Important. Something Emelyn was supposed to be, though she couldn't begin to fathom how. She wanted to, though. She wanted it to be true. Wanted to be important.

Emelyn took a deep breath, both to calm her nerves as well as steel them. She closed her eyes again, trying to think of nothing save for the color of the rising sun and the shadows of the trees. For a time all she heard was her own heart beating, and the blood rushing through her ears. As she listened to the sounds of her body, Emelyn once again heard the melody.

This time she did not open her eyes but instead tried to envision in her mind the person who was singing. She imagined she was the falcon flying through the trees, searching for the owner of the voice. When she saw the little figure kneeling in the snow, her eyes snapped open and her heart was sent racing. The melody faded, but it didn't matter—Emelyn knew where she needed to go. That is, if what she saw was true. Part of her was afraid to find out, but she needed to know. Emelyn turned towards the trees she had flown past in her mind and began to walk.

She paid little attention to where she was going and stumbled over hidden roots and rocks. She barely noticed, her eyes remaining fixed on the snow ahead. She heard the melody before she saw anyone—a lively tune that was more suited to a summer's field than a winter-laden forest. Someone was humming, not singing, she could hear that now. Then she saw it—the same little figure upon the snow, just as she had seen in her mind.

It was a girl, kneeling as she scrubbed a pot with snow. Her long, dark hair fell to the ground around her, the snow clinging to her bare feet.

"Iyen?"

The girl looked up, startled at first, then smiled when she saw Emelyn. "Hello."

Emelyn edged towards the girl. "What are you doing here?"

Iyen giggled. "Washing this pot."

Emelyn watched as Iyen rubbed snow inside the pot, her mind reeling with all the questions she wanted to ask. Was she real? Was she magic? But only one question came to her lips. "Where is Corran?"

The girl looked up again, her smile gone. She shrugged her shoulders, the way that children do when they don't want to talk.

"You know who he is, don't you?"

The smile returned. "He's my friend."

"He's my friend, too," Emelyn said. At least, she had thought he was, but maybe he wasn't real, either.

Iyen looked at Emelyn askance, the doubt apparent on her face.

"We were traveling together," Emelyn said, "but then he disappeared. I've been trying to find him."

"I don't know anything about that."

Emelyn thought the answer strange. "So you know where he is?"

Iyen stood, leaving the pot in the snow.

Emelyn tensed, afraid that the girl might leave. "Wait."

Iyen remained, frowning at Emelyn.

But Emelyn didn't know what to say. All the questions she had for the girl would sound ridiculous and would likely be met with equal coldness. She realized that the questions didn't matter; she just didn't want Iyen to leave.

Emelyn crouched in the snow and scrubbed the pot that Iyen had dropped. From the corner of her eye she could see that Iyen remained.

"What was that song you were humming?" Emelyn asked.

Iyen crouched down and watched as Emelyn scrubbed the pot but said nothing. She was silent for so long that Emelyn began to wonder if she had heard the question.

"It's a song I like," Iyen finally said. "Corran plays it for me sometimes, to cheer me up."

Emelyn stopped scrubbing and looked at her. "He plays for you?"

Dimples broke across Iyen's cheeks as she smiled. "The flute. He only plays it for me, though."

"Has he played for you recently?"

Her smile faded as Iyen fixed her opalescent eyes on Emelyn. "No."

Emelyn's heart sank at the answer, but she remained convinced that Iyen knew where Corran was. They watched each other until Iyen's gaze flicked past Emelyn. Emelyn turned.

Red robes flashed through the trees, and Emelyn rose to her feet. Magisters. Even though the glimpses were fleeting, Emelyn could tell that there were more Magi present than Percival and Aldren. She started to follow but stopped when Iyen grabbed her hand.

"Don't go," Iyen said, her eyes wide with fear.

"Why not?"

Iyen said nothing. She stared at the trees as she clung to Emelyn's hand.

"I'll be back soon," Emelyn said as she pried the girl's hand away. As she walked, the crunching of snow coming from behind told her that Iyen followed.

Emelyn craned her neck, trying to see past the trees. But the Magisters kept a rapid pace and Emelyn only saw swathes of red against the pale snow. She glanced back at Iyen. The girl was keeping up, though her face was ashen and her eyes had grown wild.

"It will be all right," Emelyn said.

Iyen said nothing, giving no indication that she had heard Emelyn at all.

Emelyn stretched out her hand and Iyen clasped it, but her eyes remained fixed on the trees ahead. They walked together, hand in hand, until they heard voices.

Iyen stopped, pulling Emelyn back.

"It's all right," Emelyn said. "There's nothing to be afraid of."

Iyen frowned as she wriggled her hand free.

Emelyn didn't know what to do. She wanted to see what was happening, but she didn't want to leave Iyen alone, especially since she looked so frightened.

A shout, angry and threatening, echoed off the trees. Emelyn turned, but Iyen grabbed her arm.

"No . . ." the girl whimpered.

Emelyn freed her arm and ran towards the commotion. Four Magisters faced a young man and woman. One of the Magi had a bald head, with spectacles perched upon his nose. He looked much like Aldren, but different. Younger. Another Magi with a long, dark braid streaked with wisps of white stepped forward.

"We mean you no harm," he said.

"Then leave us alone," the woman said, her voice trembling. She clutched a bundle of blankets close to her breast.

Emelyn's breath caught. Iyen and Corran. The same young couple she had seen in the woods, only Iyen was no longer pregnant.

The braided man spread his hands open. "I cannot do that. It is for your own good, as well as the good of all."

"Liar!" Corran said. He stepped towards the Magisters but stopped when Iyen touched his arm.

Emelyn heard a soft sniffling and turned to see little Iyen peeking from behind a tree, her eyes red and swollen with tears.

"Please," the little girl said.

"Please," Iyen said to Corran as she handed him the bundle.

"No . . ." Corran said as he took the babe.

Iyen's trembling hands lingered on the blankets as she looked into Corran's eyes. Her voice was soft, yet Emelyn still heard her speak. "Run."

"No!"

"Run!" she screamed as she pushed Corran away.

He stumbled backwards, his face twisted in anguish. He turned and ran.

"Take her," the braided man said, and the other Magi advanced.

Iyen, turning towards the Magisters, knelt and put her hands to the ground.

The Magi stopped to scribble runes in the dirt and in the air before them. The air hummed and Emelyn's skin tingled. Then the air cracked, and a bright white light flashed that momentarily blinded her. Then another crack, another flash, another moment of darkness. Someone shouted a rune and the flashing stopped, and Emelyn could once again see. The trees then shivered, bowing and waving as if caught in a storm, though the air was still. One tree bent so sharply that, with a bone-resounding crack, it splintered and crashed to the ground below. The Magi scrambled out of the way, except for one.

Emelyn looked away as the Magister was crushed under the falling branches. Little Iyen wept, her sobs wild and hysterical. Emelyn turned back just as the trees before her burst into flames. She backed away from the heat, but remained close enough to see. She didn't know if it was Iyen or the Magi causing the flames, but the braided man now used the fire to his advantage. Speaking runes and waving his hands, the Magister pulled globes of fire from the burning trees and launched them at the kneeling woman. The flames dissipated when they reached Iyen, dispersing into a spray of sparks that fell around her. But the braided man was relentless, and as he continued his assault the other Magisters approached.

Iyen's gaze darted between the three Magisters, lending her the appearance of a wild animal. Like an animal, she bared her teeth. A sharp wind blew past her, whipping her hair and knocking two of the Magi over. She looked back to the braided man just as he flung a ball of flame.

The bald man, the one that looked like Aldren, ran towards her. The ball of flame dissipated overhead and Iyen's gaze flashed back to him. But the Magi was ready. Raising his staff, he shouted runes and the patterns etched in his staff glowed golden. He struck his staff upon the ground, and a tremor knocked Iyen off balance. As she fell, the remaining Magister rushed forward and grabbed her arms before she had a chance to touch the ground.

The Magisters bound the struggling woman. Iyen screamed—a harrowing, heart-wrenching shriek that filled Emelyn with dread and sorrow. One Magister, losing his resolve, glanced at the others as he covered his ears. The bald man, looking on the verge of tears, raised his staff and struck her over the head. The screaming stopped.

Emelyn lingered among the charred ruins of the trees. She felt drained, and could only watch with an empty heart as the men in red robes dragged the woman away. Emelyn wiped her eyes, realizing she had been crying.

A glimpse of red crept into the corner of her vision. She turned to find Aldren and Percival standing nearby, watching her. Emelyn knew then what she had seen, and the cold glint in Percival's eyes told her that he knew she understood. The braided man had been Percival. The bald man, both familiar and unfamiliar, had been Aldren—both from many years ago. That was why Magisters couldn't be trusted; that was what they had done.

"Run," Iyen whispered.

Percival edged towards her, extending a hand. "I am sure you are very confused," he said, his voice calm and even. "You must have many questions. Come, let us discuss what has happened here so that you might understand."

Emelyn tensed, remembering the outstretched hands of the braided man before they had taken Iyen, before they had bound her and dragged her away.

"Run," Iyen whispered again, more urgently this time.

"Why did you take her?" Emelyn said, her voice tremulous.

Percival smiled; the same tolerant, condescending smile that now only angered her. "That question cannot be answered here, amongst the trees. Come along, and we will discuss it, as I have said."

Both Percival and Aldren walked towards her, and Emelyn remembered how the Magisters had advanced on Iyen before they had struck her unconscious, before they had taken her away to some unknown fate.

Someone touched Emelyn's hand. She looked down to Iyen's small face peering up at her.

"Run," Iyen said, her voice cracking as tears streamed down her cheeks.

Emelyn hesitated, glancing between the girl and the Magisters.

Iyen balled her hands into fists as she filled her lungs with air. "Run!" she screamed with a voice that was not her own. It was louder, deeper, the voice of a woman.

Emelyn started at the outburst and, casting one final glance at the Magisters, she ran.

CHAPTER 18

"Run!" Iyen screamed with an intensity that made Aldren's heart race and stomach sink. Emelyn, with a look of fear and mistrust, darted into the woods. Iyen also turned and ran.

Aldren's racing heart leapt into his throat as he watched Emelyn disappear among the trees. "We have to go after her," he said, starting to follow, but Percival grabbed his arm.

Percival's eyes were cold, stern. "We need our supplies."

"There is no time."

The grip on his arm tightened. "You are suggesting we set off into the woods after a girl—a girl quite capable with the Art who does not wish to be found—without any supplies. You are foolish if you think you will find her quickly. What will you do, then, when the hours pass and you are forced to return here? We have little time, indeed, and you are squandering it by arguing with me rather than doing as you are told." Percival released his arm but the venom in his eyes told Aldren that he would brook no nonsense.

"Yes, my lord," Aldren said before turning and heading back towards the village. He hurried through the snow, intent on reaching their camp as quickly as possible. Small brown faces peeked at him from behind the trees, though no one approached him. Good. He was in no mood for folly. Upon reaching the camp, he walked up to Cobbe.

"We are leaving. Pack the supplies, we cannot afford delay." Aldren began gathering up the supplies and loading them onto the mule.

Cobbe frowned at him as she stirred the stewpot. "Glass-eyes speaks much nonsense. Cobbe will not leave until warm food is in belly."

"Emelyn has run off," Aldren said as he continued packing. "We need to find her before she comes to harm."

Cobbe pressed her lips together. She looked at the stewpot a long while before letting out a heavy sigh. She picked up the pot and carried it over to a nearby Wylkin sleeping on the ground. She nudged him with her foot and handed the pot to him, then waved her hands as she shooed him away. The man blinked in confusion, staring at the stewpot in his hands. Then he smiled, nodded, and tottered away with it.

Cobbe turned and helped Aldren pack. Together, they swept up the supplies and tied them to the back of the mule. Once they had finished, Aldren picked up the reins. He tugged, but the mule did not move. He glanced at Cobbe, but she only shrugged and waved her hands, encouraging him to continue. Aldren tugged again. The mule's ears twitched, but still the animal did not budge.

Blasted creature. Aldren removed his glasses and rubbed his eyes. Emelyn had always handled the mule; he had forgotten how ornery the beast had been back when they purchased it. He tugged on the reins again, but the mule stood fast. He looked to Cobbe for help, but she had wandered off to tend to her pig. Aldren looked around and saw a multitude of Wylkin peering at him from behind the trees, but no one stepped forward to offer assistance.

Aldren's patience was wearing thin. He was the High Magister, second to the Grand Magister himself; he would not be thwarted by a dumb animal. Aldren picked up a twig from a bundle of kindling lying by the fire. He snapped off a piece and, speaking a rune, flicked it at the mule's haunches. The bit of wood flared orange as it burst into flame and landed on the animal's flank. With flaring nostrils and wide, fearful eyes, the mule bolted.

Aldren rubbed his brow as the animal disappeared into the forest. With a heavy sigh, he started after it but stopped when a Wylkin stepped in front of him.

"Red-robes not welcome in den any longer," the Den Mother said.

Aldren cast her a cursory glance. "We are leaving at once, I assure you."

The Den Mother narrowed her eyes, but said nothing.

Aldren brushed past her and ran to where the mule had disappeared. It was gone, leaving behind a trail of tracks in the snow. He ground his teeth. Now both the mule and Emelyn had run off. He was tempted to run after the mule, just as he had wanted to run after Emelyn. But he knew it would be foolish—the mule could run much faster than he. Instead he went back to find the Grand Magister.

As he walked, Aldren noticed that the landscape had changed. Where the Wylkin village had once been was now only snow and trees. He looked around, but the little houses were nowhere in sight. Not welcome anymore, indeed. Whatever ability the Wylkin had to make themselves hidden was now, it seemed, being put to use. It was unsettling, and Aldren's sense of direction suffered. He searched the ground for his tracks, hoping to follow them back to Percival, but the snow was smooth and undisturbed. He scanned the trees, searching among them for familiarity, but there was nothing. He stood still, unsure of what to do.

A snuffling approached and Cobbe appeared, riding her pig.

"Glass-eyes wastes time," she said, waggling a finger. "Tells Cobbe that we are soon leaving, then runs off, playing in the snow like a child."

The relief Aldren had felt upon seeing Cobbe was replaced by a twinge of annoyance. "I was not playing. I was trying to find our supplies. The blasted mule ran off and I . . . lost my way."

Cobbe's frown turned into a grin, and Aldren thought she looked much too satisfied with his misfortune than was proper.

"Come," Cobbe said, steering her pig past Aldren. "We will find other red-robe."

When they found Percival, Aldren explained what happened, preparing himself for the Grand Magister's scorn. But Percival simply listened and, after Aldren had finished, remained silent as he looked around.

"We must continue north," he said at length.

Aldren hesitated. "What of the supplies?"

"And how would you propose we track the beast? Whatever these . . . people . . . have done to hide their village seems to have also wiped away all tracks. We will do what we can to find the mule, but it is paramount we reach the Tower without delay. All else is secondary."

All else, including Emelyn. "She will not survive in these woods. Not alone." Aldren kept his voice gruff, hoping to hide the tremor he knew was there.

Percival's eyes softened. "It is regrettable, but she made the decision to leave. She will have to bear the consequences."

Aldren clenched his jaw, keeping the words he wished to say unspoken. Yes, my lord. Those were the words he should speak, the ones he told himself to speak. But they would not come. Nor, he feared, would they come again.

CHAPTER 19

SNOW-LADEN BRANCHES slapped Emelyn's face and arms while her legs and lungs burned. She didn't care. She strained to hear any sound, but all she heard was her own ragged breathing and the snow crunching beneath her feet. She ran. For how long, she no longer knew. Fear spurred her forward, sustaining her with strength and energy. But even fear had its limits, and Emelyn soon found herself doubled over as she caught her breath. Her stomach constricted and she heaved what was left of last night's meal onto the snow. She spit the acid from her mouth before picking up a handful of snow and sucking on it until the nausea subsided.

Once she had recovered, Emelyn looked around. The woods were quiet, the snow undisturbed save for her footprints. No sign of red robes, no indication that the Magisters had followed. Emelyn held her breath, straining to hear, but there was only the wind in the trees and the blood in her ears.

Why hadn't they come? Emelyn thought she should feel relieved. She had sought to escape the Magi and it would seem that she had. Why, then, was she left with a knot in her stomach? Had they let her go? Had they wanted her to run? She didn't know why the Magisters would want her to run, but her escape had been too easy, and she wondered if they had been unable to catch her or if they simply did not care. Emelyn didn't know which answer she preferred.

Yet it wasn't only the Magi Emelyn was searching for. The little girl that had prompted her to run was nowhere to be seen. Emelyn scanned the trees for a glimpse of dark hair, of a brown leather dress with colorful beads.

"Iyen?" she called, but all was quiet.

The fact that Iyen had not followed her distressed Emelyn far more than the mysterious motivations of the Magisters. If not for Iyen, Emelyn would not have run. Now, because of her, she found herself alone in a wintery wood. She had no idea in which direction she ought to travel, nor any idea of how to survive. She had no knife; she didn't even have her staff. All Emelyn had were the clothes on her back and a faint inkling of plants that might be edible.

Stupid girl. After all that had happened, after all the strange and dangerous creatures she had seen, she was still foolish enough to go running off, unarmed, at the behest of a child she did not know and, from what Aldren had told her, was nothing more than an apparition. Perhaps it was a trap—an illusion of an innocent girl that led the unwary astray to their doom. It wouldn't have been the strangest thing Emelyn had seen in her travels, and she had fallen for it without hesitation.

Emelyn leaned against a tree. She felt like crying, like screaming and pulling her hair. Instead she stood there, listening to the wind whisper in the trees. What should she do now? She stared at her tracks in the snow that led like a road back to Bog's little village, back to the Magisters and to Cobbe. The tracks wouldn't remain for long; either the wind or newly fallen snow would cover them and, once they were gone, she would not be able to find her way back again.

She should go back. She knew nothing of surviving in the woods. But Emelyn remained leaning against the tree. As fearful as she was of being alone in the woods, as uncertain she was she could survive, Emelyn realized she didn't want to go back. The memory of seeing the Magisters capturing Iyen, binding her like she was a wild animal, haunted her. She realized, with a startling vehemence, that she would rather die alone in the woods than become a plaything for the Magisters. She had been a servant once; she would not become one again. Not unless she chose it, and she suspected that a choice was not something the Magi were willing to offer.

The wind stirred, whipping Emelyn's hair around her face, and she felt a calmness descend. Whatever uncertainty her future held, it was hers to discover, without aid or interference from Percival, Aldren, Cobbe, or Miss Cook. For the first time in her life, Emelyn felt free, and she knew then that she would never go back. Turning away from the snowy tracks, she began to walk.

As a little girl, Emelyn had often dreamt about running off into the woods and making a home for herself among the ferns and tall trees. In her dreams, she had always lived alone, thriving in the wilderness as if she had lived there all her life. There was no fear in her dreams, no question of when her next meal might be. The trees had always been her friends and companions, protecting her and sheltering her from the outside world. Emelyn tried to dig up the comforting feelings she had always felt in such dreams, but they were nowhere to be found. She was hungry and cold; afraid of what might be hiding in the woods, afraid of starving to death. Most of all, though, she felt lonely.

As she walked, Emelyn realized that never before had she truly been alone. She had grown up in a household of servants with ever-present, if distant, masters. There was Fallow, with Mr. Hibberly and all the other shopkeepers she frequently had contact with. She had thought before that she had known loneliness, yet there had always been someone there. Even after leaving Fallow, she still had the Magisters and Corran, even Beryl, the innkeeper that had been so kind to her. Although she had felt alone in the world, there had always been someone nearby, looking after her. Here, in the woods, there was only snow and trees. For the first time in her life, Emelyn was truly alone, and she didn't find it as appealing as she had in her dreams. Now, instead of feeling free, she only felt small and lost in a very big world.

She stopped and looked around. Wisps of snow fluttered lazily on the wind as though deciding whether or not to fall to the earth. She peered at the sky, but the sun was hidden behind clouds, and Emelyn no longer knew the direction in which she traveled. It didn't matter. She had nowhere to go, what difference did it make now?

Emelyn pulled her coat around her, trying to keep out the wind. She had only taken a single step when a rustling noise from behind caused her to stop. Images of the Magisters advancing through the trees flashed through her mind, and Emelyn turned to face them. Instead she was faced with a pack-laden Ferrin crashing through the brush.

The mule trotted up to her and nuzzled his nose into her arm. Emelyn patted him on the head, smiling as she felt his coarse, bristly coat.

"Where did you come from?" she said, watching the trees for signs of the Magisters. They wouldn't have let the mule run off on his own, not with all of the supplies fastened to his back. But there was no other movement behind the trees, no red robes or the tapping of staves. Emelyn frowned. Something must be wrong. Worry crept into her mind as she wondered what had happened to Cobbe, her friend. She picked up Ferrin's reins, staring at the creases in the leather. Aldren and Cobbe were both clever foragers, she was sure they would be fine. Her self-assurances did little to ease her worry, but they would have to do—she couldn't turn back.

Emelyn walked for as long as the light lasted. Once it had faded, she stopped to make camp, tethering Ferrin to a tree before tackling the supplies. The sacks piled upon the mule's back were heavy, and Emelyn struggled with unloading them until her arms shook and sweat dripped from her brow. Once she had finished, the sweat froze on her skin, causing her to shiver. She needed a fire.

She dug in the snow, gathering fallen pieces of wood before assembling them into a pile. The wood was wet and would not easily catch flame, and she wondered how she ought to proceed. Starting fires in the kitchen at home had always been simple, but the wood had been dry and a tinderbox ready to hand. Here there was neither. Aldren had always tended the campfires during their journey, and Emelyn knew he used the Art in some fashion. Cobbe had, on occasion, built some of the fires, though Emelyn never knew how she had managed it. After seeing some of Cobbe's kin and the way in which they kept their village hidden, Emelyn wondered if the woman also had some ability with the Art.

She stared at the wood, knowing that she, too, would need to use the Art should she wish to ignite it, but she didn't know how. She tried the exercise that Aldren had taught her to set the tip of a stick aflame, but that ended as it always had: with a blinding headache. Rubbing the pain from her eyes, she tried to wish the wood alight, like the wishes she made upon a falling star as a girl. But nothing happened.

Emelyn ground her teeth, as much from frustration as to keep them from rattling with the cold. The sky had grown dark, and there was no moonlight to light her way. All she could see were vague silhouettes of the surrounding trees. Emelyn looked at the pile of wood as her heart sank. Why did her ability never come when she needed it?

The snow cascaded through the sky, blanketing the wood even as Emelyn struggled to light it. She reached out to brush it off but snapped her hand back when the wood moved. Shadows. It was dark; her eyes were playing tricks on her. Yet as soon as she finished the thought, the wood shivered again, knocking a clump of snow to the ground.

Emelyn leapt to her feet, her heart racing. It was probably a squirrel, or a mole, crawling up out of the ground. She didn't know how a mole might burrow out of the frozen ground, but it was the best explanation she could find and she didn't want to entertain other, more uncertain, possibilities.

Then out from the twigs and branches popped a tiny head. Not a rodent's head, but that of a person, only much, much smaller. Emelyn stood frozen, watching as the little person grabbed hold of a piece of wood and pulled its body out of the pile. Once free, it turned to Emelyn and grinned.

Emelyn flinched as the creature looked at her, but relaxed when she realized it wasn't hostile. Wary, she leaned in for a closer look. The creature's body was smooth and pale, showing no signs of gender, and exuded a gentle light. The creature hopped down to the ground and, with a single swift kick, knocked the remaining snow from the wood. It waved one of its hands in an elaborate flourish and the wood flared alight with wild, silvery flames. The creature turned back to Emelyn and threw her another wide grin before darting away into the darkness.

Stunned, Emelyn sat down, watching where the creature had disappeared. The flames crackled and warmed Emelyn's face and frozen body. She could have cried, then, out of happiness and relief, but she was too tired and too hungry to spare the tears. Whispering thanks to the mysterious little creature, Emelyn rummaged through the supplies. She made a simple stew of onions and dried meat. It wasn't as tasty as Cobbe's stew, but she was too hungry to care. With her belly full and her skin tingling with warmth, Emelyn made a bed out of supply sacks and promptly fell asleep.

The fire was still burning when the dawn broke through the trees. Silvery flames danced and flitted as strong and bright as the night before. It was a pleasant experience to wake warm rather than cold and shivering. Emelyn prepared a breakfast of mashed roots. It tasted dreadful; she didn't know how Cobbe managed to make the things palatable. But she choked it down, knowing that, sooner or later, she would have to eat them when the tastier provisions had run out.

Once breakfast was over, Emelyn began loading the supplies onto Ferrin's back. As difficult and tiresome unloading the supplies had been, loading the sacks onto the mule's back was far worse. Emelyn huffed, hoisting them with sore, shaking arms. She struggled to place the sacks properly, and on more than one occasion a heavy bag would fall back to the ground with a hollow thud. Emelyn's heart sank each time a sack fell, and she wondered how she would find the strength to lift it again. But find the strength she did, and, after what felt like hours of struggling, she managed to load all the supplies and tie them down.

She had forgotten about the cold as she worked, but now the air chilled the sweat that ran down her body. Emelyn returned to the fire and remained there until her shivering subsided and she felt warm again. She gazed at the pallid flames, regretting the need to leave. With a heavy heart, Emelyn kicked snow onto the fire. As the flames flickered and died, she wondered if she would ever see its like again.

Leading Ferrin, Emelyn plodded through the snow. She was tired, and, with no destination in mind, had no need for haste. She examined the trees as she walked, taking care to observe discerning traits and landmarks, anything she might recognize should she pass that way again.

She also examined bushes that looked like those Cobbe had always been drawn to. Emelyn thought about rummaging through the supplies for an axe or something she could use to dig up the roots to see if they were the same that Cobbe had harvested. But she couldn't bring herself to untie the heavy packs, dreading the moment when she would need to unload Ferrin again.

As the sun dipped below the treetops, Emelyn's mood sank with it. She didn't want to stop to set up camp. The sky was clear; there would be a moon that night. She could keep walking. For how long, though? She knew she wouldn't be able to walk through the entire night; she needed food and rest. Maybe she could just walk a little further, until she found a nice place to stop. Someplace sheltered from the wind. She tried not to think about how she was going to light a fire.

A fluttering passed overhead, and then a bird alighted on a nearby branch. Emelyn smiled, recognizing the falcon from Roelith.

"Where have you been?" she said as she walked towards the falcon.

The bird preened its feathers before stopping to turn a single black eye upon Emelyn. After a few moments, the bird took flight, briefly, landing again in a nearby tree.

Emelyn watched the bird, waiting for it to take to the sky and disappear, but it never did. She wandered to the tree, finding the falcon perched on a low branch. Just as she arrived, however, the falcon again took flight, landing, once again, in a nearby tree.

Emelyn frowned, feeling as though the falcon was toying with her. Then she felt silly. It was just a bird; they didn't toy with people. Yet even as the thought entered her mind, so did the memory of the tiny person that had lit her fire the previous night. Deciding that there were stranger things in the world than a mischievous falcon, Emelyn followed the bird, grateful for a reason to keep moving.

The falcon flitted from tree to tree, and Emelyn, now committed to the endeavor, followed. The chase continued even after the sun had set, and Emelyn strained to see the bird in the moonlight. Her limbs were heavy and sore, and the pain in her stomach reminded her just how long it had been since she had last eaten. But the longer Emelyn followed the bird, the more convinced she became that the falcon was leading her somewhere. She didn't know how such a thing could be possible; all she knew was this was not a manner in which wild birds behaved.

She stumbled through the night, eventually coming upon a darkened cabin. She stopped and hid behind a tree while peeking at the house. Faint firelight flickered in a window, beyond that all was dark and still. Emelyn looked to the trees, trying to find the falcon but instead saw a long, shadowed spire stretching into the sky. Her stomach sank. A Magister Tower.

She wanted to run, to take herself as far away as possible. But she remained still, staring at the flickering light in the cabin window. Emelyn didn't know how she'd get another fire going on her own. The arrival of that little creature had been luck; it likely wouldn't happen again. What would she do, then, out in the cold? It would be warm in the cabin, but she was hesitant to go and knock on the door, not knowing who lived there.

Footsteps shuffled from within the cabin. A minute later, the door opened. Emelyn tensed as a man stepped into the moonlight

"Hello?" he called.

She crouched down, not wanting to be seen.

The man stood still, his head cocked to the side. Emelyn held her breath, hoping she would not be heard. The night was bright; he had only to look out to see her. But the man remained still, his head to one side as if listening to sounds that only he could hear.

As though confirming her thoughts, he spoke. "I can hear you out there. Your breathing, your footsteps. Make your intentions known, or else be on your way."

Emelyn froze, unsure of what to do. Her mind told her to run, to get as far away as possible from the Magister Tower. But something in her heart kept her still.

The man sighed. "I'll not stand out here in the cold waiting for your answer. Come inside to get warm if you like, but know I'll not tolerate any mischief. I might be blind, but I can still crack open your skull if I've a mind to." He turned and stepped inside the cabin.

Emelyn remained still. That the man was blind gave her no comfort; she was quite convinced he spoke truthfully of his ability to crack skulls. She had no assurance that no harm would come to her should she step into this stranger's house.

Stranger. Emelyn was certain she didn't know this man, but there was something familiar about him she couldn't place. Such an inexplicable feeling made her uneasy and kept her anchored in the snow as she wondered what to do.

The wind gusted, tearing at Emelyn's skin with icy fingers. She shivered with the cold just as her stomach constricted, reminding her of her hunger. She crept towards Ferrin and tied his reins to a tree. Why was she still being so quiet? He knew she was there. Yet Emelyn couldn't bring herself to walk normally.

She snuck towards the door and crept up the steps, cringing when they creaked under her weight.

"The door's unlocked," the man said. "Come in and be done with it."

Emelyn felt silly with all her caution, yet still she hesitated, her hand hovering over the door handle. *Stop being a ninny. Open the door or leave.* Taking a deep breath, Emelyn pushed the door open.

"I've never known anyone to take so long in deciding whether or not to come inside." The man sat in a chair near the hearth, whittling a piece of wood with a knife. A feeble fire stuttered around glowing coals, threatening to go out.

"Poke the fire if you want," he said. "There's wood by the hearth if you're cold. I'm afraid I don't get company, so I don't have a chair to offer you."

"That's all right."

The man stopped whittling at Emelyn's voice. "You're a girl." He sounded mystified, his voice losing much of its previous gruffness.

Emelyn fidgeted. "Yes," she said, feeling silly but not knowing what else to say.

"What's a young girl doing wandering such a place in the stark of night?"

"I . . . got lost," Emelyn said, feeling like she couldn't explain the real reason.

"You've not been traveling alone, I hope?" The man put his knife to the piece of wood, whittling it by feel alone.

Emelyn's gaze fixed upon the wood, the strange feeling of familiarity striking her once more. "No," she said. "We . . . were separated."

"I see."

Emelyn walked to the hearth and threw a piece of wood onto the glowing coals. Picking up the poker, she prodded the fire into life again before turning around to look at the man. He was in his middle years, his brown hair showing streaks of grey. Tied around his eyes was a strip of cloth, worn and in need of washing. His skin below the cloth was broken and mottled with old scars, and Emelyn wondered what had caused his blindness.

"I take it you've not seen a blind man before," he said, the bitterness heavy in his voice.

"I . . . I'm sorry. It's just . . . you seem familiar to me, somehow."

The man grunted in what might have been a laugh. "I imagine I've lived here in these woods longer than you've drawn breath. I know no young girls."

"My name is Emelyn."

The man whittled in silence for a while before answering. "Corran. That used to be my name. I've not much use for it anymore."

Emelyn's heart raced as she looked upon this man she did not know. "I . . . I knew a Corran, once," she said, unsure of the answer she was hoping to hear.

But the man said nothing, continuing to whittle in silence.

"I used to live in Fallow, before . . . I left."

The man stopped whittling and turned his blind gaze towards Emelyn. "Fallow?"

"Yes. Do you know the town?"

The man set down the wood and knife. "Yes, I lived there, once. Long ago . . ."

Emelyn opened her mouth to ask another question, but closed it, knowing there was no need. The Magisters had been right; everything they said was true. The Corran she knew had not been real, merely a memory of the man now sitting before her. Emelyn kneeled on the floor, fearful her legs would not support her.

"I . . . I had a wife . . . a daughter," Corran said. "I've not talked about them to anyone."

"Iyen," Emelyn whispered, mostly to herself.

Corran's head snapped up. "Yes . . . how could you know . . . ?"

"I . . . know of her."

He grew silent, his shoulders drooping under an unseen weight. "Then you know what I've done."

Emelyn licked her lips, nervous of saying the wrong thing.

"Is that why you've come here?" Corran's voice grew harsh, angry.

"No . . . I . . ."

Corran stiffened in his chair, his hands balled into fists. "You come from Fallow, you know of my wife. Why are you here? You couldn't have come all that way, found me here, by mistake. Tell me why you've come before I throw you back out into the cold."

Emelyn's lips trembled, saddened that this man was so angry with her. "Because I knew the memory of you," she said, hearing how ridiculous she sounded. "I've seen your wife as a little girl, as a young woman, as a mother protecting her child. You, as a young man, protected me from dangers I still don't understand. I don't know how I've come here, but I agree that it wasn't a mistake."

Corran fell silent and cradled his face in his hands. "Then you do know. You've seen it, just as I've heard it outside my windows for years."

"I don't know what I've seen. Not really."

"You've seen moments in her life, Iyen's life, both happy and sad. I've lived in this house for years, I've forgotten how many. But rarely a day goes by that I don't hear her laughter and mine, playing together as children, as we used to. Those are the good days where I can sit in my chair and remember."

"And the bad days?"

Corran hesitated. "The bad days are much more difficult. Especially that day . . ."

"The day they took her?"

Corran nodded. "I hear her screams. Even now in my

head I hear them. On those days I wish for death, but I know that death would be too kind for me."

"Why do you say that?"

"Because I failed her, my wife, my daughter, both of them. You saw what happened. She placed the baby in my arms, told me to run. And I did, I ran as fast as I could; even as her screams echoed through the trees, I ran. I felt such shame, then. Like a coward, fleeing to the shadows. But the shame I felt was nothing compared to the shame and despair I would later feel. I wish now that I had kept on running, as much as it pains me to say it. But at least then I would have only lost one of them, instead of both."

"You mean your daughter?"

"Yes. I ran to Fallow. I needed to find a safe place for her so I could go back after Iyen. I couldn't leave her with the Magisters. I had heard her screams . . . I couldn't leave her . . ." He fell silent, wringing his trembling hands.

After regaining his composure, Corran continued. "There was a house in Fallow, on the outskirts. It was large, well kept. Figured the people there were well off . . . that they had the means to look after a child for a short time . . ."

Emelyn stiffened, the story sounding all too familiar. "You left her there."

"It was only to be for a short time, until I had rescued Iyen. I . . . meant to return."

Emelyn slumped onto the floor, her body shaking.

"But I was a fool," Corran said. "An arrogant, stupid fool. My wife was capable of remarkable things, wondrous things. Yet they still managed to take her. I thought . . . I thought I could just knock some heads, save her. She would fight, too, and together we'd get out of there, fetch our daughter before fleeing someplace else." He shook his head. "Such a fool."

Emelyn remained silent, struggling to calm the sea of emotions storming within her.

"I don't know why they didn't kill me." Corran's voice was flat, emotionless. "Perhaps I was beneath them, not worth the trouble. I've spent years wondering why they didn't. I expect I'll never know."

Emelyn watched Corran as he sat slumped in his chair. Part of her wanted to hug him, part of her wanted to yell and scream at him. But most of all she wanted to understand. "What happened?" she whispered, amazed that she had managed to speak at all.

Corran scoffed, a bitter laugh that broke Emelyn's heart.

"I went to their Tower, the one near Fallow. I was yelling, screaming that they release her. When they wouldn't, I swung my staff at one of them. My eyes . . . they burned terribly, and then everything went dark."

The fire crackled as silence hung between them.

"I don't know where I was when I woke, but someone was there, tending my wounds. I remained there a while, waiting for my sight to return, but it never did."

"And your daughter?"

Corran hung his head. "What could I do? I was struck blind, left to the mercy of a stranger's good will. How could I return to Fallow when I didn't even know where I was? How could I care for a child and provide for her when I couldn't even care for myself? Even now I depend on others for my survival. How could I, in good conscience, bring a child into such a life, always depending on others to get by? I would not do that to her, make her destitute, a wretch on the side of the road to be pitied as we begged for charity. As much as it pained me to admit, I realized that Siyan was better off where she was. One cannot survive on love alone, and love was all I had left to offer."

Emelyn bit her trembling lips, fighting back the tears that welled in her eyes. "Siyan?"

"My daughter. That is what we named her."

Emelyn bit her lip so hard that she could taste the metallic tang of blood. But it didn't matter. Tears rolled down her cheeks and dropped onto her clenched hands.

"You are crying," Corran said, his voice soft.

Emelyn didn't know how he knew, unless he could hear her tears falling to the floor. But now that he did know, Emelyn could no longer contain it. All the emotions she had struggled to hold back now burst forth in loud, wracking sobs.

Corran sat still as she wept, making no move to console her. When she calmed, he held out his hand.

Emelyn, wiping the tears from her cheeks, looked at his hand. Why was he being kind to her? Hesitant, she reached out and took his hand in hers.

"Why are you crying, child?"

Emelyn looked at his hand with bleary eyes. It was warm, rough, the sawdust from the wood he had been whittling still clinging to his fingers. What should she say to him? How would he react when he knew who she was?

"I never knew my parents," Emelyn found herself saying. She felt distant, detached, as though her body now acted under an authority of its own. "I was also left on the doorstep of a household in Fallow, a big house on the outskirts of town. The people there were well off, though with no children of their own it often felt barren, lifeless. The housekeeper raised me, and, while she might not have loved me, she was usually fair, though I sometimes wish her hand had not always been so heavy. I was looked after, given a basic education, and I know I have no warrant to complain. There are others who are not so fortunate and, given my situation, it was arguably more than I deserved.

"But I grew up wondering why my parents had left me, why my guardian couldn't love me, even just a little bit. You say one can't survive on love, and maybe you're right. But I think I would have liked the chance to know the love of a father rather than receive a proper upbringing at the hands of strangers."

Corran's hand trembled before he jerked away. "Siyan? Is it possible?"

"I never knew that name. Emelyn is the name I was given. I know of no other children that were left on doorsteps in Fallow, so, yes, it is possible."

Corran sat frozen in his chair and Emelyn wondered what she should do. Should she leave? Was she no longer welcome, the daughter he had abandoned so long ago?

Corran eased himself out of the chair, as if uncertain his legs would hold him. Emelyn rose with him, unsure of what he would do. With outstretched hands he searched for her and, having found her, pulled her into a tight embrace.

"Thank you, my love," he whispered.

Rigid, Emelyn stood in his arms, not knowing what to do, how to react.

Corran held onto her for a time before releasing her. Then he wrapped his hands around her face and, leaning down, tenderly kissed her forehead.

Emelyn had thought she hadn't any more tears to spare, that she had already cried more than any one person could. Yet still they came, a lifetime of hurt and sorrow, streaming down her fevered cheeks. She wrapped her arms around her father and together they stood, embracing by the flickering firelight.

CHAPTER 20

EMELYN STIRRED THE pot hanging over the fire. The night had grown long, and she hadn't eaten since that morning. After they brought Ferrin inside and unloaded his packs, Emelyn had pitched whatever she could find into the pot, not caring how it would taste. She imagined her boots would be rather tasty right then, as hungry as she was. As she cooked, Emelyn glanced into the narrow room where Ferrin was stabled. Corran was tending to him, brushing his coat and feeding him roots from the packs. Her father. It still seemed so strange, finding Corran—the real Corran— only to find that he was her father. Emelyn didn't know if she fully believed it yet, it all seemed too remarkable to be true. But then, the entire journey had been too remarkable to be true.

Despite the mismatched array of food Emelyn had thrown together, the aroma rising from the pot made her stomach grumble, and she decided that supper was ready.

"I only have a single bowl and spoon," Corran said, after she had called him to eat. "I don't get company, as I've said."

"That's all right, there should be some in the supply sacks."

Emelyn poured some soup into a pair of bowls, putting one into Corran's hands before slurping hers down.

She neglected her spoon, drinking directly from the bowl instead. She finished it within minutes and poured a second helping.

Corran was more reserved in his appetite, navigating the spoon from the bowl to his mouth with careful deliberation. Emelyn's heart ached to see him; not only for his blindness but also for the pain he had borne all these years.

"You say you don't get visitors, but you also said you depend on others for survival. What did you mean by that?"

Corran's spoon froze halfway to his mouth. "There is someone who looks after me, but they aren't one for socializing. Not in the traditional sense, anyway."

"Who is it? Do they live nearby?"

Corran set his bowl onto the floor. "They do live nearby, yes. As for who . . . well, you've already met her."

Emelyn considered a moment. "Iyen?"

Corran nodded. He was quiet a long moment, then he said, "It was some time before I knew. Back when I was struck blind, I thought the person tending me was simply a kind stranger. But I realized later that it had been her. It had always been her."

"How did you know?"

"It wasn't until much later, after I left the place where I had recovered. I set out, wanting to remain close to the Tower in case Iyen ever escaped. But I was still not used to being blind, not used to being unable to travel on my own. I stumbled, a lot, and wandered aimlessly until I found someone to give me direction. I considered myself fortunate that just as hunger or fatigue threatened to overtake me, there was always someone there to offer me food or an arm to lead the way. Again, I thought they were kind strangers, until the day I heard her. Iyen. Only it wasn't my wife but the little girl I knew so long ago. I could hear the clicking of the beads she had always worn on her dress. I thought maybe my ears were playing tricks on me, or that it was someone else who wore beads like hers. But then she spoke . . . her voice, her laughter; I knew then that it was her.

"I never truly understood the extent of her abilities. I mean, I knew she could do remarkable things, but just how remarkable . . ." Corran shook his head. "She was always uneasy with herself, of what she was capable. I never wanted to discuss it with her for fear of making her uncomfortable, of upsetting her. I regret it now, not pursuing the matter. Maybe I could have helped her. Or even if I couldn't, at least . . . at least I would have known my own wife better."

Corran was quiet a moment.

"After encountering Iyen as a little girl," he continued, "I started paying closer attention to the people I met. I still cannot say for certain who might have been her and who might have been a genuine stranger. It seemed like there was always someone different. I kept hoping I'd meet her as Iyen, my wife. But I never did. She only came around as the little girl and even then rather infrequently. I continued traveling. I figured fatigue or hunger or injury would force me to stop at some point, but it never did. In time, I knew I must have been well past the Tower. But I didn't have anywhere else to go, so I kept walking, always with the hope that maybe I'd see her again, in some fashion. It was months, maybe a year, maybe longer, before I came here. She led me here, Iyen the girl. Told me I'd be safe and that she'd look after me." Corran laughed—a hollow, mirthless sound. "Do you know what it's like to have a little girl tell you that they'll take care of you? Especially when that girl is the very person you failed?" He fell silent.

Emelyn looked at her hands, unsure of what to say. There was nothing she could say. Nothing could make it better.

After a lengthy silence, she asked, "Does she still come here?"

Corran nodded. "Her . . . and others. Some are friendly. Some are not. I hear them out there, like living nightmares, screaming, hunting. I recognize some of them from stories I told her, old folklore, dreams. I don't know why she's brought them into being, but I'd wager the reasons aren't good."

"I've seen them too," Emelyn said. "In Fallow, it's why I left there." With the Magisters. But Emelyn didn't speak her thoughts, worried that Corran would be upset to hear of her traveling companions.

Corran cocked his head. "In Fallow? You've seen them, even there?"

"Yes. It was frightening. I'd never seen anything like it before."

"So it was a recent occurrence?"

"Yes."

Corran fell silent, deep in thought.

"Does it mean something?"

"I don't know. I can't be sure of anything regarding Iyen's abilities. But . . . I didn't know her power was so great. I didn't know she could . . . project . . . such things over such distances."

Emelyn frowned, confused. "But she led you here from Fallow. That's a long way."

Corran shook his head. "She's not in Fallow. Not anymore. She's here, in a Tower not far off."

Of course. Emelyn shook her head, feeling stupid. The creature of magic. She sometimes forgot that the creature and Iyen were one and the same.

"They brought her up here from the Tower in Fallow," Corran said. "I don't know why. To lock her up, maybe, refusing to let someone with her power roam free. I always thought . . . I liked to think . . . that she led me up here with her. That we traveled here together, in some way. It was a silly notion."

Emelyn stared at the empty bowl in her hands before returning to the pot to fetch more soup. She wasn't especially hungry any longer, but she didn't know what to say to Corran, and stirring the soup helped to fill the silence. Emelyn sat back down on the floor, fiddling with her spoon when a thought occurred to her.

"How do you know she is here?"

"The girl and I speak, sometimes. She doesn't like to talk about herself, about what happened. But sometimes she'll give small hints, and, after she's gone, I've nothing else to do other than consider every word she has ever said."

"But how can you be so sure she's in the Tower? Have you been there?"

"No. But she's there. I know it."

Emelyn poked at her soup. She needed to tell him. She put the bowl on the floor.

"There are Magisters traveling to the Tower," she said, her stomach sinking. "They found me in Fallow. I . . . traveled with them, up until a couple days ago. They mean to stop whatever she's doing to cause the disturbances."

Corran nodded. "It is to be expected. Where there are Towers, there are always Magisters. The only strange thing is that there have been no Magi here for a very long time. At least, as far as I'm aware."

"You're not upset that I was traveling with them? Especially considering their plans . . ."

Corran gave a weak, tired smile. "I'm grateful they left you alone for as long as they did. I have nightmares where I dream that they had taken you, locked you up in one of their Towers just as they did your mother. I'm grateful they kept you safe in all the turmoil that was around you and in the journey up here. I've no doubt that it was your mother that led you here, just as she led me here so long ago. But if not for the Magisters, you might have never gotten so far. For all the pain the Magi have inflicted, they have, at least, done this one thing." Corran fell silent, growing restless in his seat.

"I'm curious," he said, "Do you . . . also have abilities? Like Iyen, your mother?"

Her mother. It still sounded strange. "Yes, but I can't control it. It never seems to come when I want it to."

Corran nodded. "Your mother also struggled with her abilities. She could control it well enough with what she called 'little' things, like making a flower bloom or an icicle melt. But there were times—when she felt frightened or threatened—that she was able to do things that I think surprised her, scared her, even. I'm not sure that even she knew the extent of her ability."

Emelyn remembered Iyen's fight with the Magisters, wondering how frightened she must have felt then. "I want to see her, before the Magisters come. I want to meet her, if possible."

Corran looked at the fire as though he could see the flames flickering against the stones. "We'll leave at dawn."

When daylight broke, Emelyn and Corran loaded the packs onto the mule before setting out. The morning was clear, crisp, the Tower looming above the trees with stark clarity. Emelyn offered an arm to Corran, helping him through the snow as he held Ferrin's reins. They kept a leisurely pace, for Corran's sake, or so Emelyn told herself. She didn't want to admit how nervous she was, or acknowledge the underlying dread she felt at the thought of traveling to the Tower. They were to see her mother, a woman driven mad by the Art. Emelyn had no idea of what to expect, either from Iyen or the Tower itself, and such uncertainty unsettled her.

She looked at Corran. His skin was pale, haggard, the beginnings of a beard clinging to his chin. Emelyn wondered if he shaved himself, or if Iyen tended to that as well.

Such a strange surge of emotions she felt as she looked at him, her father. Finding him was nothing like she had imagined. In her dreams, she had only felt happiness upon finding her parents, a sense of completeness. Now she mostly felt confused. The happiness was there, but also anger, hurt, pity, and . . . regret? Emelyn wasn't sure if the regret was her own or an emotion she felt on behalf of the man holding her arm. His regret was palpable, following him around like a dark cloud.

"Have you ever been near the Tower?" Emelyn asked.

Corran's grip on Emelyn's arm tightened—she wasn't the only one nervous. "No. My last visit to a Tower did not end well. I have kept clear of this one."

"What do you think we'll find?"

Corran shook his head. "I don't know. Iyen has never given any hints as to the presence of Magisters, nor have I ever been disturbed by any. But that doesn't mean they are not there. Towers are built to house Magi. It makes no sense that they would leave this one abandoned."

"What do we do if they are there?"

Corran was quiet a moment. "I don't know."

They walked in silence for a time. Emelyn watched as the Tower grew closer, looming ever higher above the trees. As tall as it was, it didn't seem to be as imposing as the one near Fallow. But then, she had never been so close to that Tower, so she couldn't be sure. They walked the entire morning, and around midday Emelyn's skin tingled while the air hummed around her ears.

"We're drawing closer," Corran said.

Emelyn nodded before remembering he couldn't see her. "Yes."

When they came to the stone walls of the Tower, Emelyn stopped.

"We should leave the mule," Corran said.

Emelyn took Ferrin's reins and tied them to a nearby tree. She then offered her arm to Corran and together they walked to the base of the Tower.

"What do you see?" Corran said.

"The Tower . . . it doesn't seem to be as big as the one near Fallow," Emelyn said, her neck craned back as she looked upwards. "And it looks . . . worn. As though it's been here a long time. The stone is crumbling in places, and ivy is growing thickly on the walls." Emelyn hesitated, taking a moment to realize what was wrong. "Why is there ivy growing in the middle of winter? All the leaves should have fallen."

Corran tilted his head. "Magic."

Emelyn knew he spoke the truth, but whose magic was it? Iyen's or the Magisters'? They walked around the base of the Tower, looking for a way inside. There were no doors and no windows—at least, none low enough to crawl through—just an unending stone wall covered in a curtain of ivy. Emelyn reached out, touching one of the green, glossy leaves. It shivered under her touch, warm like skin. She snatched her hand back and rubbed the eerie warmth from her fingers.

"I can't find a door," she told Corran.

"Maybe it's hidden. Have you looked behind the vines?"

Emelyn had tried peering through the thick foliage and, having touched a leaf, had no desire to rummage her way through the vines. "Yes. I still can't find anything."

Corran fell silent, apparently having no other suggestions to give.

Emelyn continued to wander around the Tower, craning her neck, trying to see a door through the ivy without touching it. But the foliage was so thick in some places that Emelyn could no longer see the stone behind it. Gritting her teeth, she pushed the leaves aside and exposed the woody vines that had attached to the stones beneath. There was no door. Emelyn moved on, pushing aside the leaves where they were the thickest. Still no door. She grew frustrated. Did Magisters even use doors? Maybe they used the Art to grant them passage. The idea was daunting.

For a third time, Emelyn searched around the Tower, pulling back the ivy to see what lay behind. She was growing used to the warm, leathery feel of the vines and was not as squeamish in pulling them back. She did not dwell on how the ivy seemed to pulse in her hands, or how it seemed to resist her efforts to clear a path. She dove in, pulling the vines away from the wall as hard as she could.

A shadowed hole of a doorway peeked from behind the woody stalks of the ivy.

"I found something," Emelyn called to Corran.

When there was no answer, Emelyn turned and found herself engulfed in the ivy. The leaves around her shivered, as if pattered by raindrops even though the sky was clear. Despite the cold winter air, Emelyn felt warm among the leaves and might have been comfortable within the foliage had it not been so odd.

She pushed her way out of the ivy and, making a mental note of the door's location, walked around the Tower until she found her father.

He stood tall and rigid, his hands clenched into fists. He turned his head toward the sound of her footsteps as she approached. "Are you all right?"

"Yes," Emelyn said, feeling guilty of the worry she had caused him. She picked up his hand and placed it on her arm and felt the tension drain from his body.

"I was worried. I thought I heard you call out, but I didn't know where you were."

Emelyn's guilt deepened. It must be hard for him to simply wait, helpless if anything should go wrong. "I know. I'm sorry. I've found an entrance. It was well hidden. Come."

Emelyn led him back to where she had found the door. "There's a lot of ivy covering it, but we should be able to pass by." Taking Corran's hand into her own, she led him through the thick foliage.

Corran gasped. "The leaves, they're warm. Feels like . . . skin."

Emelyn said nothing, not wanting to think about it. She pushed aside the vines as she led Corran to the doorway. She hesitated at the threshold. It was dark inside. The air smelled clean and earthen, like rain on pine, though with an undertone of rot. She took a deep breath and stepped inside.

Sunlight filtered through the ivy at the doorway and through a few cracks in the wall. All else was dark. As Emelyn stopped to wait for her eyes to adjust, Corran ducked through the doorway after her, though the entrance was tall enough for him to pass unhindered. He wandered through the darkness, seemingly unconcerned. Once Emelyn's eyes had adjusted to the gloom, she followed.

The room was fairly small, given the size of the tower, and had the look of a modest entry hall. At one end was a set of double doors; the other end held a stairway that disappeared into darkness. The room was surprisingly warm, as if a fire had been burning even though the Tower looked to have been abandoned for some time.

Emelyn walked across the room to the doors. She pulled on a handle, but the door would not budge. She pulled again, rattling the door on its hinges, but it must have been barred from the other side. Emelyn's heart sank.

"We'll have to take the stairs," she said.

Corran nodded and placed his hand on Emelyn's shoulder.

She walked over to the staircase and began the ascent. With each step taken, the light streaming through the doorway dimmed, and Emelyn soon found herself immersed in darkness. Her heart flopped in her chest as her palms turned clammy with sweat.

"I can't see. It's too dark."

Corran removed his hand from her shoulder. "It's all right. Just keep your hand on the wall and continue up the stairs as slowly as you like. We are in no hurry, and I am right behind you."

Emelyn nodded, no longer trusting her voice. She put one foot in front of the other, creeping up the stairs on wobbly legs. She tried not to think about how far up the stairs they had come, or how far a fall it would be should she lose her footing. It was strange—never before had she feared the dark, having lived most of her life in a darkened basement. That was when she was familiar with the darkness, knew what was in it. Here, anything could happen.

She took another step and her stomach lurched into her throat when her foot met with air rather than stone. She stumbled and her foot found the floor.

"We're at the top," she said, letting herself breathe again.

Nearby, a sliver of light shone like a beacon, and Emelyn walked towards it. The light dimly lit a long hallway, with a door hanging on its hinges at the far end. Emelyn pushed the door open and peeked inside.

The room was snug, circular. Rows of books lined the walls, the shelves interrupted by a narrow latticed window that cast diamond-shaped patches of light onto a vibrant red carpet. In the middle stood a desk, too large and too ornate for such close quarters. Upon it lay heaps of scrolls, stacks of books, a scattering of feathered quills, and a single, unlit candle.

Emelyn's heart leapt when she saw it and she stepped inside the room, walking towards the desk. A figure slumped against the wall crept into the corner of her vision and Emelyn turned, her breath catching in her throat.

Corran's grip on Emelyn's shoulder tensed. "What is it?"

"It's a Magister," Emelyn said as she drew nearer. "I . . . I think he's dead."

"What killed him?"

"I don't know."

"Look."

Emelyn, taking a deep breath, crouched near the Magister. She covered her mouth and nose with her hand—the smell was . . . pungent. With shaking fingers, she poked the Magi; his body was cold, little more than skin and bones. Emelyn pulled her hand back.

"What do you see?"

"I . . . I don't know . . ."

"Is there blood?"

Emelyn looked. "No . . . I don't think . . . wait." She gritted her teeth as she placed her fingers under the Magister's chin. His skin was leathery, pulled tight over his skull. "There's . . . dried blood on his face . . . from his eyes and nose." Emelyn recalled Iyen's altercation in the woods with the boys, how she had made one of them weep blood. "What does it mean?"

Corran was quiet. "I'm not sure. Maybe poison killed him. Maybe magic. Hard to say."

"Did Iyen do this?" Her mother—a woman with a broken mind and seemingly capable of killing at a touch. Was it a mistake to come here?

"We should move on."

Emelyn stepped away from the body and fetched the candle from the desk. She didn't know how she would light it, but should the opportunity present itself, she wanted to have it handy. Stuffing the candle into a pocket, Emelyn returned to Corran so that they could leave together.

There was another door on the opposite side of the room and Emelyn walked over to it and pushed it open. The hallway outside was dark, but the light streaming from the room illuminated another set of stairs leading down. The place was a maze. With Corran's hand on her shoulder, she stepped out into the darkened hallway and started down the stairs.

She clung to the wall, using it to steady herself as she walked down the steps. Emelyn caught herself holding her breath on more than one occasion as she strained to hear any unusual sounds. Yet for all of that, she felt calmer than she had walking up the first flight of stairs. She didn't quite understand it. She would have thought that seeing a dead Magister would have put her even more on edge, further solidifying her fear. But it didn't, quite the opposite, in fact. It was as though the worst had already happened and she had come out of it unscathed. At least she hoped that was the worst of it.

Edging her foot outward, Emelyn searched for the next step but found only level ground. She crept forward, still not trusting that she had reached the bottom of the stairs. But there were no steps and Emelyn wondered what to do next. She was in an unknown room in a Tower she knew nothing about, without any light whatsoever to help her navigate.

"It's dark again," she whispered to Corran. "I can't see."

Corran once again removed his hand from her shoulder, stepping away to see what he could find on his own. Emelyn followed his lead and walked forward, her hands stretched out before her. She shuffled through the darkness and bumped into a table. Nearby, there was a clattering and breaking of glass.

"Sorry," Corran said.

"Are you all right?"

"Yes."

Glass crunched under Corran's boots as he continued walking. She did the same.

With her hands outstretched, Emelyn felt the wall before she walked headlong into it. She made her way alongside it until she found a door.

"There's a door," she said to Corran.

"Keep talking so I can find you."

Emelyn didn't know what to say, so she kept repeating "over here" until Corran found her. Emelyn found the door handle and pulled it open, relieved that it wasn't locked. Yet her relief was short-lived when the room beyond proved to be just as dark.

"Are you all right?"

"It's still so dark. I wonder if we'll get lost in here."

"You will be fine. We've come too far to turn back now."

He was right. She walked through the threshold, following the wall with her left hand. The way was long and straight, and Emelyn figured they must be in a hallway. The air stirred, cooling her face, carrying with it the scent of rain and pine. Running her hand along the stone, Emelyn once again felt the strange leathery leaves of the ivy that had been outside.

"Do you feel that?" she said.

"Yes, we must be getting closer."

Getting closer to what? Emelyn continued down the hallway. As her hand brushed against the ivy, the leaves emitted a pale light. They were in a narrow passageway, barely broad enough for two people to walk abreast. At the end of the hallway was a portal, pallid light glowing beyond it. The shattered remains of the door laid strewn about the threshold, decrepit and crumbling under Emelyn's boots. She peeked around the corner and into the room beyond, and her breath caught in her throat.

"What do you see?" Corran asked.

Emelyn didn't know how to put into words what she saw. She stepped through the doorway, pulling Corran in after her.

CHAPTER 21

THE AIR STIRRED. If not for the darkness, Emelyn might have thought she was outdoors. But the breeze was not what held her attention. A great white tree stood in the middle of the room, glowing with a ghostly light. Silvery leaves fluttered in the air, growing from gnarled branches the color of bone. The base of the tree was twisted and misshapen, rising from the rubble of the broken stone floor. Emelyn stared in wide-eyed wonder. It was beautiful—a thing of ethereal splendor that made her want to weep. Yet it was also frightening. The way the tree had twisted in its growth hinted at something sinister and perverse. Just as Emelyn admired its beauty, she also wanted to turn and run, to hide her eyes, hoping never to see its like again.

A clicking of beads echoed from the darkness and Emelyn turned as Iyen emerged from the shadows. She ran to Emelyn and Corran, her small face beaming up at them as she took their hands.

"You came," she said, as if they had been invited to tea.

Emelyn, not knowing what else to say, said, "Yes."

"Iyen." The affection was plain in Corran's voice, and Iyen's smile deepened.

"What is that?" Emelyn asked, turning to look at the tree.

Iyen's smile faded. "You should probably go."

"Why?"

Iyen was silent, her gaze fixed upon a point in the darkness. With a gasp she ran off, disappearing into the shadows.

Emelyn watched the darkness where Iyen had vanished, but the girl did not return. She looked again at the tree, to the grotesque twisting of the pale wood. She started towards it but stopped when another form emerged from the shadows.

The woman Iyen regarded them, her chin raised and eyes cold. "You shouldn't be here."

Corran tensed. "Iyen," he said, his voice heavy and strained.

Iyen narrowed her eyes and Emelyn was glad he couldn't see the callousness of her gaze.

"You shouldn't be here," she repeated.

"We came to see you," Emelyn said.

Iyen turned her gaze upon Emelyn, her eyes as black as the surrounding darkness. Emelyn fidgeted, wondering, once again, if they had made a mistake in coming here.

"Why?" Iyen said.

Emelyn swallowed the lump in her throat. "Because you are my mother."

Iyen remained unmoved, watching her with a cold detachment that broke Emelyn's heart. "I am no one's mother."

"Iyen, please," Corran said.

Iyen's lips peeled back into a snarl. She reached out and grabbed Corran by the neck. He didn't resist, even as his neck turned black and blood trickled from his nose.

"Don't, please," Emelyn said.

The air stirred and Iyen's face twisted with pain and rage. She released her grasp before turning and stalking back into the darkness.

Corran crumpled to the ground, his body shaking as he wept. "You should have let her kill me."

"I couldn't . . ." Emelyn began but stopped, realizing that anything she said wouldn't matter. She turned away, her gaze drifting back to the twisted tree. There was something strange about the way the shadows played on the surface, of the contours she thought she saw. She walked towards it, watching as the silver leaves shimmered above like stars. So beautiful.

When Emelyn lowered her gaze to the base of the tree, her stomach sank. There, within the wood, was a woman's body. Her form was twisted and bent, as though struggling under the weight of the branches that sprouted from her back like broken wings. With trembling fingers, Emelyn traced the lines of a face petrified in torment and pain. The wood was hard and smooth, like the keys on Mistress Mansell's piano.

"Mother?"

The tree beneath her hands shivered, sending a few silvery leaves fluttering to the ground.

Emelyn closed her eyes against welling tears and rested her forehead against the tree. "How is this possible?"

Whispers echoed in the darkness, and Emelyn turned to find a group of silvery forms take shape. These weren't like the apparitions she had seen before—these were diaphanous, fleeting, as if constructed of little more than smoke and moonlight.

"She is capable," a man's voice said. "Much more capable than the others, and with an understanding of what she is doing."

"Yet she is not cooperating," said a second voice. "She claims she cannot do that which we ask of her."

"Either she is lying," a third voice said, "or is truly incapable. In the case of the former, she will learn to obey. If it is the latter, then she can only benefit from our guidance. Do as you must."

The figures dissolved, replaced by others.

"Her threshold is . . . remarkable. It has been difficult replicating that day in the woods. It is as though she is holding back. She is not responding as expected to the stimuli. I am at a loss on how to proceed."

"Pain is not the only stimulus. Her mind evidently has barriers that are not easily broken. It is there you must focus your efforts."

"What would my lord suggest?"

"Fear should be a proper motivator. She likely felt fear for her family, if not for herself, the day we seized her. Explore the matter further and report to me what you find."

The figures dissolved then reappeared.

"My lord," the man's voice was hurried, fearful. "Something has gone dreadfully wrong. We were exploring various stimuli, as instructed. I believe it has worked—all too well. Her power has grown considerably, but her mind . . . it is broken. She cannot be reasoned with. Magister Hauer has been injured while Magister Jennison . . . He is dead, my lord."

"Why did you not take precautions?"

"We did, my lord. At least, I thought we had. We had not been expecting such results so suddenly."

"Then the blame lies with you. Now that you know what you are dealing with, I am sure you will be all the more careful in the future. It is imperative that we fully understand the way these people wield the Art. You will proceed as instructed."

"Yes, my lord."

The figures vanished but the whispering remained, fleeting through the darkness like disembodied spirits.

" . . . madness . . .," the voices rasped.

" . . . beyond control . . ."

" . . . kill us all . . ."

"She will kill us all," a man's voice said as the luminous forms reappeared. "She must be stopped, lest she bring the entire Tower down upon our heads."

"Agreed. Construction of a Tower has begun in the north. I have developed restraining runes that should prove strong enough. She will be relocated there and you will follow."

"M . . . my lord?"

"Someone will need to tend the runes. As this failure is your doing, you will accept the consequences. Try to do so with a modicum of grace."

"Y . . . yes, my lord."

The figures dissipated and the darkness grew quiet.

Emelyn stared at where the figures had been, trying to make sense of it. "They did this to you?" she whispered, but no one answered.

A scuffling of boots drew Emelyn's attention. She turned, expecting to see more ethereal forms. Instead she faced Aldren and Percival, their lightstones glowing from their leather straps. Emelyn took a step back.

"Do you fear us now, child?" Percival asked as he approached her.

"I've seen what you've done." Emelyn placed her hand upon the tree. "You did this to her."

Percival cast a cursory glance at the tree, his expression calm. "She did this to herself."

"Liar!" Emelyn's rising fury startled her—never before had she felt so angry. "I saw what you did. You tortured her! Why?"

Percival thinned his lips and folded his hands, like a parent dealing with a petulant child. "We did what was necessary in order to learn of her abilities with the Art. Such information is crucial to our society, our way of life."

"You didn't have to take her . . . to hurt her . . ."

"I do not take pleasure in such things, but I am afraid it was quite necessary. She had proven to be thoroughly uncooperative, we had no choice but to force submission so that we could assess her abilities and the potential threat she might have posed."

Emelyn fell silent as she considered the Magister. "You took them, didn't you? Her people, the forest people. That's why they left, isn't it?"

Percival blinked. "Their reasons for leaving are their own."

"But you did take them. There was talk of 'the others' and how Iyen was stronger than them."

Percival narrowed his eyes and Emelyn suspected she knew more than he would have liked.

"A remarkable people," he said, "the forest people, as you like to call them. A simple society with a simple culture, yet somehow every one of them has capability with the Art. Truly astounding. Nothing refined, mind you. Most are unaware of their power, using it unconsciously for mundane matters such as lighting a fire or shooting a straight arrow while hunting. It is how they escaped our notice for so long. But then a young girl with unusual eyes and unusual capabilities caught our attention. We then . . . revisited our observations with her people, to understand the extent of their abilities."

"But why take them? If their abilities were so mundane, what threat could they have possibly been?"

"Admittedly, the threat posed by an average savage was likely very little. But we needed to be sure. We also needed to understand the way in which they used the Art, as it differed from our own. We needed to understand if it could be refined, improved, taught to others. It is through such study that Magisters have come into being. It is through knowledge that men have come to wield the Art at will, and it is upon that knowledge that our society is built. We owe it to ourselves and to society at large to continue in that pursuit of knowledge."

Madness. Emelyn closed her eyes, forcing herself to take a deep breath. She was having difficulty seeing, difficulty thinking straight, and she needed a clear mind when dealing with Percival. "Why didn't you take me, too? You knew who I was all along, didn't you? Who my parents were?"

"Indeed, but we did not know if the power would manifest in you. Your blood is, after all, only one half of your mother's; the other half is mundane. We did not know whether you would develop any capability with the Art, so we decided it best to leave you as you were until such a time your abilities manifested, should that ever occur."

Emelyn looked at him askance. "You were watching me?"

Percival spread open his hands. "'Watching' is too strong a word. 'Occasional observation' would be more appropriate."

Emelyn stared at the Grand Magister, wondering if he was attempting to be humorous. "Is that why you helped me in Fallow? Told me of my parents so that I'd follow you, all to continue your 'occasional observation'?"

Percival gazed at her, immovable and unblinking. "Yes. It was an opportunity to observe you more closely and I seized it. It also removed you from an unknown variable, namely your mother's influence through the Art. Her power had grown greater than anticipated and I did not know what effect that might have on you. It would not have been wise to leave you on your own, amidst all the turmoil she had been causing."

Emelyn glanced at the tree, her heart heavy with sorrow. "So you weren't at all concerned with helping me or keeping me safe? You only wanted to know if my ability would manifest?"

"We never wished you ill. But our mission was never to gather up the townspeople to keep them safe. It was a matter of priorities, and you fell within that range of priorities."

In other words, no, they had never cared about her or keeping her safe. Emelyn continued to gaze at the tree, at the tormented and twisted form of her mother. "And when my power manifested, what then? Were you going to do to me what you did to her? All in the name of furthering knowledge?"

Percival was quiet a moment. "I was hoping to enlist your cooperation—something I never obtained from your mother."

"And if I didn't cooperate?"

"Then I would have done whatever was deemed necessary."

Emelyn glanced at Aldren. The younger Magister shifted his feet, his gaze darting from the tree, to Emelyn, to Percival. He looked liked he wished he were someplace else. She wished they were someplace else. She wished they'd leave them alone.

"What are you planning to do with her?" Emelyn said.

Aldren stiffened, but Percival remained calm.

"She cannot be allowed to continue," the Grand Magister said. "We brought her here so that she could not inflict more harm upon others. But she has managed to break her runes of restraint, killing yet another of our brethren. She is becoming a liability and a danger that I can no longer justify protecting."

Emelyn's stomach turned to ice. "You're going to kill her."

Percival's gaze hardened. "It is not something I wish to do, but she has left me little choice." He thrust a hand towards the tree. "Look at her! She has lost her humanity.

She cannot be reasoned with. She is like a rabid animal, and the only merciful course of action is to put her down and end her suffering."

He was the cause of her suffering. Emelyn looked at the tree. Hiding behind the ivory trunk was little Iyen, peeking from behind the twisted wood with wide, fearful eyes. "You will not touch her," Emelyn whispered.

"I am afraid, my dear, that the decision is not yours to make."

Fury erupted in Emelyn, her body shaking. Her vision dimmed and the world turned black, yet she could still see. Shimmering auras of silver and white illuminated the frame of the twisted tree, of the Magisters, and of Corran still lying crumpled on the ground.

"You will not touch her!" Emelyn's voice was not her own; it echoed and reverberated off the walls, causing the stone to tremble around them. But she was not afraid. It was as though, after all this time, she finally understood. At last, she was seeing clearly.

"So be it," Percival said as he brought up his staff.

CHAPTER 22

ALDREN GREW NERVOUS when Emelyn's grey eyes darkened and turned black.

"You will not touch her!"

Though she had not shouted, her voice resonated in Aldren's skull and he resisted the urge to cover his ears.

"So be it," Percival said, raising his staff.

No . . . Aldren's heart sank, for it was a scenario he had seen before. Not again.

Emelyn knelt to the ground and placed her hands upon the floor. Her fingers scraped along the broken stone, yet could not find purchase. She grimaced, rising to her feet. As she rose, the ground quaked, forcing the Magi to support themselves with their staves. Cracks widened and tore across the floor, while pale snakes writhed up from the ground. Aldren blinked. Not snakes, but roots from the great white tree twisted and churned, crushing the stone into pebbles and exposing the soft earth below.

Once again, Emelyn knelt and put her hands to the ground.

The earth was soft, cold, like the soil of a freshly tilled field. All was dark save for the shimmering silver auras around the Magi and Corran and, more spectacularly, around the tree. Each branch, each leaf and twig, glimmered with light. From the ground, small pearls of light blossomed, gleaming in a bright flash before vanishing again. It was like floating in a sea of stars. Calm, beautiful. Then, memories of what had happened, of what was about to happen, and Emelyn's anger flared anew. The need to touch the soil deepened, as inexplicable as it was. She submitted to the impulse without hesitation, without question, clenching her soil-filled hands into fists.

Aldren dragged his staff through the loose soil. As soon as he drew a rune, however, a root rose from the ground to destroy it. He clenched his teeth. This would be difficult. Nearby, the Grand Magister had given up trying to scrawl runes on the ground and wove his staff through the air. Aldren knew he ought to do the same, to begin inscribing offensive runes, rather than defensive. But he wouldn't. Not yet. Not until he knew there was no other way.

The air grew warm and stifling, like trying to breathe through a thick woolen blanket. Percival completed his rune and a faint light flared near the tree only to flicker and stutter before extinguishing. The air was too wet, too heavy. Beads of sweat broke across Aldren's brow; his limbs grew heavy and lethargic. An invisible weight pressed upon his chest, and he gasped for air. Stars speckled his vision and, from the corners of the room, the shadows moved.

Aldren turned, thinking the shadows mere constructs of his imagination, but they remained—darkened forms that crept and clawed. Aldren gripped his staff, trying to raise it. But the wood was leaden, and the sweat on his palms caused the staff to slip from his grasp.

Sweat dripped from Emelyn's brow as the warm air clung to her skin. It pressed upon her, constricting her breathing. It was like being swaddled too tightly in damp cloth. But it didn't frighten her. Emelyn found comfort in the closeness of the air and strength in the sense of confinement of her body. Just as the air pressed upon her, Emelyn could feel her own energy pressing back. It was a pulsing sensation—an ebbing and flowing of power that filled her with a strength of body and mind.

She inhaled, feeling the thick air slick down her throat like oil. Detached, she watched as the shimmering forms of the Magi slowed and grew lethargic. She smiled and leaned closer to the ground, smelling the mustiness of the earth as the air pressed upon her. It was like she carried the world on her back, and she reveled in her strength.

The ground shuddered, sending a tremor up Emelyn's arm. Her grip on the soil slackened as the tremor shivered along her spine to her skull. White light flashed and then all was dark.

Aldren heard the cracking before he saw it, felt the rumbling in his chest before he knew what was happening. Shadows scrambled towards him, their sinuous hands long and grasping. He stood frozen, immobilized by pathos and fatigue as though the thick air had sapped his will and strength. The cracking grew louder, the rumbling moving from his chest to his legs. Aldren turned his head—a small movement requiring great effort—and watched in a bleary stupor as a nearby wall crashed into a pile of rubble.

Sunlight streamed in and, with it, cold, fresh air. Aldren gasped as if he had been trapped underwater. The stickiness of the cloying air fell from his body just as his sweat froze, sending a chill that spurred him to action. He picked up his staff and turned to meet the encroaching shadows only to find that they had gone.

Emelyn had fallen, lying in a heap beneath the tree that, in the sunlight, had transformed. The pale silver leaves were now green and glossy while the white bark blushed with a golden hue. Aldren licked his lips. Emelyn's own power, while substantial, was new and unrefined. The power of her mother, however, was another matter entirely. The fact that Iyen had managed to transform herself was a clear indicator of how great her power had grown, and Aldren was not eager to see that power firsthand. She would want retribution. After what they had done, she would want blood.

The pale roots no longer writhed within the soil, and Aldren scribbled a rune around himself, hoping it would be enough to offer some means of protection. Percival did the same. This was a mess. All the same mistakes were being repeated; mistakes he had vowed he would not make again. He wished he knew how to pull himself out of this hole he and Percival had dug.

A white mist crept along the ground, emanating from the base of the tree. It rolled across the broken stones and upturned soil, eclipsing the forms of Corran and Emelyn as it spread across the room. Roiling and churning, it reached the feet of the Magi and surrounded them, though it did not breach the runes they had drawn. A promising sign, though Aldren would prefer the mist was gone entirely. He cast a rune of air to disperse it, but nothing happened. Fire—still nothing.

Movement from the tree drew Aldren's eye. Out from behind the golden trunk stepped a young woman, her long, white hair gleaming in the winter sun. Patches of grey and white fur clad her pale body while in her hand she carried a long ivory spear. She looked like Iyen, yet different—like a ghostly visage of a distant ancestor. She walked towards the Magi, a hint of a smile tugging at her lips.

The Grand Magister wove a hand through the air as he drew a rune. Before him the air shimmered, like the rippling of sunlight on water. On spoken command, the glimmering shot forward, darting towards the woman like a knife. She smiled and vanished into swirling mist before the air could reach her.

A deep, throaty laugh resonated near Aldren's ear. As he turned, a sharp switch burned across his cheek. He clasped a hand to his face, his fingers coming away slick with blood. The woman was nowhere to be seen. She was toying with them. A quick glance at Percival showed he also had blood running down his cheek. His face was ashen and grim. He was angry now. Aldren's hope of a peaceful resolution dissolved.

Aldren swung his staff, twirling runes into the air that whipped the wind into a flurry. He hoped that the gusts, together with his circle of protection, would keep the spirit away. But a sharp stab on his arm, another trickling of blood, told him he was wrong.

The woman reappeared near the tree, a smirk twisting her delicate features as blood dripped from her spear. She ran her finger along the blade, discoloring her fair skin with the Magisters' blood. Reaching up, she plucked a leaf from the tree and rubbed the blood onto the glossy surface. With another smirk, she flicked the leaf into the swirling mists.

Emelyn awoke to a world white and shifting. The air, crisp and fresh, cleared her clouded mind. She sat up and poked her head out of the mist. The room was filled with light, the branches overhead gold and green. Everything was brighter, sharper, as though a layer of dirt had been wiped clean.

Nearby, the Magisters faced a fur-clad woman wielding a spear. Emelyn blinked, uncomprehending. Then she remembered—her fury, the stifling air. She remembered watching the Magi grow lethargic and the delight she had felt because of it.

She cradled her head in her hands, gripping her hair with dirt-encrusted fingers. After all her struggles with her power, she had finally gained control of it only to almost lose herself. Now, in the light of day, it seemed too much to bear.

The mist swirled and eddied around her knees. Get up. Emelyn pulled her hair, fighting the urge to lie down and hide. Get up. Putting her hands to the ground, she pushed herself up.

The white woman plucked a leaf from the tree and cast it into the mist at her feet. She laughed, languid and sonorous and wholly without mirth. Then she was gone, dissipating like smoke in the wind.

The mist roiled where the woman had stood, rising and congealing into the shape of two men. Their robes were white, adorned with intricate embroidery that sparkled like diamonds. One of the men had a long white braid, the other a pair of luminous spectacles. Emelyn recognized these men, as, she knew, did the Magi.

As Aldren watched his own pallid reflection rise from the mist, his resolve wavered.

The shade of Percival smiled. "We mean you no harm." His voice was coarse, rasping like rusted door hinges. "Come, let us help you." The shade raised his staff, sending a ball of flame towards the Magi.

Aldren raised his own staff in defense, speaking a rune that dissipated the fire as it reached him. Just as the flames dispersed, another was upon him, then another. Sweat dripped from Aldren's brow as he struggled to keep up. Then, as suddenly as it had begun, it stopped.

A smile twisted the shade's colorless lips. "Your capability with the Art is remarkable, if rudimentary. Help us to understand so that you, too, shall gain greater understanding." He nodded to his companion.

Aldren's reflection stepped forward and raised his staff. "Please, try to relax."

The room darkened and turned black. Aldren spoke a rune for light, but nothing happened. He looked around but saw no one. "Hello?" His voice echoed off the walls, carrying with them a wavering of fear. He spoke the rune again, trying to illuminate the lightstone at his hip. Still nothing.

A child's voice whimpered in the darkness. "Father?"

Aldren froze as he searched the shadows.

From nowhere, a circle of light appeared and into it stepped a boy. He looked about four or five, with golden hair and eyes like a twilit sky. He looked at Aldren and smiled. "Father."

Aldren hesitated. He knew with absolute certainty that he did not know this boy, that he had no son in the world to call his own. Yet, with equal certainty, he knew the boy spoke the truth—this was his son and he could feel his love for him filling his heart. He was dreaming.

"Father, I skipped a stone on the water three times! I threw it just like you showed me."

Aldren knew he had never done any such thing, yet he could see the memory plain in his mind—the pond nearby their home and the hours he and the boy would spend there fishing and throwing stones. "That is wonderful, son." He heard himself speak the words, even as his mind reeled at the possibility.

The boy beamed up at him and took Aldren's weathered hand in his own.

Aldren looked down at the dimpled hand clasping his fingers and his resolve failed. His son. It had all been a dream—his life as a Magister, all of it. His child was what was real, and only now was he waking up.

Shadows coiled in the darkness behind the boy, gathering and shifting like a flock of birds. Aldren watched it, disliking its sinister look. "Be gone," he said, as if shooing away a stray cat.

The shadows crept closer, pulsing and heaving like a great beating heart. Wisps of darkness reached towards the boy, grasping at him with sinuous hands. Aldren wanted to shout, to take the boy and leave. But his voice failed him and his limbs were leaden.

The boy beamed at Aldren, unaware of the dark hand that reached out from the shadows, grasping his neck in its vile embrace. The boy did not flinch as the hand constricted, nor cry out as his blood pattered onto the floor.

"No . . ." Aldren whispered as the boy's eyes grew dark and vacant, his small hand falling lifelessly from his own. "No!" Aldren fell to his knees, gathering the body of his son in his arms. He wept violent, wracking sobs that threatened to tear his own body apart.

"Aldren . . ."

The voice was vague, distant. Aldren ignored it, clinging to the body in his arms. Leave him . . . let him die.

"Aldren!"

Aldren looked up to find Percival gazing down at him, his brow furrowed and eyes stern. "Get up."

Aldren looked at the ground. There was no boy, no blood, no shadows. He wiped at his eyes—the tears, at least, had been real. "What . . . ?"

Percival grabbed his arm. "There is no time. Get up!"

Aldren staggered to his feet, blinking at the circle of runes around him, at Percival's circle, now abandoned. "You left your circle," he murmured, unsure of the implications.

Percival pursed his lips but the harshness in his eyes softened.

"You are making this difficult for us all," the shade of the Grand Magister rasped. "You would do well to be more forthcoming."

Both shades rushed at the Magi, attacking Aldren and Percival in unison.

Aldren raised his staff in time to counter a blow from his shadow. His movements were rote, unconsidered, his mind still clouded from the horror and confusion of the dream. It was not real. But it had felt real. The way the boy had looked at him, right before his blood had spilled to the floor . . .

A sharp crack to his head brought Aldren to his knees, his staff falling from his hands. Stars sparkled as the edges of his vision grew dark. Get up. The clashing of staves echoed around him as the Grand Magister continued to fight. Get up, you fool, and help him. Aldren tried to push himself to his feet, but his legs were liquid and would not obey.

Helpless, he lifted his head, peering at Percival with bleary eyes. A flurry of staves and a haze of white—it looked as though the Grand Magister was fighting mere mist. Flashes of light erupted as Percival cast simple runes at his attackers, but to no effect. Aldren grasped at his staff. Ignoring the throbbing pain in the back of his skull, he used it to hoist himself to his feet. His head pounded and his vision dimmed, but he was upright and Aldren took that for a small victory.

The Grand Magister's staff whirled as he parried and blocked, all the while murmuring runes to try and hinder the ghostly figures. But for every move the Grand Magister made, it was mirrored in the two pale figures—they parried every blow, blocked every rune. Their colorless lips moved as they spoke runes of their own, and Aldren could no longer tell which attacks belonged to whom.

Aldren drew a rune in the air with his hand, trying to knock the staff from his counterpart's hand. The attempt failed, drawing instead the ire of his reflection. Mimicking

Aldren, the shade drew and spoke a similar rune and Aldren's staff was wrenched from his hand. Without its support, his legs buckled and Aldren fell back to his knees. This could not be happening.

Movement pulled Aldren's gaze and he turned his head, meeting the brilliantly blue eyes of a young woman. Iyen.

"Please . . ." Aldren murmured. "Stop this madness."

She lifted her chin and turned to look at Percival and the ghostly Magi. With a stirring of wind the figures dissolved and Percival leaned upon his staff as he caught his breath. Aldren felt hopeful until, from the mist, the white woman returned. She charged towards Percival, her spear raised. Aldren cried out.

Percival brought up his staff, but was too late. In a fluid motion, the white woman brought down her spear, breaking the Magister's staff with a resounding crack. Percival reeled and fell. Before Aldren could breathe, the woman was upon him, the tip of her spear at his throat.

"No!" Aldren cried, reaching out with his hand.

The woman turned her head and fixed her colorless eyes upon him.

"Please . . ." Aldren whispered. "Please."

A mirthless smile stretched across her pallid face; a smile that shriveled Aldren's heart and chilled his blood. She leaned upon her spear, plunging the tip into the Grand Magister's throat.

Emelyn watched in mute horror as blood bubbled from Percival's throat, running in rivulets down his neck to the ground. Nearby, Aldren crumpled into a heap, burying his face in his hands. It was time to leave.

Emelyn turned and waved her hands through the mist until she found Corran. He hadn't moved since his encounter with Iyen, and Emelyn wondered if he was even aware of anything that had been happening. She grabbed him by the arm and tried to pull him up.

"Leave me be," he grumbled.

"Get up, we're leaving."

"I'll not leave her again. If she wishes me dead, then death is what I deserve."

"I'm not leaving you—"

"Begone, girl!" Corran wrenched his arm from her grasp.

Any other time such an act might have hurt Emelyn's feelings, but now it only made her angry. She crouched down in front of Corran and wrapped her hands around his worn and haggard cheeks. "Father, I'm not leaving you. Get up, please."

Corran sighed, the lines in his face softening. He nodded and allowed Emelyn to pull him up.

With her arm around his waist, Emelyn began leading Corran towards the crumbled wall when movement caught her eye. The white woman, having finished with Percival, now walked towards Aldren. Emelyn slowed, watching as she waited for Aldren to get to his feet, to fight her off, to escape, to do something. But he remained on the ground, staring at Percival's body as the woman approached him.

Emelyn hesitated. He was a Magister, he could take care of himself. But still she remained. Look at what he did to your mother, what he helped turn her into. He deserved whatever was coming to him. Maybe he did, but as Emelyn looked at the Magister kneeling on the ground, she only saw a man that had been kind to her; a man that had looked after her when she had been hurt. She didn't want to leave him behind any more than she wanted to leave Corran.

"Wait here," she said to Corran as she turned and made her way through the mist.

The white woman was kneeling next to Aldren, studying him as she might a curious insect. Was she waiting for him to act? Or was she simply enjoying the moment, reveling in seeing him defeated? Emelyn looked away. She walked to the trunk of the tree and placed her hands on the pale wood.

"Mother, stop this." Emelyn didn't know what else to do. She could call on her power; she knew that she could, now. But she didn't want to. She was afraid of losing control of herself, as she had before, and she wanted this to end without anybody else getting hurt.

A figure moved in the corner of the room and Emelyn turned, meeting the gaze of Iyen.

"Stop this," Emelyn repeated. "Please."

Iyen's eyes narrowed and her gaze flicked over Emelyn's shoulder.

Emelyn turned to find the white woman looking down at her. She was tall, at least a head taller than Emelyn, and her eyes were as cold and colorless as glass.

"Stop this," Emelyn whispered, holding to the hope that the conflict could be resolved peacefully.

The woman swung her spear, bringing the blade to Emelyn's face.

Emelyn dodged the blow. She darted around the tree as the spear thrust at her again, a sharp pain in her side telling her she had not entirely succeeded. Emelyn's heart raced, her mind reeling. The woman was quick—there was no time to stop, no time for Emelyn to focus her power.

The air shimmered and grew sharper, colder. A loud *snap* cracked from behind, but Emelyn didn't stop to look. She ran through the mist, making her way towards Aldren who was now on his feet, waving his staff. The air continued to shatter behind Emelyn even as she arrived, breathless, at Aldren's side. He was haggard and pale and looked as though he had aged ten years.

"Get behind me," he said, grabbing Emelyn by the arm as he pulled her behind him.

Emelyn did as she was told and got out of Aldren's way. Once behind the Magister, she watched as the air shimmered around the white woman before solidifying and, an instant later, shattering into a cloud of shards. Undaunted, the woman moved through the shards. If they cut her, she did not show it, nor did her skin rend or bleed.

Emelyn crouched behind Aldren, putting her hands to the ground. She focused on the earth at the woman's feet, turning it soft, viscous. The white woman slowed as she sank into the mire. She put her own hands to the ground and, once the earth hardened, pulled herself up onto her feet. Emelyn sharpened her focus, but the ground didn't soften beyond a thick mud. Not that it mattered—the woman had stopped, raising her spear back over her head.

The spear arced through the air. The tip of the weapon had nearly reached Aldren's head when he spoke a rune and deflected it. But his attention had been diverted and that was all she had needed. Like a cat she leapt through the air, knocking the Magister down as she landed on top of him.

Emelyn tumbled out of the way, scrambling for the spear the woman had thrown. With the weapon in hand, she turned back, finding Aldren prone on the ground as the woman sat atop him, his arms pinned down by her knees. Her hands were wrapped around his neck, his skin darkening beneath her fingers.

"Stop." Emelyn's voice quavered, and she cringed at her own weakness. Pursing her lips she raised the spear, bringing it to the base of the woman's skull. "Please, stop."

The white woman ignored her. She squeezed her hands around Aldren's neck and blood trickled from his nose.

With sweat-slicked hands, Emelyn tightened her grip on the spear. Mother, please. Closing her eyes, she steeled herself for the thrust . . .

Music lilted through the air—mournful yet sweet, like a memory of love long since past. Emelyn opened her eyes just as the woman removed her hands from Aldren's neck. She rose from the Magister's body and turned towards the music. Standing alone in a corner of the room was Corran, holding a flute to his lips. The white woman watched him, her arms hanging by her sides, her head tilted as if enthralled. She took a single step and then stopped, as if walking were painful, difficult. Slow and labored, she took another. She had only walked a few paces when the wind gusted, dispersing the mist covering the ground until she, too, evaporated like smoke.

Emelyn watched where the woman had stood. Was she really gone? Was it all really over? Aldren stirred and she kneeled down, relieved to see that he still breathed.

"Are you all right?" she asked, helping the Magister to his feet.

He groaned. "I will live. The question is, are you all right?"

Emelyn forced a weak smile. "Some scratches, I'll be fine."

"That is not what I meant."

Emelyn's smile faded. "We should go."

She bent down and picked up Aldren's staff. She tried not to look at the Grand Magister's body, but still she saw it—the pooled blood, the ashen skin. She looked away.

Handing Aldren his staff, Emelyn walked across the room to where Corran stood. Lilting strains echoed off the walls, fading and returning like a chorus of ghostly pipers. As she reached him, Emelyn touched Corran's arm and the music stopped.

"Has she gone?" he asked, his voice heavy.

"Yes."

Corran nodded.

"How did you do that? How did you know what to do?"

Corran fidgeted with the flute. "I didn't. I just . . ." He took a deep breath. "I used to play for her, you know. When she was upset or frightened, I would play for her and it would always cheer her up, take her mind off her troubles. When I heard all the commotion I just . . . I just wanted to play for her again, to ease her pain, to tell her I love her . . ."

Silence hung between them as Emelyn tried to think of what to say.

"She's still there," Corran whispered, almost too faintly for Emelyn to hear. "She's still my Iyen."

Realizing there were no words, Emelyn took Corran's hand and led him from the room.

CHAPTER 23

THEY CLAMBERED OVER the rubble as they made their way out of the hole that now gaped in the side of the Tower. Emelyn helped Corran navigate the uneven terrain while Aldren hovered nearby. He looked as though he wanted to help, but he never did. It was just as well. Several minutes, a banged shin, and skinned palm later Emelyn and Corran reached solid ground.

Outside, the sun shone in a clear blue sky, gleaming against the snow in blinding brilliance. Emelyn felt like she had been inside the Tower for years and was surprised to find the world unchanged. But it had changed. Everything had changed.

Nearby, a line of smoke twined upward.

"That would be Cobbe," Aldren said upon seeing the smoke. "We left her out here to wait."

Emelyn nodded and walked towards the camp. Before long, Cobbe came running through the snow to meet them.

She hesitated when she saw Emelyn, looking at her with narrowed eyes. Then a smile split her face and she nodded.

"What is it?" Emelyn said.

"Silver-eyes is Silver-eyes no longer. Will now be called Eyes Like Water."

"'Eyes Like Water'?"

Aldren shifted his feet and cleared his throat. "Your eyes are blue now, Emelyn."

Emelyn glanced up at the blue sky above. Eyes of And'estar. She said nothing, leading Corran to the camp to sit by the fire.

Cobbe had been busy while the Magi had been in the Tower. Having found Ferrin tied to a nearby tree, she had taken it upon herself to unload the supplies and start supper. Emelyn was glad for it. She was hungry and her body ached. A throbbing pain at her side caused her to lift her shirt, where she found a long slash caked with blood—a gift from the white woman's spear. It was a shallow cut, but left untended it could fester.

Cobbe saw the wound. "Eyes Like Water is hurt. Cobbe fix." She hurried off to rummage through the supply packs.

Emelyn examined the broken skin—she could see each ragged tear, each tiny hair that poked through the blood. She remembered the leaf that had once been dead and lifeless that she had made green again.

She put a hand to her wound and imagined it whole. She imagined the pain gone until warmth spread through her side and the throbbing subsided. Removing her hand, she found the wound closed and scabbed over.

Cobbe, returning with a handful of roots, appeared crestfallen at the sight of the healed wound. Then she shrugged and, returning to the cooking pot, threw the roots into the stew instead.

Emelyn looked up and met Aldren's eyes. He had been watching; he had seen what she had done. Unwavering, she met his gaze, wondering what he would do.

But the Magister said nothing. He looked away and accepted the bowl of stew Cobbe now offered him.

Mealtime was quiet, tense. Only Cobbe seemed untroubled, swinging her spoon as she ate, as though she enjoyed the silence. Emelyn, however, grew weary of it.

She turned to Aldren. "Why did you do it? Why couldn't you just leave her alone?"

Aldren seemed unsurprised at the sudden questions. He placed his bowl of stew on the ground, took off his glasses, and rubbed his eyes. "We did as we thought was best," he said after a lengthy silence. "There was much we did not know of your mother's ability, nor that of her people's. We needed to know. It was . . . our obligation."

"An obligation to torture her? To break her mind? Ruin her life?"

Aldren stared at his hands. "Mistakes were made."

Emelyn scoffed, if for no other reason than to keep the tears at bay. "Mistakes?" She thrust a hand at the nearby crumbling Tower. "You saw what happened to her, what she became *because of you,* and all you can say is 'mistakes were made'?"

"It is all I can say because it is the truth. We did what we thought was best, what was *needed.* Yet how it was handled was a mistake, one I did not wish to repeat."

"And the Grand Magister?"

Aldren hesitated. "The Grand Magister had . . . difficulty . . . in seeing any other way."

"And what do you see?"

Aldren peered at the Tower looming against the darkening sky. "I see my greatest sorrow embodied in the construction of that Tower." He paused. "Throughout history, the construction of a Tower was one of great celebration. It signified not only the expansion of our power, but also the expansion of civilization. Where a Tower was built, society has always thrived . . . until now. This, our Thirteenth Tower, hidden away at the edge of the world, is the Magisters' greatest shame and greatest failure, and I weep for my Order."

Emelyn watched him in silence for a time. "And what of me? Will the Magisters also come for me, to see what they can learn?"

Aldren looked at her with sad, tired eyes. "I cannot speak for my brethren, but from me you have nothing to fear."

Emelyn said nothing, turning instead to Corran. He had remained silent through the conversation, but Emelyn knew he was listening. She placed a hand atop his own, but he kept still. Emelyn wept inwardly for him. She wondered what he had been like before he, too, had been broken. She stood and left the campfire, wishing to be alone.

The sun had set and Emelyn walked in darkness alongside the Tower. The moon had not yet risen, but Emelyn could still see with startling clarity. She circled the Tower until she came to where the wall had collapsed. Within, the pallid branches of the tree glowed like moonlight. Emelyn sat in the snow and, burying her face in her hands, she wept.

Someone touched her shoulder and Emelyn looked up into Iyen's small face.

"Why are you crying?" the little girl asked.

"For you. For Corran. For everything that's happened; everything that could have been."

"But it's all right."

Emelyn wiped her eyes. "No, it's not."

"Yes, it is. You are alive; you have *woken*. Fear no longer chases you. You are strong, now."

But Emelyn was still afraid. "I don't feel strong."

Iyen's face dimpled. "You will."

"What do I do? Where do I go?"

Iyen said nothing, her smile deepening before she darted off into the trees.

Emelyn remained by the Tower until daybreak when she and Aldren retrieved Percival's body for burial, along with the other Magister that had perished within. It was unpleasant business, but necessary.

After the task had been completed and the supplies were loaded onto the mule's back, Emelyn found Corran standing near the Tower. She hesitated a moment, then asked, "Will you be all right here?"

"I will. She will need someone to look out for her, to keep her calm, to help her remember who she is. I can do that. It will . . . be nice to be with her again."

Emelyn looked at him, her father, as ragged and worn as the shabby strip of cloth that covered his damaged skin and blinded eyes. She reached up and touched his temple, wondering if she could heal him, let him see again.

He touched her hand and pulled it away. "Don't. I . . . it's better this way."

Emelyn swallowed and nodded, even though she knew he couldn't see her. She tried not to dwell on the way his hands quavered or the tremor she heard in his voice.

"We will be here, should you ever wish to return. Be safe, my daughter." He brought his hands to her face and kissed her forehead before turning and disappearing within the Tower.

Emelyn watched him go, wiping her eyes before turning around. Nearby, Aldren and Cobbe waited. She walked over to them.

"Are you all right?" Aldren said.

Emelyn nodded, not trusting her voice to answer.

A bird soared by, alighting on the supply packs tied to Ferrin's back. Emelyn was glad the falcon had returned.

Turning to the Magister, she asked, "Will you be returning to Fallow, then?"

Aldren frowned. "I do not know. I feel like I no longer have a place there. I . . . am uncertain of what to do."

Cobbe scoffed. "Glass-eyes clever, almost as clever as Cobbe. Red-robes not needed, never needed. Glass-eyes will travel with Cobbe, much exploring, much cooking. Will be very good."

Aldren smiled, though his eyes remained sad. "Maybe so, my little friend."

Cobbe grinned.

"What of you?" Aldren said, turning back to Emelyn. "What will you do?"

Emelyn considered the question. "I'm not sure. I want to understand—myself, my mother, where we come from, who we are. I want to find her people. *My* people . . . I'm not sure where to go or how to find them, but I need to try." She glanced at the Tower. "I need . . . to keep moving."

Aldren opened his mouth to say something but then closed it again. After a moment, he nodded and extended a hand. "Be well, Emelyn."

Emelyn looked at his hand and hesitated before finally taking it in her own. She smiled. "My name is Siyan."

Acknowledgments

I'd like to thank Mårten Aronsson for reading through my first draft and still managing to find nice things to say about it; Ray Rhamey for his insightful editing; and Ferdinand Ladera for the beautiful cover art. I'd also like to thank everyone who has helped me along the way in providing suggestions, advice, and constructive criticism. You know who you are, and thank you.

Most of all, my thanks go to Anders Nyström, without whom this book would not have been written.

ABOUT THE AUTHOR

Sara C. Snider was born and raised in northern California, but now lives in Sweden with her partner and two beastly cats. You can find her online at: www.saracsnider.com.

Siyan's adventures continue in *A Shadowed Spirit*.
From the back cover:

She used to be called Emelyn. She used to be nobody. Now she is Siyan—a creature of magic known as an And'estar. But Siyan doesn't understand what that means, just as she can't control the power that has woken within her.

Addigan worked her entire life to master the Art of magic and become a respected Magister, only to fail her final test. Scarred and desperate to prove her worth, Addigan pursues rumors of trees of power and a mysterious people called And'estar.

When Siyan heads into the dense and dangerous forest searching for answers, she doesn't realize Addigan is coming for her. In this twisting chase of hunter against hunted, Addigan must choose how far she is willing to go to prove herself. And Siyan must let go of everything she knows—and everything she loves—if she is to gain control over her power. Even if it kills her.

In a journey that follows the intertwined lives of two women, *A Shadowed Spirit* is a mystical tale that redefines the boundaries between life and death, dreams and reality, and what one is willing to sacrifice to achieve the happiness she seeks.

Read on for a preview of the first chapter.

A SHADOWED SPIRIT

CHAPTER I

SIYAN CALLED THE WIND. Above her, the branches of a towering oak began to sway, rustling in the breeze like a hoarse whisper. She smiled, enjoying the cool spring air against her cheeks. Then her smile faded and pleasure turned to determination. She focused her attention and willed the wind to be something more—to cause the branches to lash with storm-like fury. But even as the thought entered her mind, the focus faded and slipped from her grasp, and the breeze stilled and died. Siyan clenched her jaw.

It was the same every time.

She studied the branches, now still against the clear morning sky. Control of her ability continus to elude her. Her power came easily enough with simple things—calling a gentle wind, turning a faded leaf green—but she was capable of so much more.

Siyan could control the weather and change the earth beneath her feet. Heal wounded flesh. She had done all of these things, but they had been during frantic moments of fighting for her life that had, at the time, seemed as simple as anything. Now, when she tried to repeat such feats, she couldn't do it. She didn't understand why, and that troubled her.

She toed a narrow edge by remaining near a city where so many Magisters lived. Magisters had taken her mother and tortured her until they broke her mind. They might have done the same to Siyan had she not escaped their grasp. Even though it lay several leagues away, the tall spiraling stone Magister Tower seemed to cast a heavy shadow.

The morning had grown late, so Siyan turned her back on the tree and walked through the grassy field as she returned to the Falconry Guild. It was a drab place with russet-colored stone buildings and hard-packed earthen grounds. Plant life seemed to shun it, keeping to the surrounding fields and giving the Guild a wide berth. It looked out of place in such green surroundings, like someone had dropped it there and then forgotten it.

Siyan crossed the expansive courtyard, surrounded by tall towers echoing with the calls of falcons and hawks. A couple of men traversed the grounds, each carrying a falcon on a gloved fist. She stayed clear of them, weaving between wooden posts and poles as she made her way to the other end of the compound, taking care to nudge the occasional stuffed leather decoy out of her path with her foot.

When she saw Master Sorrel speaking with a visitor, Siyan turned and hurried away. He was undoubtedly boasting of the prowess of his trained birds. Men from Roelith would often visit the Guild, touring the grounds as Master Sorrel regaled his birds' capabilities, which he promised would make any man into a superior hunter. But only if they joined the Guild, whose yearly fees were, of course, a modest investment that any serious huntsman would be pleased to pay. She edged along the courtyard, hoping to remain unnoticed.

"Siyan!" Master Sorrel cried and waved her over.

Siyan closed her eyes and let out a breath. Why couldn't

he call over one of the men? She wasn't in the mood for this particular little performance.

As she approached, Master Sorrel said, "I was just telling Mr. Jash—"

"Please," the man said. "It's just Jash." He had copper-colored hair that had been pulled back in a short tail. A rapier hung from his belt at one hip, and a flintlock pistol at the other.

"Ah, yes," Master Sorrel said. "I was just telling *Jash* here that falconry is extraordinarily simple. Be a dear and demonstrate just how simple it is."

Siyan tightened her jaw, wondering what Master Sorrel would do if she told him no. Yet he was still her employer and, despite these embarrassing demonstrations he insisted upon, a good man. He had given her a job when she had needed one, and he paid her well—better than some of the men in his employ. Glancing at Jash, Siyan then looked to the sky and whistled.

From the roof of the tallest tower, a falcon took flight. Siyan put out a leather-clad arm, and the falcon circled ever downwards, perching at last upon her limb.

Master Sorrel laughed and brought his hands together in a thunderous clap. "You see?" he said, turning to Jash. "Falconry is so easy that even a woman can do it!"

Siyan bit the inside of her cheek. She wished for the day Master Sorrel would stop parading her around like a prized pony.

Jash looped a thumb in his belt and smiled, his gaze lingering on Siyan. "Clearly. And where did you find such a woman?"

Siyan shifted her feet, uncomfortable under his gaze.

Master Sorrel waved a hand. "Before me, she was nothing. A pathetic vagabond. Now she is a mighty huntress! All because I taught her everything she needs to know of falconry."

That was all false, of course. Master Sorrel hadn't taught her a thing of falconry, other than how to put on the leather sleeve that protected her skin from sharp talons. The falcon resting on her arm was wild and had never—much to Master Sorrel's distress—seen the inside of his aerie. Siyan had saved the bird from a trap two years ago, and he had been following her ever since.

Fal—that was what she had taken to calling him—seemed tame around her, but he was still a wild animal that largely came and went as he pleased. The fact that Siyan was able to use her power to interact with him didn't really diminish that. She certainly didn't compel him to return to her—nor did she truly understand why the bird obeyed her commands. That he did any of these things only made Siyan all the more grateful for his presence. She only wished Master Sorrel wasn't so eager to exploit her and the bird.

"Impressive," Jash said.

Master Sorrel drew himself up and pointed at the flint-lock pistol hanging at Jash's hip. "Far more impressive than hunting with one of those things. Abominable creations. More likely to kill you from misfire than hit your mark. You'd be better off using it as a paperweight and leave the hunting to my birds."

"And such fine birds you have," Jash said. His gaze lingered on Siyan, pushing her discomfort to the edge of alarm. Why was he looking at her like that, with that half-smile as if he were privy to some secret? She wanted to leave.

"The finest!" Master Sorrel said. "You'd be hard-pressed to find better."

"I agree completely," Jash said, "and see no need to continue the search."

"Wonderful!" Master Sorrel said. "I can draw up the papers today, officially marking your enrollment in the guild, which will give you access to our birds and to training. I… uh… assume you'll prefer to pay the enrollment fees at once, correct?"

Jash pulled his gaze from Siyan to look at him. "Of course," he said, causing Master Sorrel's face to light up. "Once I speak to my patron, that is." He glanced at the Magister Tower and then winked at Siyan.

She froze as her stomach clenched into a knot of ice. Had he something to do with the Magi?

"Oh, I see," Master Sorrel said. His voice sounded distant, difficult to hear over the thundering of Siyan's heart. He mentioned something about drawing up the papers and having them ready for Jash's return, and Siyan felt sick at the thought of seeing him again, his patron in tow.

Siyan stared at the man. Had he been searching for her? She wracked her mind, trying to remember an encounter, a strange look that suggested she had been recognized, but nothing stood out. Jash smiled at her. He bowed low, keeping his gaze locked with hers.

"Have you gone daft, girl?" Master Sorrel's sharp voice pulled her out of her thoughts. He waved his arms at her. "I said off with you now. Shoo!"

Siyan cast another glance at Jash and then lifted her arm and Fal took flight. Keeping her back rigid, she turned and hurried away. Siyan resisted the urge to look back, feeling as though Jash's gaze was on her until she opened the door to the servants' quarters and stepped inside.

She leaned against the door as she took a deep breath in an effort to calm her racing heart. Jash had recognized her. She didn't know how or where—all she knew was that his glances were more than passing admiration. And the fact he seemed to know Magisters just made everything so much worse. Why was he here? What would he do when he left?

Siyan peeked out the door, but Jash had gone. She stepped outside, looking around, but saw only Master Sorrel.

"Didn't I tell you to get to work?" he said. "Why are you standing there gawping like that?"

"That man, Jash. Is he still here?"

Master Sorrel pulled the waist of his pants up over his protruding gut. "No. Said he needed to go find his patron. I told him I'd take that pistol of his as collateral for the dues, but he wouldn't have it. And I was being generous, too. Those things are all but worthless. Everyone knows that."

Siyan's gaze moved over the field and to the road that led towards Roelith, but Jash was nowhere in sight.

"I have an errand I need to run," Siyan said as she headed towards the road.

"Errand? I don't pay you for errands, girl!" Master Sorrel called after her.

"I won't be long!" Siyan called back. She rustled through the grassy field until she reached the main road and there, further down the way, walked a copper-haired man. Siyan swallowed as Jash rounded a bend and fell out of sight. Part of her wanted to let him go; she shouldn't be following a man potentially in league with the Magi. But she couldn't leave. She needed to know. So she followed him.

A sinking dread settled in Siyan's gut as she drew closer to Roelith. Why had she stayed here so long? She hadn't really intended to. It was only supposed to be temporary—she'd intended to stay long enough to earn some money to buy some supplies before she headed back into the forest to find her mother's people. But then nearly two years had passed and she still hadn't left.

She told herself it was the comfort of routine, the security of steady work and decent wages. The others at the Guild even seemed to hold a measure of respect for her and—having once felt invisible when she had worked as a housemaid—that meant something to Siyan.

But there was more to it than that. She was afraid of what she might find should she go searching in the forests.

She knew what she wanted it to be. She wanted to find her mother's family—a clan of forest folk that lived somewhere out in the wilds. She wanted to find love and acceptance, a place to call home. She wanted to understand herself and this power that eluded her. But she knew from past experience that what she hoped to find was not always what came to pass, and she was afraid of going out there and having her heart broken all over again.

Siyan quickened her step, trying to ignore another deeper, uncomfortable truth that continually nagged at her mind.

She felt drawn to the Magister Tower.

There was an energy about it—a tingling on her skin and a humming in her ears. She had felt the same energy when she had approached her mother's Tower, and she felt it now. It was faint, given the distance to Roelith's Tower, but it was there. It pulled at her in a way she couldn't explain. Almost like an intense curiosity, though she knew better than to go anywhere near it.

She lost sight of Jash once he reached Roelith and passed through the gates. Siyan hurried after him and, once in the town proper, she stopped and looked around.

Massive stone houses with tall arched windows and wrought iron balconies loomed overhead. People bustled up and down the streets, while fountains bubbled from one of the many gardens that followed the city wall. Jash was nowhere in sight. She scanned the roads, hoping to find his distinctive coppery hair, but saw nothing.

Her heart sinking, Siyan turned off the road and followed narrow alleys and side-streets until she got to the well-maintained, though primarily empty, road that led to the Magister Tower on the outskirts of town. She had hoped she'd been wrong—that she was just imagining Jash having recognized her. Yet when she passed through Roelith's eastern gates and saw a coppery-haired man on the road ahead of her, Siyan's stomach clenched into a hot little ball. Her palms began to sweat and she wiped them on her breeches. She shouldn't be so close to the Tower. She needed to turn around and head back to the Guild.

And yet she kept on walking. Why was Jash going the Magister Tower? Who was he going to meet? What would they discuss? The pull from the Tower seemed to intensify along with the prickling on her skin. Siyan had never come this close before. She'd thought about it and all the things she'd like to say or do when she got there, but she'd never dared.

What would she find if she did? In Fallow, Magisters had taken the forest people into their Tower where they were never seen again. Would she find forest people here, locked up and forgotten by the outside world? Maybe that's why it had been so difficult for her to leave. Maybe, deep down, she thought she should be locked up with them.

Siyan bumped into someone and staggered back.

"I'm sorry," she said and then noticed the man was wearing a Magister's robe.

"Quite all right," he said.

Siyan froze, unable to breathe. When had the air suddenly become so stifling?

"Are you well?" he said and reached towards her.

Siyan's entire body tensed as she staggered back another step. Overhead, the clear sky clouded over.

"Do you need help?" he said as he took her arm.

Siyan yanked her arm away and lightning flashed in the darkened sky.

The Magister looked up just as rain started to fall. Her heart racing, Siyan turned and ran.